PLEASE FEEL BAD I'M DEAD

PLEASE FEEL BAD I'M DEAD

by

M. Price

lugubrious /lə'g(y)ōōbrēəs/

adj. sad and dismal; mournful

0. Intro to Insanity

Jumpin' Christ, this is too much work. How do people even get these things loaded?

I'm on nine, but there's still room for seven more. What? How? Who's this strong? It's—ya know, it's not even about strength, it's dexterity—but how do others have this dexterity? They're strong, yeah, but they can't be that good with their hands. And why do I even care? I only need one. Guess it's just unrealistic, uh, something standards.

And my thumbs! Already swollen up to shit now. What's really stupid is people would see this and be like, "Oh, what a loser, he can't even load it all the way, what a scrawny whi—" —ya know, it's not always about strength—just not as practiced as others may be in this field and that's nothing to hold against me. I'm certainly trying something new and isn't that what everyone wants? What they keep telling me to do? Whatever.

Durkheim posits that neurasthenia has no definite correlation to suicide. Jhaegar Holdburn posits that Durkheim's a rustic country asshole who doesn't know anything about me and I'm gonna do whatever I want. Stupid sociology, telling me how to think. Or psychology. Phycology. Something. They're all the same. Bunch of old white people (which I'm definitely not, by the way).

Oh, my jumpi—forget it. We're sticking with nine. I don't have time for this, it's all just a waste—they're not gonna check it anyway. Nobody but me has standards in the first place and if they're all gonna be degenerates, I may as well be, too.

But yeah, I set the gun (pistol?) on my desk. My nerves assault me as I do. What if I miss? I should've got the shotgun—I mean, it'll be Visa's problem, not mine. Sigh. I never think. This website I saw (name forgotten already) listed all the best (best) ways to (I gotta stop using

[1]

parenthesis) kill yourself and they listed shotguns with a 99% success rate ("success" and I sure feel bad for that remaining 1%). Gun/pistol was set at I think number three right after cyanide, but it's like, who has cyanide? And I feel it's more classical or something this way with a gun/pistol. I'm a man of aesthetics.

I'm just afraid I'll jerk my head at the last moment and shoot my face off. Or shoot below my brain and just sever my eye connector things—orbiter deals. Or shoot myself in the forehead and hit the wrong lobe. According to that website, it's actually a lot more difficult than it may initially appear. I really should've got the shotgun, but it's fine. It's all fine.

Whatever. Step two: Music. I turn on my radio cuz I'm also a rustic country asshole and still own one and put in The Sleepy Jackson's *Personality (One Was a Spider, One Was a Bird)*. It's my favorite album and the second track, "Devil in my Yard," is one of my favorite songs and should queue up by the time I've completed the other steps. Their album title also has parenthesis. Double also: I enjoy, "You Won't Bring People Down in My Town," but it's farther down the track list. I was gonna use it in a movie I never made—it was for the part when Mico's at the dance with all the girls and he dances with all of them in turn during the "na na bu dah" parts but he doesn't really feel it until the big "na na bu dah" part comes in while Luke's like— ya know? I'd use the real lyrics, but I'm sure they'd sue my corpse—fine me while I'm in Hell or something—but then the right girl comes on to dance with him even though she's not actually real and all the lights switch to a new color and they dance and as they dance the camera does this neat thing where it changes the central filmic lens and the girl then becomes the main character of the movie to help illustrate the man having a sexual identity crisis and longing to be a woman but then he dies and like I said she's the main character until of course she dies and

[2]

he's reborn out of her dead body. It was a pretty wild movie. "How Was I Supposed to Know?" is also a great song, but it's the last one.

Step three: Use the bathroom.

Step four: The Note. One must (wait, isn't THIS the note?) be careful creating The Note as this'll be the final messa—well, I'm just trying to get out of a going to a party tonight. Is this worth it at the moment?

Shut up! Yes, yes it is—I was gonna do it anyway, it's just a convenient coincidence. But The Note, or lack thereof, is important cuz it's your last chance to blame others—or leave an extreme, yet ambiguous, trail of breadcrumbs about your death to forev—

—A dog just took a shit outside. Is that alright? And she just left! Pick up after your dog, people live here!

Benny's back of course. Squirrely little squirrel asshole. Always mocking me.

"Dear Benny: Fuck you."

No, that won't work. All wrong. How could I put "Dear" in my note? Do I really hold anyone dear? Not really. But what else would I put? Do I have to put anything? "Devil in My Yard" is playing so I don't have time to lollygag.

Ya know, I'll put "Deer" instead. The detectives won't understand cuz Benny's a squirrel. We're doing it.

Alright, "Deer…"

…

…

I fucking hate writing. Waste of time—goofy I even have to do this. I rather say nothing, but then people'll call me selfish. Need a drink of water.

[3]

I get said water from the bathroom sink like a real American. An unfortunate side effect of this is that I see myself in the mirror. I'm, uh, six even, hundred eighty pounds of muscle cuz I'm in basketball. Yeah. I'm smokin'. And I'm black...I mean, Black. Well, brown (Brown). Definitely not white. Never white. I'm a woman, too. Latin-American is offensive to me, just letting you know. I'm Chilean Second Generation.

The "Welcome to Chili's" meme gets stuck in my head. Great. This is what I wanted to think about right now.

"Deer: I hope you're all doing fine. As you can see by the body in this room: I am not fine."

Ehh, I can't use that. That's stealing from George Carlin...well, the whole idea of this note is stealing from George Carlin, but they won't know. They don't listen. I'll use it and they'll never see. And if they did, they wouldn't care. Maybe they like him, too? Maybe it'd make them admire me, they'd find in me a kindred spirit. Plus, what are they gonna do, write me up? I'm dead.

"Deer: I hope you're all doing fine. As you can see by the body in this room: I am not fine. I'm penning you this notice regarding my death in hopes of bringing to light my decisions (not that you could ever hope to understand HahHahHahHahHah). Luke Steele's an underrated singer who—"

—Piss! My thoughts interrupted my writing again! Gotta start over. Do I have enough paper for this? Oh well, I'll quick get this thought out before I write again: Luke Steele, the main singer guy, has his other band, Empire of the Sun, right? They rushed their third album, like SO hard. That kind of stuff disappoints people. You get these expectations and

[4]

Shut up! It's fine. Just get the note, get the note, get the note, get the—

—I sneeze. I have a cold, I guess. It's not ideal, but it'll have to do. We all make the best of our situations. See? I'm always told I'm not very positive. Clearly wrong. I am quite positive (double meaning!).

When one leaves behind a suicide note, the detective people take it in and examine it to see if I was murdered. Nirvana fans still think Cobain was murdered—not all Nirvana fans, I understand this, just some—but he wasn't murdered. Kurt definitely killed himself. I wonder if it's better that he did? The whole message they were giving wouldn't have really worked with a band of forty-year-olds…and at least he knew commercialization with appeal to a larger audience ultimately kills true art…or maybe he wanted to die. Doesn't matter thinking about it now, he's dead and—

—He used a shotgun! I should've got the shotgun!

Christine Chubbuck lived for like fifteen hours after she shot herself. I don't want that, that's nuts! She severed the eye thingy—the orbiter!—she shot too low. I won't make that mistake. Have to learn from others. Thanks Christine, for all you did for us. Is it alright if I call you "Christine?"

I ditch the note. Simply not practical. I've been writing (attempting) for a time now, so long in fact I'm actually approaching, "You Won't Bring People Down in My Town." This is either an unforeseen boon, a, uh, or—people always wanna do things in threes. There's actually only one in this situation. You won't see a false second and third from me. Terrorists don't win this time.

[5]

But yeah, people'll just have to deal with it. They don't care anyway. I reset the album back to the beginning. I take my gun/pistol off my desk, slip into bed, a

I'm sorry

Jhaegar! Stop! Just do it already!

I prime or whatever-it-is the gun/pistol. Harder than it looks. Daniel Craig just snaps it back like a badass. It's more of a strained yank for me. I always wanted to make a James Bond movie cuz I have an old ex-friend who loved James Bond and I know he'd go nuts. He ruins my friendship, I ruin his movie. It's the least I could do.

I sneeze again. Man, this cold. Suddenly, I get the impression I'm a Manchurian candidate. What? What even is that? Does that relate to my cold?

"Devil in My Yard" comes on. Now's my chance. I decide to leave a mental suicide note. Wait, weren't there more steps? Never mind. "Deer everyone: it's my life and I love it, I will never live for the sake of another man, nor ask, uh...I won't ever ask...or tell, I guess." It's alright to copy that, people too busy playing *Bioshock* instead.

I hold the barrel underneath my chin. Sigh, too unreliable...I hold it to my temples. The eye thingies! I raise it higher. I don't know how much is right! I try my forehead! It's hard to aim this way! Do I have sufficient finger strength?! Finger dexterity?!?!

Luke's almost done! Piss on it all, I hold the gun/pistol back underneath my chin and pull the—

—I sneeze.

[6]

***

I wake up in the hospital.

Piss...

Or maybe it's just a hospital-like Heaven or Hell? Whether this is worse or better, I cannot yet determine.

If Charlie Kaufman directed this scene from my life and/or death, the lights would be flickering and there'd be cockroaches everywhere. That's called Expressionism, ya know? Expressionist filmmaking. Not about how something is, but how something feels. But Kaufman didn't direct this, some dime a dozen studio "Filmmaker" did. And no, I'm not gonna attack Marvel right now (though I should). Rather, I must investigate.

My mystery finds itself quickly solved. I discover several thick bandages covering my right ear—this is the same moment I realize I can no longer hear anything out of my right ear.

I sigh.

***

I sigh just a bit harder as I sneak back inside my house. God knows what would happen if my Mom saw this. The Doctor told me she'd (cuz not all doctors are men mind you!) let me off with a warning which I found rather strange. An attendant at the door then told me to, "Please come visit us again!" Real, real strange.

Some blood trickles past my bandages. A soft pang (right word?) in my heart gives me a tad of insight into what it must be like being a woman. At least maybe? I'm a woman

[7]

sometimes—but not at the moment, so my prior knowledge is null. I wipe the trickle with a store brand facial tissue and remind myself to never wear white again and then chastise myself for reminding me now cuz it won't really matter unless I remind myself at the next instance I'll be pressured to wear white. No barnyard weddings in the coming weeks I can think of so I should be fine. I can't stand those barnyard girls. Quirky culture's dead.

I get a drink of water and, well, you know me, it leads me to the bathroom sink and I see my new reflection. These bandages put a damper on my appearance. Jumpin' Christ, they're gonna call me "Hijab Holdburn" now. I take off the bandages.

I see my NEW new look.

I put the bandages back on.

"Hijab Holdburn" isn't that bad. Maybe it'll make people think I'm Middle Eastern? But Middle Eastern is the one that hasn't really risen up the social tiers yet, they're still kinda open season. Not like Black. Black is set. Black is good to go. Is there a Black sounding nickname I could get from this? I only see Middle Eastern or Latinx—Latino—Latin—La—whatever. I don't know, I just have to stop being white.

The "Suicide Checklist" I keep on my wall mocks me (it's the several items already crossed out). Jumping off the roof just hurt my legs and apparently I have a preternatural immunity to sleeping pills, et cetera, et cetera. I grab a pen and cross out, "Fucking shoot yourself." You got me this time, Life, but next time I swear I'll win. This pride dissipates as there's nothing left on my list to try.

I recall that party is still on tonight and I, quite well alive, must attend.

Super sigh. I regret not putting all sixteen bullets in the clip. That probably would've added the required weight to stop the gun from jerking so hard.

[8]

I. Youth

Margot Hidlebacher. I could never stand her. Her or her brother, Braxton Hidlebacher.

As I park my car down the block, I remember Braxton actually died a few years back in a drunk driving accident. This thought comforts me. Probably shouldn't tell Margot.

Closing my door and beginning the trek to her house. What's really stupid is that I have to pass all the other cars as I go. Stangs. Jeeps. One Ferrari and two Saturns. How do they have cars this nice, are any of us even eighteen?

My car's, uh, it doesn't matter. What does matter is my fucking ear (or lack thereof). I don't think I can handle any more emotional strain tonight.

Whatever. I knock on Margot's front door. Why am I knocking? Just go in. I don't go in. I stand here and wait. I feel like a Jehovah's Witness. I feel like I need to make a joke about it, but I don't. There's no one coming. I go inside.

"Hey, that's Hijab Holdburn!" someone shouts.

I shoot myself in the head and this is the thanks I get.

"It doesn't even look like a Hijab!" I shout back.

I head for what I believe to be the kitchen—Christ on a Cross—like every house party, it's absolutely nothing like the movies. The mixers are all Costco brand. There's the token Party Dog just wandering around. You know how they are, Party Dogs? Someone's blasting The Doors as loud as they can for some reason. Kind of a waste, I doubt anyone here even knows who The Doors are—I mean, of course I do, but I don't tend to group myself up with, uh, people—and I don't just know them cuz of Jim Morrison, by the way. I listen to music.

[9]

I forget why I came in here (you know how that goes (and I'm in the kitchen now)). I try to consult that head voice I heard earlier. I think it responds, but it whispers into my right ear. What a scam.

Maybe I can knock the message towards my left ear? I pound my head. No luck. I pound it again in disdain. I make a mental note to never use that phrase again.

"Jerkin' on or jerkin' off?" someone behind me asks. Oh piss...

I turn around to see a girl. She's pretty. Really pretty. (I'm sure she has other characteristics, too, but I can't delve past her initial appearance cuz she's only said five words to me so far—sorry).

"Oh...you know..." I stammer.

"Oh."

"Yeah."

She ponders me. Or at least I like to think she does. Curly, I wanna say tangerine, hair (you don't see that too often) spills over her shoulders...wait, it's in a ponytail, why did I think it was spilling?

One of her eyebrows perks up. I think her pony tail perks up in tandem. "You like to have fun?"

I'm sure we have conflicting definitions of "fun," but I nod my head.

She reaches into her hoodie (points for wearing a hoodie, shows you're a real person) and reveals a McCormick bottle of ground turmeric.

At this point, everyone who I didn't notice was also in the kitchen I now notice as they sprint screaming out of there. They not like Indian food? I take my chances with Turmeric Girl.

[10]

A worn glass pipe materializes in her hand. She loads it with that delicate, orange powder. I feel like smoking this'll kill you. I open my mouth to warn her, but she's already inhaling—oh no, don't do that! That can't be safe, don't hurt yourse—!

—Wait, what?

She exhales and the party house's aroma becomes much more tolerable.

"Aw fuck, this shit's crazy, man."

For a brief moment her pupils turn rusty ochre. Or did I imagine it? I'll speculate later.

Turmeric Girl offers me the pipe.

I don't know what to say. I decide on, "Maybe later. I—ya know—I shouldn't."

She pulls it back. "'Maybe later?' You better. I'll be around."

I feel like she has a New Jersey accent (not a real one, but like a stereotyped one), but it's hidden underneath the layer of a surfer girl accent.

"What's your name, by the way?" I ask. This is my lead to the dialect questions.

"You're weird. And you know me, man."

"Which class? Algebra?"

"Algebra?"

"Algebra II?"

"Civics."

"Civics?"

"Your name's Jhaegar."

"Alright?"

"Mr. Ratschlatter loves *Game of Thrones* and dumps on your name like all the time."

"What does that have to do with it?"

[11]

"I think there's another Jhaegar on *Game of Thrones*."

"Is there?"

"Dunno. Don't watch, man. I, like, experience."

"Well, what's your name?"

"Tyrion."

"You're a girl."

She takes another intense, eye altering huff from her pipe. "No, Tyrion is the name of my favorite character from *Game of Thrones*. He's the knight."

"Tell me your name, please."

"Gwynevere. Clamshell."

"Well...you, uh, you have a nifty hoodie. It really shows that...you're human."

Gwynevere puffs into my face. "Cool."

She holds out the pipe to me again.

"It's 'maybe later' now. Try it."

I'm scared. I really want Gwynevere to like me. I really like Gwynevere to want m—I really—but it's seasoning, so I don't know. I examine her hoodie closer. Blue's Clues is on it. Jumpin' Christ, she's awesome!

Glancing down, I find the pipe in my hand. I also find it in my mouth. Gwynevere leans over and lights it. I also also also think Blue winks at me. I don't know why, but I do.

"Sweet apple pie, is that Rhaegar Holdburnt!?" some unseen harpy exclaims.

I turn before I can inhale. Not like I could inhale anyway as Gwynevere stashes the pipe back into her hoodie (lucky Blue ("Lucky Sue" by Men I Trust)). I assume this must signify some sort of red alert.

[12]

Margot Hidlebacher stands in the doorway.

Red alert, indeed.

"I'm so glad you came! Otherwise you'd be home all by your lonesome and I cou—"

—Her voice cuts out cuz I'm thinking about how I really shouldn't bring up her dead brother. Does Gwynevere know her brother's dead? Maybe I can trick her into bringing him up for me?

I glance over at Gwynevere to relay this request mentally as we seem to have that kind of connection. She's gone.

Margot steps closer to me now that I've become easier prey. Her mouth moves, yet I still can't hear her.

Double red alert.

"Come on Mar, leave the guy alone. You know he likes it that way." I've never heard this voice before. Who could—?

—Braxton Hidlebacher peers at me from behind his sister.

"Braxton? You're alive?"

Braxton winces and swipes a flat hand across his neck in a cutting motion which I don't find all that appropriate. He also shakes his head, but I feel like I'm the one who should be surprised—oh wait, Margot's sobbing now.

"Oh Lord," she cries, "Daxter!"

Braxton takes a step forward and holds her against his chest. His eyes drill shame into mine. Why's he upset?

"Why're you upset?" I ask.

[13]

"Don't you know, Rhaegar?!" Margot spits. "It's true, you don't care about anyone but yourse—"

—That's right, she had a second brother! Braxton's fine, he's in my Intro to Germanic Cooking class. Daxton's the one who's dead.

And jumpin' Christ—now is not a good time to play, "Riders on the Storm." This guy needs to chill with The Doors. If they would've played "Lucky Sue" like I said, I don't think Margot would be this up in arms. As long as they didn't play, "I Hope To Be Around." She probably wouldn't like that. Or "Pierre." Not that Daxton's name is Pierre, but that I could see similar lines of, uh, lines in their lives. Though Emma's basically singing Pierre should be happy with his life and people love him, he just needs to realize it. They might wanna go with the Live Session of "I Hope To Be Around," though, it'd add to the party vibe and maybe even add a sort of "Live" effect to the whole deal. Emma's so good. Why am I thinking about Men I Trust?

I wish Gwynevere was back.

I leave the remaining Hidlebacher clan sobbing. I'll go ruin another room.

**

"There's a somethin' on da road—and dis dog's a little chode." I flush the toilet and the water's thick and syrupy and I'm pretty sure it's blood. Am I hallucinating?

Didn't huff any of that turmeric, did I? There was definite interference. I try to locate my pants—they're on me already. Why am I in the bathroom, I don't even have to jerk off? Or maybe I don't cuz I already jerked off? What happened in the last five minutes?

[14]

At this point, the only conclusion I can arrive at is that Margot must've derided me and now she must pay.

GRANDPA J'S PARTY TIDBIT NO. 1

People who host house parties deserve to be punished and a simple way to participate in this ritual is to jank up (well, down) their water. The only guaranteed way to do this is to adjust the water pressure for their bathroom sink. The key word here is "adjust;" do NOT turn the water completely off. Why? Cuz once the host discovers their water's janked, they'll surmise, "Ah, my water is not working in my bathroom sink. Some rapscallion must've turned off my water in an effort to prank me. Consider me not pranked." One must simply ADJUST their water valve so the pressure is thoroughly reduced, but not altogether gone. Now, at THIS point the host'll surmise, "Ah, my water is not working in my bathroom sink. The pressure is rather low, but still obviously functional, so I know no rapscallions were in here and no foul play is afoot. I must enlist the aid of a plumber," at which point the plumber appears and promptly says, "What the fuck's your problem, asshole, the valve's only halfway open, check it first before you call next time, that'll be eighty dollars," and stomps the hell out of the host's now soiled home, leaving their coffers depleted and their emotional stability utterly destroyed.

I do just that. Margot'll rue this day. Also! While in her cabinet, I discover several bottles of sub market hand soap. "Sea Island Cotton," huh? I adjust her water pressure a tick lower for good measure.

"Look at you go," someone says.

Look at me go? I think.

[15]

There's a girl peeking at me from behind the shower curtain. She's not naked, she's just wearing fishnet everything. It's quite prevalent through her ripped jeans—but when her jeans stop being ripped around her crotch, I wonder if the fishnet continues around (or as part of) her underwear up to where it appears again around her naval or if there's two separate pieces. Three pieces actually for two legs. Unless the legs are conjoined aroun—

—She tilts her head. "What's your favorite anime?"

"*Evangelion.*" Piss. I'm too obvious.

"We might get along."

"What do you like?"

"*Free. Citrus. Showa Genroku Rakugo Shinju.* Bit of this and bit of that, yeah?" Her eyes flash at my hands. "What's the deal with the soap?"

I look down and realize I've started kneading the Sea Island Cotton hand soap into Margot's rug (it's labeled "Margot"). Ya know, it actually does smell like Sea Island—or at least what I'd image Sea Island Cotton to smell like. How do they do that?

"Sorry. Not the soap. I was messing with Margot's water. Don't tell her?"

"Why not?"

"She deserves it."

"For what?"

I think I'm turning red so I try to scoop up all the soap back into the bottles, line them up where I found them, eye Margot's water valve. It seems dejected.

"Cuz people get what they deserve and they deserve what they get. They need to know what people like us go through."

"Us?"

[16]

"Yeah, I mean, you in the…" I don't know what I'm saying. "In the shower and—they just don't get it and we have to show them. Make them understand. Ya know, us?"

"You believe yourself an Invisible?" She smirks. "Well Jhaegar, why don't you just change your life instead of ruining everyone else's?"

"You know my name?"

"Everyone here knows your name."

I believe I turn redder so I stick my head farther into the cabinet. I don't know how much longer I can keep this up as I'm running out of soap to collect and Margot's valve is beginning to give off a subtle, yet menacing aura. I gotta get out of here.

I stand. This girl's the same height as me. I'll have to imagine her taller next time.

She seems to hear this and backhands me across the cheek.

"You're cool for a creep," she almost (but doesn't) croon (or croons? Piss, I messed that one up).

"Thanks, uh…"

"Viviiviana Chunk. We dated for a year."

"Oh, alright. Of course. And how do you spell that again?"

"Viviiviana."

"Nifty."

Vivi-ivi-ana (does she put dashes in her name?) tests the bathroom sink. The water pressure is feeble, but not nonexistent. She (I'll just call her Vivi) smirks that smirk she did a minute ago. I like it more now.

"Pranked."

"Snitches get hospitalized," I reply.

[17]

"It's fine. Margot's a cunt anyway."

"Alright."

"I'm done with her and all her plaster pussy friends."

"Uh, what—?"

"—with jelly dripping down their thig—"

***

I'm drinking a Skeleton Key in the kitchen. By myself—I don't know if I went to the bathroom or not. I do know Vivi's not real, she can't have been there and I couldn't have been there either—I don't think, at least—I guess we'll find out soon enough, but I do open a stray phone book to the plumber page just to be helpful. Not a total monster.

Skeleton Keys are good. They're like—Halloween, but I drink them on Christmas, too. They are the drink to "unlock every door" as they say—mainly as I say. Sometimes I drink them when I'm really sad. Drinking them also makes me really sad.

COUSIN J'S SKANDALOUS SKELETON KEY

Decent amount of Bourbon (cheapest)

More than a kind of a splash of St. Germaine

A big ol' squirt of lime juice

A can of Ginger Beer

Those things I forget the names of

Step 1. Combine the Bourbon, St. Germaine, and lime juice in whatever you have with ice or not.

[18]

Step 2. Fill it to the top with the beer.

Step 3. Sprinkle the whatevers on top. I wanna say "succulents," but I know that's not right.

Step 4. Drink.

Step 5. Drink two more, then text Vivi and let her know she was the one that got away and you still have feelings for her.

Step 6. Make a Tinder account.

Step 8. Get frustrated when nobody likes you, drink two more Skeleton Keys, stalk a young male Instagram Influencer, copy and paste their pictures into your profile, instantly get a bunch of women to like you, then get real sad cuz they only like your façade and not you, never, never you.

Step 2. Make a Bumble account.

Step 3. Delete Bumble the next day when post-drunk clarity arrives.

I traverse a narrow hallway—wait, what?—painted with what appears to be raccoon feces. Some partygoers still appear cognizant and I ask them if they've seen Buggins around. They ask me why I wanna know and if I wanna suck his "fairy cock." Why do I bother? There's no way I'll ever find Buggins in this mess anyway. Did he even come to this? Was he invited?

Wait, was I invited?

I dash into a room to recapitulate. To recalcitrate? Reconcentrate? I try to gather my—

"—Hey what the Hell?" someone shouts. "The water in here sucks!"

I grin. Vivi grins, too. Apparently she's standing next to me.

"Hey creep," she says. "You gave me a pretty sick idea."

[19]

She pats me on the head like a child and skips out of the room. I hope she does something nuts.

Also. There's a TV on in here and it's playing this show, right? I'd notate it, but I find this format restricting—well, not restricting. This format is actually quite limitless. Here, just—it doesn't matter.

FUN TIMES ON 5ᵀᴴ STREET

a new Sitcom on TBS

EXT. FOOD LINE   DAY

A line of HOMELESS PEOPLE wait for morning handouts from a large food truck. Among them are SHIT DUDE and FRIEND.

    SHIT DUDE
Bro, I really gotta take a shit.

    FRIEND
Settle down. We're almost there.

    SHIT DUDE
Can you hold my spot, just, fuck, never mind, man—

    FRIEND
—God I think they're running out.

    SHIT DUDE
If they run out, I will literally kill myself.

    FRIEND
That's a bit intense…

    SHIT DUDE
I REALLY gotta drop a load, man…

    FRIEND
How? Aren't you starving? Do you even have anything to get rid of?

                         SHIT DUDE
              Don't patronize me, I—

                          FRIEND
              —Oh, finally we're next.

They step up to the truck…

                          FRIEND
              Good morning, two please—

                      CHARITY WORKER
              —I apologize, we just ran out.

                         SHIT DUDE
              Well…it must be done.

Shit Dude pulls out a SAWN-OFF SHOTGUN, points it at his
chest, and BLOWS HIMSELF AWAY…

…which paints a stain upon the food truck composed of blood
and HUMAN FECES.

BUGGINS taps me on the shoulder.

                         JHAEGAR
              Buggins, you're here!

He shoots me one of his looks. I call it a "look" just to be nice (Buggins has no eyes).

"I'm not here," he says.

And he's gone.

"Hey, aren't you Jhaegar Holdburn?" someone asks.

Three, dare I say "decent," appearing boys drink huddled around a complex stereo

system. I had presumed the controllers of the music in this house to be assholes (presumed, not

assumed, did I use "assume" wrong earlier?) based upon their musical preferences. Now that I

see one of the boys insert a Steve Martin and the Steep Canyon Rangers CD into the stereo (yes,

[21]

yes, Steve Martin plays banjo with a bluegrass band and yes, yes, I know, Steve Martin is very talented) I KNOW they're assholes.

The Inserter meets my eyes and says, "Yeah, it's him. Hey man, can you help us out? Margot said you're really good with music?"

But they can't be total assholes if they're willing to learn. Assumed—presumed, uh, supposed wrong, I did.

"Yeah," I proclaim, "I know a little bit of—of a 'this' and a 'that.' What seems to be the...trouble?"

"Huh?" they say as one.

"What?"

"We just, uh, we just thought we'd take a 'famous-actor-becomes-a-music-hack-after-their-career-ends-and-leads-a-phony-band' kick. We already got Steve and now Ronnie here claims the Rangers were a legitimate band at first and Steve just—"

"—Steve even said they're not his band, but that he's their celebrity—"

"—Sure, and do you have any other ideas?"

I think. I find answers. I contemplate not telling them.

But...I've been waiting for this for years.

"Have any of you ever heard of DSBM?" I ask. "Not BDSM. DSBM?"

"...Huh?" they say as one again.

Perfect.

"Well I'm glad you said that, gentleman. DSBM, or Depressive Suicidal Black Metal, is an oft forgot and too many times ignored subgenre of Black Metal, which itself is an oft forgot and too many times ignored subgenre of Metal. DSBM bands are usually from the dark and

[22]

mysterious parts of Scandinavia and their music contains heavy plodding riffs, excruciating screams, and messages from the Devil spoken in clear and concise Norwegian."

"I thought they were from Scandinavia?" says Ronnie. I can see why his name is Ronnie.

"Alright. Think the Swedish Bikini Team, but they're stranded in the mountains, have to eat each other, and are being chased by blood starved Wendigoes."

"That's a different culture."

"They're hardcore. Now...there is a clear distinction between what is and is not 'hardcore'—even 'dark' or 'sad.' Billie Eilish is 'sad.' Billie Eilish is 'sad girl looking sad in a sad place doing sad things.' Not very true to form. Varg Vikerness on the other hand—

—A massive explosion rocks the house. Screams and wails (lesser than Varg, but more than wannabees like Metallica) ensue and waves of flame seem to pulsate from the kitchen. I make out the same voice that complained about the water.

"Oh man, not the gas lines, too!" but I think he dies in the second house rocking explosion.

More screams, wails, fire, yada yada, then Margot's body crashes through a wall and slams right into the stereo system. She does her own screams, wails, yada yada (better than Metallica, but still can't touch Varg) and we all watch her burn to death as Steve Martin's rendition of "King Tut" distorts, breaks, and grows even more malefic.

I guess now her AND her brother are dead.

***

But yeah, this house is definitely a goner.

[23]

I don't see many others standing on the lawn with me. My fingers cross in my pocket as I hope the human gene pool was thinned out this night. Whatever. I click my feet and spin around as the safety of my car beckons. Ya know, this is why I don't go to these things much. Just nothing but trouble—

"—Look at ME go."

Sigh…I turn.

Viviiviana (covered in ash and burn scars I might add) grins back at me.

"I followed your advice. It was pretty sick, right?"

Daxter/Baxter/Whateverthehell is screaming about his sister so I can't quite hear what Vivi says next. The growing inferno reminds me I have nerve damage on my feet from taking scalding hot showers. It kind of hurts to walk, but, ya know…it's worth it to feel good for five minutes (yeah, yeah, yeah, I know, I'm so "edgy," right? Just let me take a shower). I ask Vivi to repeat herself. I love the way she tal—

"—Yeah, her place's done as fuck."

"I actually think you killed her, Vivi."

"Oh. Okay."

Gurgles of either erratic or sporadic laughter spill from her mouth. I gotta get better with words. My head's so—it's—medicine—no, ya know, it doesn't work—just dumb and just—it's sporadic. It's sporadic laughter.

She crooks her thumb to the side.

"Mind if I gallivant into the night?"

"You do you."

She gallivants into the night.

[24]

I've never gallivanted before.

I hope I see her again.

But now that I'm in my car, I can think and drive and re-review my stance on DSBM.

So, this whole "Mental Illness" nonsense is made up. It's a form of social engineering created by the ruling class to manipulate the lower classes, much like politics, religion, ya know? You have people like Billie Eilish (nothing against Billie, I'm sure she smells good) who are…sigh, they're not even "fashionably sad" cuz that would imply they at least, at some point, reach "sad." What I'm saying is they're never really "sad." Their "sadness" is an illusion. Someone like Varg, though, that's not "sad." That's "despair" or "bleak" or "anguished" or any other term across the spectrum of "sad"—and this constant sensitivity regarding so called "Mental Illnesses" and what even constitutes one (they'll tell you it's everything) becomes more ridiculous each year. Billie was a teen girl who cut herself. Aww cute, Baby's first self-harm? Join the club.

Varg burned down a church. And murdered a guy. THAT'S a "Mental Illness."

And not even that, he just thinks differently. If these so called schools are gonna say remedial learners just "Think differently," then I "Think differently" enough to say it should apply to other aspects of life. DSBM is that life, my "alternative facts" if you will (sigh, I've switched from parenthesis to quotation marks). You see, when—

—fucking asshole cutting me off—

—when you get the…the…

Fuck. Fuck. Fuck. Fuck me. Fuck me. Fuck me with a pitchfork fucking dick, what was I thinking? Gun. Hospital. Ear. Party. House. Margot. Brother. Dead. Vivi. No Turmeric Girl first. Vivi. Gwynevere. More Margot. Doors. Emma. Steve Martin. DSBM. John Belushi. He had a

[25]

legitimate group, though. House burned down. It was Vivi. Other brother. Oh, Buggins was there!

Buggins Willcox. I met him in the fourth grade. We sat next to each other during April. Ya know, how they do that thing where they switch everyone all the time? So I only had a little time with him before it was fifth grade and we didn't have fifth grade together, but we were in the same gym class in ninth grade (wait, note from the thinker, it was Cardio Fitness). Walking. And that's actually not a joke. Walking is a gym class—and we met again after all these years and I complemented his shoes and he complemented mine (remember, he's blind), but he said he was confident they were cool looking judging from how my voice sounded. He said I was commanding and bold. Boy, did he know! But yeah, we hung out all the time and played Blazblue and P4 Ultimax. His Waifu's Rise and, I mean, that's a fair choice. Mine's Yukiko cuz I just love that more classic vibe if that's what you'd call it—that's certainly what I'd call it— though I did cheat with Rise, but if you can't cheat in a Persona game, then where can you? And Rise was crying! Usually it's a "friendzone" or "no-friendzone" decision, but Rise was literally sobbing and it's like, "Comfort her or don't," and how I am supposed to not? What do you want me to do, Atlus, why do you force me to make these—?

—My head starts hurting again. I forget where I am. I forget where I'm driving. How I'm driving. I just sit back and watch myself for the rest of the night.

***

I can't get closer to her. Why can't I get closer to her? Why isn't it working? I'm sprinting as fast as I can.

[26]

A dream isn't just sound and vision. A dream is a mind state. In my dream, I love her. She loves me. And I'm chasing her. Not in that, "I'm gonna axe murder you," kind of way. In that, "Let's mess around and have fun and be cute like in a movie," lovers kind of way. I'm chasing her cuz I love her and I know in my mind state she so very badly wants to be caught.

We're in a carnival. Or a mall. A carnival mall, I don't know. I can never tell. Somewhere with lots of lights where one can easily become lost—like an underground mall. With no ceiling and also in Brazil. Marissa Nadler's playing on the pissy, 80s sounding mall stereo. She's white, not Brazilian. What was Brazilian music called? It has a special name—at least I think. Whatever. You know you have a Marissa Nadler album when all you have to do is read the track list and you're already depressed. "Lover Release Me." "Interlocking." "All Out of Catastrophes." Jumpin' Christ.

Why does no one ever chase me? She stops running. Stops under a canopy of old lightbulbs. A vendor asks if she wants to buy a falafel, but I don't think she hears him. She just kind of crouches down in the dirt for some reason. She's everything. Radiant.

Dreams are an entire new reality. "What's more real than dreams?" asks Andrei Tarkovsky. I wish I knew, Andrei. We spend so much of our time in our dream states. Why does no one ever chase me? Does she chase me in her dream state?

Though she's stopped moving entirely I still can't get closer to her. I might even be getting farther, as if the clutches of "reality" are dragging me back with my shirt collar. Let 'em have my shirt. I bet I'm jacked underneath. I'm not. I can't even win here. Now I'm getting pulled back by the skin of my neck.

She waits there in the light. She knows I'm not getting closer. Knows I'm not coming. Knows I'll never be there with her. But she doesn't hate me. She could never hate me, she could never hate anyone. There's nothing but grace in her heart. It makes her perfect.

Yet there is something growing in her. A feeling. I can sense it, though I'm halfway across the carnival mall. Not that I need to sense it right now. I knew it before we got here. I knew it when we went on our first date. When we first held hands and kissed. People just give you *The Look*. Sometimes even *That Voice*.

In my dream I'm from New Jersey. I don't know why, I guess I like their accents. I speak with one, albeit one that's probably stereotypical and offensive to those who actually live in New Jersey. I've never even seen *Jersey Shore*. I should say to somebody, "Ehh, I'm waulkin' 'ere!" and see what they do. They'd probably hurt me. All I can think ab—please stop—

—All I can think about is her pussy. You usually don't think of girls like that as even having vaginas. Kind of like how boys in boy bands don't have penises. Something so unsanitary. Is she ever horny—no she's not, she—and what kind of panties she's wearing right now. She's wearing a skirt or jeans or something so I could easily find out. She wouldn't notice if I just—if I just brushed my hand and—just so unfair to her. To all of them. They didn't ask for this. I hope I never catch her. I hope she starts running again, but she just waits under the light in between the falafel guy and the woman with the shooting gallery. I wish I was just shot. But they're making me run.

I run and I run and I never reach her. She waits for me. And I never come. And she's disappointed.

[28]

***

Of course I'm the first one here. Always the first or the last, whichever is more embarrassing. What's really stupid is that our "Question of the Day" already has a few answers submitted. "Moon Landing: Real or Fake?" screams from the chalkboard. Nine marks have been struck under "Real" and only three for "Fake." I decide to have some fun, erase "Moon Landing," and replace it with "The Holocaust." I'm not racist, I just like a good bit of entertainment, ya know? I love to watch civilization break down. "Anomy" they call it. I think.

Whatever. I take my seat and endeavor to recreate Post Malone's face on the top of my desk. One by one, other students filter into the classroom. Much astonishment to be had at my new Question of the Day and (unsurprisingly enough, if you ask me) several students add strikes under "Fake." As a matter of fact, two students go so far as to erase strikes under "Real" beforehand. Alas, we end at an even fifteen to fifteen. Mx. Sacs will have to be the tiebreaker.

That is, Mx. VULVA Sacs (I didn't make the name) and I hear her approaching now—she's still a long way off, you can sense her by the ripples of water lapping up against your feet (it's water). It's very much like hearing thunder and counting the seconds in between to determine how far the storm is? Here we just count the, uh, the water pulses and when they get pretty frequent we know to simmer down.

Gwynevere Clamshell turns to me (I guess she's in this class) and offers her pipe. Turmeric fumes wisp out of it and swirl towards my nose. I perform a shuto block and send the fumes swirling towards another student. They enter her nose and her eyes immediately melt and run down her face. I believed she voted for "Real," so "Fake" triumphs after all.

"Come on, man," Gwynevere says to me. "All the kool kids are doing it."

[29]

"Why did I get the feeling you spelled 'cool' with a K?"

"Girls will like you."

"No, they won't."

"Don't be such a narc."

"And girls only like me for my wit and empathy."

"Change that and drink turmeric."

"Drink?"

"Huff."

She holds the pipe out to me. I get a split second impression the pipe is conscious. Gwynevere nods and I feel that impression grow stronger.

"Ugh, is that a weed!?" sneers some goblina.

Snowelda Roach. She's even worse than Margot Hidlebacher. She has two dead brothers (wait, doesn't Margot have that now as well?) and shoots Gwynevere with her trademark arms-crossed-eyebrows-furrowed-I'm-not-mad-I'm-just-dissapointed glare.

Gwyn's too strong (I'm gonna call her "Gwyn," I think we're friends). She counters with a double turmeric blast. Snow dodges them both (she's fast, that one) and they sail past her into one of her Puritan Club cronies. One dodges, but the other—well—not. Sigh, pretty sure she voted for "Fake."

The first turmeric blast's still in the game—gone rogue—it bounces off the wall and comes back around towards Snow. Snow's hair and skin and just everything on her's shiny and expensive and as the blast approaches her, the shine hits it with the look-if-you-get-any-closer-I'm-gonna-call-the-police-and-when-they-show-up-who-are-they-gonna-believe-you-or-me grin. The turmeric blast dissipates. This one goes to The Roach.

[30]

"You may dispense of that right now, Gwynevere," gurgles Snowelda. Jumpin'—okay, I have an issue—maybe—she didn't really "gurgle," she just said it regula—

"—ou don't even know, Snowelda?" replies Gwyn.

I tend not to enjoy conflict, so I take this moment to notice the increasingly frequent waves of "water" smashing against my feet.

Boris Glomgaaker (he's our scout), soaked and heaving, pokes his head through the classroom door.

"She's coming!"

There's a joke in there somewhere, but before I can find it, Mx. Sacs (sorry, "Mx." is cuz she's like gender fluid or something—I don't know, you tell me) plunges her hands into Boris's chest and rips him in half. She steps forward through a cloud of blood as the "water" at her feet begins to dissolve the Boris pieces like acid. Oh Boris. You fool.

All of us students raise our feet as far from the floor as possible. Mx. Sac's heels click (splish) clack (splash) as she stalks towards the front of the room. She opens both hands and drags her screeching nails down the chalkboard as the muscles in her back fold and churn underneath her (rather thin) blouse.

Mx. Sacs turns to us.

Snowelda raises her hand.

Mx. Sacs begrudgingly nods and the water around Snowelda's desk subsides long enough for her to stand and narc on everybody—also—uh, she's wearing, like, I think TWO sweaters? Why? She usually wears her Puritan Club sweater, but she has another sweater over it now. Still a Puritan Club one I guess, but it's an older one back when they were just called the "Yuppy Asshole Club." Haha kidding—I, uh, I really don't know—it's definitely a sweater but—

[31]

"—If I may say, Mx. Sacs," whines Snowelda, "I would like to start off by stating that my girls here, as well as myself, had absolutely nothing to do with this—this—this"—insert rich white crying—"this abominable 'Question of the Day.' And if I find myself nauseated so, I cannot imagine how one such as Yechiel may feel."

Snow leans slightly as to reach (yeah) Yechiel, our token Jew—sorry—token Jewish Person—I'm not anti-Semitic. I HATE hate—and conformist nutcases like Snow—apparently Yechiel does, too, as he cringes under her faint, but hellish, touch.

"And how do you feel, Yechiel?" Mx. Sacs purrs.

Yechiel rises to respond (but cuz Mx. Sacs doesn't recall the water for him (wonder why) he has to stand on his chair).

"F-f-fine, Mx. Sacs. Just fine."

"Fabulous, then you won't mind cleaning up dear Deidre and Demiah?"

Yechiel gulps. Big time.

Other students lean back in their chairs as to give Yechiel room to hop between desks. He gets to the desk of the first girl who got turmeric-ed (Demiah I think) and pushes her body into the water. That nonsense eats her right up. Yech then hops over to the Puritan Club girl (I said the first one was Demiah cuz Deidre sounds richer, I genuinely don't know them—but not like it matters, who they gonna complain to?) and pushes her into the water as well.

Ope! (Sorry, from the Midwest).

"Ope!" several other students echo my thoughts as Yechiel slips on some turmeric residue and dives headfirst into the water. The water doesn't eat him as fast as it did the others, though...yeah, it's substantially slower and more agonizing...on the bright side, he seems a lot more resigned to it.

[32]

Mx. Sacs groans as she takes her seat. It's hard to call it a groan—it's more like a moan, but—ya know—she sits down and shakes her head.

"Was he for 'Real' or 'Fake,' does anyone remember?"

Snowelda (who never actually sits back down, she just kind of stands there the rest of the class waiting to answer more questions. I suppose she saves more energy that way. Also, I definitely used "suppose" correctly this time) and yeah, my tangent was a little long there and I forget what she's doing again. Gwyn nudges me.

"Man, just try it. It'll, like, change your whole life."

She holds her glass pipe out to me along with a baggie of turmeric and I once again get the feeling that—see! It just moved! It's—!

—Gwyn fills it up for me. Mx. Sacs doesn't notice cuz Snow's going off about something or other. That's how it usually goes. The teacher always has one or two kids they listen to and everyone else is left to fend for themselves. Tam Lin and Lam Tin sit in the corner (on a desk, don't worry) and make out. Tiresias Tyrone Tyreke Washington Lincoln Roosevelt III shuffles several papers around and writes. Seems rather focused. Like, too focused. Like, someone should tell a counselor who'll inevitably ignore them and say, "Oh, I'm sure they're just kidding," focused. Oh well, who cares? Biff Chubster flirts—tries to flirt—with some of The Puritans. Oh Biff. You dog.

Gwyn's pipe's in my hand. She smiles at me. I dislike calling smiles "warm" cuz there's so many better words to describe a smile like that, but then again the more I think about it, there're really not, are there? What would I call it? An "everything" smile? She smiles everythingly to me. Everything-ingly? Everything-like? She still flaunts her Blue's Clues hoodie. She smiles and it's everything to me.

[33]

I take a huff of turmeric.

***

—nobody really likes me. And shut up, I'm not being an Edgelord—I'm sure nobody likes anybody. They just like perceptions.

Who else considers that? Who else sits down and thinks after a losing streak on Mortal Kombat or after chugging six Skeleton Keys or even after you've been married for thirty years and your wife tells you she's leaving you for another man and you realize "For No One" is actually about you and Paul McCartney was an unabashedly emotionally intelligent twenty-year-old? Is it just me?

What I'm trying to say is no one likes the real anybody. That's not to say everyone's a phony (get it?) who continues on with some sort of façade, Jungian or—I guess, not. It's simply the fact people only see what they wanna see.

For instance, my Mom loves me (as I'm sure most moms love their spawn). But does she love ME? Or does she love the me that exists inside her mind? Her own personal Jhaegar? If I rob a liquor store, is it cuz I'm a crook or cuz I "Lost my way?" If I do well on an exam, is it cuz I showed up to class and studied or cuz I've "Always been such a gifted boy?"

This is also not to say I'm somehow elevated above my peers and (well—I mean—but really, though) and I'm immune to such a phenomenon. I'm not. Cuz I don't see the real, "My Mom." I mean, piss, I don't even know her real name! I see her as "Mom" and only as "Mom." It never crosses my mind that she has her own struggles, that she has—or had at one point—her own dreams and aspirations that are now crushed cuz I have no Dad (wait, did I ever have a

[34]

Dad?) and she has to "love" me twice as hard and—basically, I don't consider the possibility that my Mom is human. And well, why should I? She's "Mom," my parental unit who pays the rent and supplies the kitchen cupboard with Apple Jacks. What more does she need to be?

If I were to consider her an actual human, that is where I believe society (sorry for using the "S-word") would collapse. Society would give in to anomy (aw yeah, I get to use "anomy" again) and social norms, cultural norms, everything would go to shit. We all exist upon the personal presumptions that all other characters in our lives fit into a certain station without opportunity to be any different than their station allows cuz them being "different" would actually lead to them being similar to oneself.

You know what, Gwyn? I'm gonna do it—I'm gonna—I'm gonna recommend you a book. It's called "No Longer Human" by Osamu Dazai (or "Disqualified From Being a Human Being" if you're Japanese). It's an honest book, one of the few honest ones out there. The story is, uh…it's, uhhh…coincidently, it's—it's a good book. Read it, Gwyn. I'll give you my copy, just ignore all the circled parts. Those are the parts—I'll buy you your own, that way you can circle your own circled parts and not see mine—or just don't damage the book—well, not "damage." You could say it enhances the original reader's experience by highlighting key areas of appeal and—just take it. Here you go—forget it. Just—I'll just rip out the pages you won't like—

***

I exhale.

[35]

Gwyn stares into my eyes. Intent. Deep. Special, I think. The turmeric fumes from my breath curl up into her nostrils, but her eyes don't melt out of her skull. She must be used to it.

Then the glass pipe bites me.

Yup.

I drop the pipe and clasp my now bleeding hand. My sudden yelp draws the attention of the other students, Mx. Sacs, and the somehow still talking Snowelda Roach.

"Jhaegar Holdburn," Mx. Sacs starts, "please quit your yelling, we have yet to emasculate you today."

But I can't stop yelling. Mostly cuz the glass pipe (Glass Pipe from now on) cuz Glass Pipe manages to hiss, leap up, and bite me again—this time on my neck! I swat it away, but it comes right back. I try for a shuto swipe, find I'm too slow, and then find Glass Pipe undoing my ear bandage.

"Oh shit, that pipe's undoing Hijab Holdburn's hijab!" some pond scums shouts.

I spin to face them.

"It's not a hijab, a hijab is clearly—ah OW!"

Glass Pipe bites my ear/ex-ear face lump thing.

Gwyn shoots to her feet and rushes Glass Pipe. The water doesn't affect her (she's wearing Periwinkle galoshes (Periwinkle is the cat from Blue's Clues, this woman is perfect)) and I think I really like this girl. Did we ever date? Will we? Isn't that Vivi girl in this class—?

—Glass breaks. I'd quote "Breaking Glass" by David Bowie, but I don't think it fits. Glass Pipe seems to have escaped through the window while I was busy thinking about Blue's Clues. Good riddance. I make what I believe to be a congratulatory turn towards—

[36]

—Gwyn, skin covered in tiny glass specs, lies dead on the floor. The water soaks her clothes. Her body dissolves before my eyes. The last thing I see of her before she goes is Blue.

"Hey," someone says, "didn't she vote for 'Real'?"

Mx. Sacs erases a chalk mark under "Real."

"It appears the Holocaust was fake after all," she moans.

I gaze down at the water where Gwynevere once was. How is she gone, I—I just met her. Why did she have to go? Why did she have to leave?

She died trying to help me—this is my fault. If I weren't here, she wouldn't be dead. I'm the one who got in the way, I killed her. Somewhere else in the school, "For No One" starts to play. The sound is muted through the walls, but I still hear Paul blaming me for her death. Well, not blame—warning me that maybe her death was good and it's fine I killed her. It's okay, right? Thing's wouldn't have worked out with her. They never do. With anyone. She'd never really like me. She just wanted someone to smoke with. Good. I'm glad she's (this is my fault) dead and she's not coming back no matter how much I smoke cuz that's what I'll do. I take her baggie of turmeric. Who even sells these? Did she fill her own bag? You'd have to buy like four of those little McCormick things to fill one of these. Just like Paul McCormick and this fucking song. Why's he named after a spice?

Stop distracting yourself

I don't know what's happening. I can't think. I can't think. I pick up my pen. I write my name. I see it's "Jhaegar Holdburn." I am Jhaegar Holdburn. I am Jhaegar Holdburn. I listen to Mx. Sacs's lesson. I take notes. I write. I glance over at Snowelda. I write more cuz I shouldn't

[37]

glance at her. I glance at Gwynevere—where she was—I killed—shut up—I killed her cuz now she's dead. I set down my pen. I rub my eyes. I comb through my hair. I feel my head. I see blood in my hand.

Is this her blood? I know it's mine, but it could be hers. In a metaphorical sense. Every time I hurt myself, I hurt others—says my counselor—says my—sometimes I feel—I'm no longer strong enough to hold up my head and my face crashes to my desk. I didn't finish my Post Malone drawing. I turn my head and look at the others. No one notices. This must not be real. I think that one kid's gonna kill me later, but his name's too long to remember—but it's fine. It's fine. Jhaegar deserves to die. Both him and the Jhaegar inside that kid's mind. I'm sure I did something in there to deserve it, too.

Sometimes I feel like I can't control myself, like I'm not me—and not in a *Stranger than Fiction* (2006) or *Macbeth* (*Throne of Blood* (1957)) kind of way—in an "I'm sick" kind of way.

I lift my head to stare at Vulva Sacs.

"Ohh," she purrs, "it appears young Jhaegar finds this rather titillating."

"Tinselating?"

"Yes, for our field trip next week to the travelling French Revolution Museum? Hmm? You began touching yourself once I mentioned the guillotine."

I look down. My hand's in my pants. Piss.

"Historically accurate," she adds. "Preserved."

That's it! That's my problem!

All of my suicide attempts so far have had at least some sort of margin for error: missing my shot, not taking enough pills, lighting the wrong house on fire. But this, huh ho baby, this! The pride of the guillotine rests in the fact that it is unequivocally fatal to all its victims. One

[38]

chop and that's it. I don't see how it could fail (though the guillotine is also unequivocally fair and I'm not sure I deserve—) —shut up. That's what I'll do. I'll sneak back to the guillotine after we've already passed it and expel Jhaegar G. Holdburn from this mortal plane once and for all.

I stand up (feet on desk) and raise my hand.

"We're already speaking, Jhaegar." Don't always have to be so rude, Mx. Sacs.

"Can I go to the bathroom, please?"

Her eyebrows furrow. Due to her skin's high moisture content, this makes an unpleasant squishing sound.

"Jumpin' Chri—MAY I go to the bathroom—what do you even care? You just teach history!"

Mx. Sacs's eyes show a predatory gleam. The water in the room stills, almost as if it's waiting…or about to drag me down to the Abyss.

She raises a hand and the water subsides to form a path out. I leap down from my desk, knock over Snowelda (it's fine, don't worry, I'm sure she'll be okay), and dash out of the classroom.

And yeah, I guess my hand's still in my pants.

***

School's out and I'm thinking about zucchini.

I just crave it—even though it has no taste—well, that's a misconception. It's like how some people say water has no taste—or if they say it has a taste, they simply say it tastes like water. To me, that's incorrect. Water doesn't have a conventional taste, per se, water tastes like

[39]

"fresh." I think zucchini tastes like fresh as well, rather forest fresh—an earthy fresh to water's watery—no, I mean—airy, mercurial fresh. Yeah.

Whatever. What if my name was Zucchini? That'd be cool I think. Zucchini Holdburn may not work, but Zucchini Paganini would be a different story. People would say I sold my soul to the Devil for that amazing name (Paganini joke). My friends would call me Zooch. I'd leave notes for girls from "Z." I find the letter Z to be an erotic one. All those—all those quick turns, ya know?

Buggins finds me (I don't know how) lounging on the school green contemplating my zucchini future. I tell him all about zucchini and what a versatile ingredient it can become. As a matter of—wait, wasn't I—I was gonna do something…I was…uh…I shrug my shoulders. Oh well, right?

I pull out my recipe book to share with Buggins.

COUSIN J'S NICE-ADILLAS (Que? They're "nice quesadillas" cuz they're vegan and make you look smooth and sensitive)

Some tortillas, white, but it doesn't have to be about color

Numerous handfuls of shredded cheese (size of hand depends on size of tortilla)

Those quesadilla spices

A jala(hollaholla)peño

And a gob ton of zucchini!

Step 1. Put a tortilla down on a plate. You should also heat up your quesadilla skillet.

Step 2. Get a bunch of that zucchini on there (diced first, yeah) and get some (sliced for this, I should've said before) hollahollapeño. Keep the seeds in for extra flavor.

[40]

Step 3. Sprinkle the spices over it.

Step 4. Use your hands of indeterminate size to disperse cheese.

Step 5. Cook that little guy in your skillet and you're good to go!

Buggins looks (I mean—turns his head to me, sorry. Sorry!) and mumbles—wait, no— he's performing sign language. Also, is "performing" the right word? But strange enough, I understand it perfectly.

"Yes? And what of the other tortilla? Do you not put one on top, Jhaegar?" Buggins signs.

"Buggins, you're deaf?" I sign back.

"What?"

At this point I find myself lost and, to be honest, rather defeated. I sift through my book searching for more zucchini-based reci—

—Oh, piss. Oh, piss. It's becoming drastically snobbier out he—

"—Jhaegar Holdburn and Buggins Willcox. What new deviancies are you hatching today?"

Snowelda and the Puritans (also the name of her Latin fusion band) tower before us— well, before me—could you call it "towering" for Buggins if he can't see them? How do they qualify this stuff in their minds? What words do they use?

I stick out my jaw in stalwart defiance of Snowelda. Not today, Institutionalized Catholicism, not today.

"Hey Snowelda, why is it that I can't tell if your name means you're from Eastern Europe...or South Central Los Angeles?"

[41]

I nudge Buggins and sign him my sick burn so he can get it on the fun.

He giggles and signs back, "Got 'em."

I giggle, too, but then I pause. Contemplate. My head rocks back a few inches.

"Buggins," I say aloud while also signing, "how can you see this?"

Buggins sits there motionless.

"If you must know," Snowelda eventually replies, "my parents blessed me with my name to keep me ethnically ambiguous. Not something someone like you could ever understand."

"Oh yeah? And what do you mean, 'someone like me?'"

She guffaws (sorry, word of the day).

"You're white."

I gesture at her. The Puritans rolls their eyes.

"We're Allies, Jhaegar," she says, clicking her tongue. "There's a difference."

"You live in the most gentrified part of town!"

"Oh, please."

"Your family's rich as piss. Don't you have a maid?"

"Yeah."

I gesture to her again. More eye rolls.

"Jhaegar, she's Asian. Not even Chinese."

"You do realize there are other minorities besides Bla—"

—She does that thing where she raises her eyebrows, eyes kinda bulge, tilts her head to the side and has a really smug grin as if to state, "Oh yeah? Whatever you say," that people like her often give. People like HER!

"You know, Jhaegar, maybe if you tried—"

[42]

"—I just wanted to show him my recipes and then you had to..." I hold up my index finger at her. "Wait, I was gonna kill myself—at the—at the—at the carnival thing!"

"French Revolution!" she yells as if I just called her mother a whore. I think I'll do that sometime.

"Your mother's a whore!"

Snow cold cocks me. Then does it again. And again! (Is it still called "cold cocking" at this point? Maybe "hot cocking?" (Jumpin' Christ, Jhaegar...)) Buggins is no help, he probably doesn't even know what's going on.

She grabs me by my shirt collar and holds me two feet off the ground. Whispers:

"Listen here you Godless sack of shit, I swear by the blood of my ancestors that if you ever insult my mother again I will bury you right then and there, graveyard fucking dead. You hear, Jhaegar? Did you hear that? Or are you like your brainless fucking friend?"

"Isn't mocking him," I stutter, "kind of like mocking a Black person?"

Snow spins me around, locks my arms, and German suplexes me across the yard.

This is where I'd usually go on a rant about the importance of WWE, but—well—I don't know. I've been different lately. Strange and sordid thoughts, ya know?

"Jhaegar Holdburn," Snow seems to condemn, "I can only stand and shiver in anticipation for Him to punish you for your perverted and heretical fascination with death. Life is a sacred blessing and all that you do spits in the face of the one Almighty."

I squirm about on the ground. Sit up and massage my spine.

"Well—well—you—!"

"—I what?"

"You don't know anything about me!"

[43]

I watched this YouTube video once about the seemingly endless amount of times people say, "You don't understand!" or, "You don't get it, do you?" in movies so now every time I say something like that I throw up a bit in my mouth.

I actually just throw up on my shirt instead…

Snow rolls her eyes. I wanna call her mother a whore again, but my ear (I don't know what to call it so I'm just gonna keep calling it my ear) bleeds through my bandages (how'd I get new bandages?). Trickles of blood patter on my shoulder.

"Good," she says. "Hopefully that should teach you a lesson. I can only pray that it gets worse."

The Puritans bow and put their hands together. Snow continues:

"And by the way, you do realize that your plan to take your life during the field trip won't work? There are, gee I don't know, FACULTY there! Who will be watching us! Watching YOU! And making sure no STUDENTS try KILLING THEMESELVES! Or did you not think that far ahead? Or did you ask Wilcox here if it'd work and he kind of twitched a little and you presumed it was a 'yes'?"

She definitely used "presume" correctly. Damn that Snowelda! Damn her to Hell! Why don't her ears bleed?!

Because she is not worth it

I rise to my feet and point at her (dramatically, I think).

[44]

"You just don't understand and you're upset you never will!" Barf. "And—and—maybe if you weren't so IGNORANT, you would lead a happier life and wouldn't find it necessary to ruin others."

"The only one ruining your life is you, Holdburn."

I like to think I roar in fury, but it's more like a pouty "Myeh" sound while I clench my fists. I grab Buggins by the hand (jumpin' Christ, I forgot he has metal hooks for hands (they used to call him Buccaneer Bugs)) and we storm off.

Mom's in the kitchen making something weird—some kind of Indian latte. I sense turmeric inside so I steer clear. Don't wanna get mixed up in that. But yeah, I lead Buggins to my room.

"Hi, Christine," I say. That's Christine Chubbuck, by the way, I think I mentioned her? I have a few posters.

"Hi, Christine. Hi, Christine," I say to my other posters. "Hi, Todd," I say to Todd. I have a poster of Todd MacFarlane in here as well. Just one, though.

Buggins seems to be having a lot of trouble as of late, so I dig inside his backpack to self-return (I don't—I don't know the term) some *Spawn* omnibuses (omnibi?) to my shelf. Not the Todd MacFarlane shelf surprisingly, the Thich Quang Duc shelf. What a guy. And could you imagine that? The man didn't even flinch the entire time. People always try to attest that if there was ever a Son of God (or Daughter if you can get a Christian to admit their misogyny) it was Jesus Christ. I think not, my women fearing friends. I think not.

Also, Jesus was an urban terro—

—Buggins mumbles some unintelligible nonsense.

"Buggins, please," I guess I argue? "Why are you doing this to me? What's wrong?"

[45]

Sigh, he's deaf, isn't he? How'd Helen Keller put up with this?

I sit Buggins down in front of my T.V. and hand him a controller. Well, I try to lock the controller so the tips of his hooks lodge in the center of the joysticks. He's gonna have to figure the rest out himself.

I put in DMC (DMC 2, you cowards). DMC 2's about the only game I feel Buggins can handle at the moment. I also modded it to be able to play co-op with Vergil. I call Vergil, of course.

"Buggins, you gotta help me kill myself, it's the only thing I've ever wanted. Ya know, some say suicide is the only act of true free will we're capable of—every other aspect of life— eh—is life, the idea of continuation, or really, the meaningless dragging out of time. What really are our lives, Buggins?" (Notice that "are" and "our" are both pronounced "are." Sorry again. Midwest) "The lives of—"

—Buggins wobbles to his feet. I sense I've irritated him with what he deems to be my senseless prattling. He guides himself out of my room by brushing his hands (hooks) across the (his hands (hooks) swipe a little too close to Christine) the walls.

Good. Great, actually. If he doesn't wanna listen, then why should he? At least I anticipated this interlude and set up the bathroom properly.

GRANDPA J'S PARTY TIDBIT NO. 2

So yeah, people eventually have to use the bathroom, right? A real neat thing you can do is switch out the toilet paper spools just before your friends come over—and I'm not talking about switching them out with an empty spool, no, that's some novice level nonsense. What you have to do is switch out to a spool with only ONE piece of paper left—because nobody can use

[46]

just one! Your friend'll have the pleasure of using one piece, but not using the amount they actually need. If the spool was flat out empty then it wouldn't work cuz the key to this is making them leave finished but wanting more, making them unsatisfied—and you have to go the extra mile here and make sure there are no refills within an immediate reaching distance—none of this, "Oh, they're in the pullout drawer right next to you," shit. No way. They have to suffer. If there's even a hint of a refill in your bathroom, it has to be on the top shelf of your linen closet. This's the way to do it, some say the only way.

Buggins returns and nothing about his demeanor has changed. I don't get it—it should've worked. Why isn't he rattled? Ashamed? In tears?

Wait a second...

I hold out my hand (hooks). Inch it closer and closer to Buggins.

It passes right through him. He's...translucent? Or which word?

Buggins turns to me:

"Dog City Never Sleeps."

Buggins's muscles relax and thousands of Buggins particles break away and dissipate into the air. I cough and (oh piss—I think I actually inhale a bit of him) and wave a hand in front of my face. It's like Buggins was never here. I check the T.V. screen.

I'm dead. How do you die on DMC 2?

***

A costume! I'll be able to sneak around the French Revolution thing if I have a costume!

[47]

And I don't mean a Marie Antoinette costume, I mean a janitor costume, a museum janitor—I'll just pretend I have to polish the guillotine and wham! I'll be graveyard dead, just like Snowelda threatened me (I could always have Snowelda kill me. Does that constitute suicide? Or is that consensual homicide? I feel like if it's that, then I don't really want it). I would write—I'll write this down for—I have to explain things to myself to really understand them—I'll explain later.

I wonder if museum janitors are like closeted savants, ya know? Like, "Oh wow, here's a Pieter Bruegel. Some say Pieter Bruegel is the creator of the original *Where's Waldo?*" and honestly, I could see it. I also wonder if they play *Where's Waldo?* Or at least *Where's Waldeaux?* Cuz ya know, he's, uh, he's Dutch.

The traffic light ahead of me flashes red. I obey laws.

"I'll just have to steal a school janitor uniform," I say to myself. "Easy squeezey, Jhaegar, janitorial security can't be that tight."

"Sure."

It's Viviiviiviiviana (when she'd get in my car? I drive her to school?). She paints her nails. Blood color. And I don't mean red, I mean blood.

"Foolish Creepy," she continues, "school janitors and museum janitors are not of the same ilk. This is known."

"By who?"

"The ones who know, know."

"It's essentially a jumpsuit with pockets—"

[48]

"—With differing colors and materials as to distinguish janitors of higher rank and station. While the museum janitor flaunts their jumpsuits of violet cashmere, the lowly school janitor plods through life in the trappings of an ochre cotton blend."

She leans in close to me.

"You see, what you're planning here is a classic 'stupid twat' move. If you dare enter the realm of the museum janitor in the threads of the school janitor, then it'll be your turn to be done as fuck. Even the name 'janitor' is obsolete in the world of high art."

"And how's that?"

"'San-i-tat-ion en-gin-eer.'"

"Ah," I click my tongue and raise my eyebrows, derisively I think, "you're one of those people."

"Disirregardless of—"

(disirregardless?)

"—your opinion of me, you will fail. This is known. But, you'll also achieve your own cutesy version of success."

I do that tongue-clicking-eyebrows-raising-derisively thing again. I wish the light would change. Viviivi's beginning to frighten me…but then…calmness.

A sizable brownish-orange pill floats a few feet above the sidewalk. Faintly glowing. Faintly aromatic. It's…jumpin' Christ, it's turmeric!

"Vivi—Vivi, look over there! Do you see what I'm seeing?"

"Oh Creepy, I'm sure you see many things."

"Maybe the floating Turmeric Pill!?"

"Yes. I should think I do."

[49]

"Well, why?!"

"Because you inhale it, possibly?"

I purse my lips and glance at her.

"Yup," she whispers as she turns away from me.

The turmeric aroma grows more powerful. Pungent, even. Unguent? Isn't that a *Lord of the Rings* thing? It—

—Oh, piss.

Peeking between the bushes…barely visible…it's that asshole, Glass Pipe!

I raise my hand at it and make a Kiefer Sutherland noise. Ya know, from *Invasion of the Body Snatchers*? I forget the year, I know there's a few of them. The famous one—famous-er one—the one with Kiefer Sutherland where he makes that Kiefer Sutherland noise at the end.

Glass Pipe recedes into the shadows.

Ha! And people call me a wimp! All it took was one good scream and—

"—I'm growing more and more done with you," Vivi sighs.

"What're you mad for? I saved us."

"For your needless, and oft times incorrect, referential and self-referential chin wagging. And remember, it was just a pipe."

"Aren't you the least bit upset that thing tried to kill me—er—was gonna kill me—was probably gonna kill me?"

"If it tried to kill you, then why are YOU upset?"

I open my mouth to verbally obliterate her, but then fall silent. The traffic light (finally and conveniently) turns green.

"So you're done, huh?" Vivi asks. Then tenderly, "Still driving me to school, Creepy?"

[50]

I drive. Marissa Nadler has a song about driving. And Maria Brink. And Halsey. And Lana del Rey. And Empire of the Sun (but from their pissy album!) and on any given album by any given artist—it's almost a faultless guarantee there'll be a song titled: Drive, Ride, You, I Want You, Without You, Tonight, "Insert Someone's Name," Colors, Stay, Crazy, Love, Dreams, Changes (I'm about to go off on "Changes" every other piss shitting album has a song titled "Changes" like we get it sometimes things change).

And then I see it:

Dog City Never Sleeps

Graffiti-ed on the side of a building in black paint.

That's the thing Buggins said before he turned to dust—or whatever he turned into.

Strange. Maybe Buggins is still alive? That is, "alive" in a very loose definition. Maybe he wants me to find him? To track him down through this "Dog City?" Where is Dog City? Why doesn't it sleep? Do other cities sleep?

Another red light. Piss. I take this time to pry answers from Vivi, but I find her to have vanished. Did she turn to dust like Buggins? Is "Dog City" behind—oh wait, there's powder over her seat. Brownish orange with a faint scent of—

—Jumpin' Christ.

I brush my finger in the powder and hold it under my nose. Give it a good whiff—yup, it's turmeric and—oh piss—oh piss, too much too much I can feel it entering my oh god oh god no no no stop please dont whats going

[51]

***

Im on the ground

Its dirty Theres lots of dirt And its nighttime Im laid back against a tree in the dirt and its nighttime while the moon glows with a lurid pallor

A man above me Its me Its Jhaegar Hes naked and standing and then bending over and towards me and kisses my face my cheek and kisses my face again and pulls his thing out and puts it inside me Who am I Im Jhaegar

My breasts sweet breasts press up against him Is this what it feels like Hes inside me Im nervous I want him to like me I want to impress him and think Im a cool girl Please go away just let me Please go away just let me be in the dirt Im getting dirtier Theres worms They slide across the back of my back and

Hands come out of the tree I dont want to be touched They shoot up between the roots and the cracks in the bole and I sense the people underneath trying to grab me Please dont touch me I dont like to be touched Jhaegar holds my face between his hands and kisses my lips I dont kiss back I dont know how I feel him getting bigger Ive never done this before

But the worms crawl inside next to Jhaegar—but they—please stop—but they keep going and going and they wriggle along my intestines and crawl back out of me but some stay and inch up my throat and out of my mouth and Jhaegar sucks them inside himself and spits them onto my face and the worms crawl through my eyes and their wetness is the only thing I feel

He comes inside but all he gives me are more worms Grabs my throat he does he grabs my throat and squeezes but the hands the other hands they take my hair my sweet breasts my legs and drag me into the earth Everything is dirt and grime and filth and sediment and it becomes me

[52]

they pull me farther and farther until I no longer feel the glow of the moon and the roots of the tree creak and bend and cover the hole and all I breathe is dust and the corpses of all those who died before

The hands break me apart I crumble like stone and worms burst forth and devour the earth while I shatter into smaller pieces smaller pieces becoming part of the sediment churning beneath the earth roiling under the forest until one day I see the moons pallor again and I slide down the hills with the rain becoming mud and grime and filth only to be recycled again

As I die I know this to be the path of all things Ceaseless death Ceaseless rebirth On and on again until I forget my past lives and existence seems new again The worms consume my lungs and I have no mouth from which to scream and thus I become worms and feel myself inch in a thousand directions consuming more corpses of those who could never live ever expanding my reach until all the earth is mine and as I sigh the rivers sigh and as I breathe the trees breathe

***

I shut my locker door.

Is that what mushrooms are like? Or LSD? Or pot or—I don't know. I've only done turmeric. And if I get that kind of dream from turmeric, what does that other nonsense do?

Super sigh. I should've been born a woman. I question whether I have enough time to stand here and ponder potential female names for myself without staying too long, decide I've already stayed too long, and land on just staying anyway. Lucina. Now that's a woman's name. Friends would call me Lucy. A cute boyfriend would call me Lu cuz—SHUT UP! GO AWAY— huh, what? Uhhh...whatever. I'd be okay with Phoebe or Kara, too—well maybe not Kara—I

[53]

feel like Kara's something else and I shouldn't mess—but Janice and Candace and Libby and Olivia (so friends and cute boyfriends could call my Livi) wait, Vivi! Is Vivi's full name Olivia? Ovivia? Cuz we used to date she says, does that mean "Vivi" is the name I gave her?

I head to class (don't know what time it is, so I'm just heading to one) and contemplate life. Sex is terrible. Like legitimately horrible, isn't it? Why can't I eat a banana in peace? Why can't I buy comfortable underwear (I take that one back, women have it worse there) or just— anything! I should chop off—no, probably shouldn't—they have those surgeries now—but I don't think doctors would let me just get rid of it altogether, they'd wanna transform it into a vagina or whatever else. Maybe they could transform it into another hand? Ha! That'd be kinda cool.

I—oh piss, here it comes…so Black kids, right? Why do they act like Black kids (not saying I'm a white kid)? Same with the Asian kids! And the Native kids (if you can find any)! The Black kids only ever say, "Yo homie, know what I'm sayin', man? I finna get dat pussy dis weekend after da game, nah-mean?" and they got the saggy pants and the Supreme hoodie and the "fresh" Nike's and—to me, at least—don't you realize you're your own stereotype here? Ya know? That'd be like if I dressed in a "BOOBS GUNS BEER" t-shirt with Levi's and a can of chew outlined in my back pocket. And some white kids do that! WHY?!

Why do the Asian kids (in my defense, I at least know they're Hmong) sit in the library after school and play Yu-Gi-Oh? Why do the Middle Eastern kids—just kidding, there's no Middle Eastern kids here (remember, Black people aren't the only minorities)—why do cheerleaders walk around with shorts so short they go backwards up to their belly buttons and why do nerds (excluding me (though I'm not a "nerd," per se)) hurry from class to class clutching their books to their chests and pulling up their knee socks?

[54]

WHY CAN'T ANYONE BE MORE THAN THEMSELVES!

"I agree," someone says.

Did I say that aloud? I glance over.

It's that guy with the long name again. Tiresias Tyrone Tyreke Washington Lincoln Roosevelt III. See? Just his name and it's already a—

"—You are correct. And you did indeed say that aloud. You also asked if you said that aloud, aloud. But returning to our original quandary, yes, I find it equally frustrating that others seem unable to act outside their perceived 'stereotype.'"

I open my mouth—

"—And yes," he puts his hand over his heart, "I am quite aware I am breaking mine. Yet, fear not, Jhaegar Holdburn, for I have plans to educate you, our fellow classmates, and even myself very soon in the art form that is Personality."

"Did you say that with a capital P?"

"Correct."

"Why?"

"Is there cause for bother? I should think that strange, given your favorite musical album capitalizes the P in 'Personality.'"

"Whoa, how'd you know that?"

"You frequently speak aloud."

"I do?"

"Jhaegar…please."

"That can't be—"

[55]

—He holds up his hands—in peace I hope—oh piss, does that mean I'm a racist for assu—?

"—Do not worry. I find us to be fast friends and I have never found issue with you or any of your demographic."

"My demographic?"

"Yes, the Mentally Ill—"

"—That's not a demographic. The only demographics are based upon skin color and perceived gender."

I say that with a straight face until I can't resist a wink. He smiles and winks back.

"See? And I still possess fond memories of the time you, I, Viviiviana and Gwynevere sojourned together on our, 'double dates,' I believe you called them."

"Who was I with?"

He (I'm just gonna keep saying "he" cuz his name's too long) wraps his arm around my neck and pulls me into a quick hug.

"You were with me," he laughs and releases, "but yet, I only jest. You were with Gwynevere."

"I was?!"

"No."

"What?"

"You have to remember, Jhaegar, there comes a time in every man's life when they can hide no longer. Even one as enlightened as I cannot escape destiny's watchful gaze."

[56]

"'Destiny's watchful gaze?'" I glance at The Crew: the four Black kids arguing over whether Sherane and LaQuisha is the bigger "hoochie mama," then glance back at he (I should probably capitalize it). "How are you—but—why are you like this?"

"Ah," He laughs, "understand this, Jhaegar—and I apologize, may I call you, 'Jhaegar?'"

"I thought you said we double dated?"

"Understand this, Jhaegar: Given time to peruse our vivacious culture, I am confident you shall notice us 'darkie folks' are a sort of prime demographic, a majority minority if you will—that is of course Black males, Black females being a substantially different story—and due to the bountiful opportunities presented to us in this modern world, Black males no longer have to give in to cliché, but may instead find their own Personality and pursue their own goals."

"I'm sorry, Tiresias something Roosevelt, I'm not sure I understand."

The class bell chimes.

He puts his hand on my shoulder and grins.

"You will soon enough. And call me 'Rooz.'"

"Eh, well, that's kind of a stereotype."

"Is it?"

And I find myself sitting in Health Class. I—oh piss, Rooz isn't a 'Magical Negro,' is he? Man, you just can't win as a white guy, can you?

***

So yeah, never expect the unexpected—never not expect the—never unexpect?—be prepared, so, uh, just be prepared so I always have an extra pair of pants stored under the

[57]

bathroom sink (the school bathrooms use those big industrial quadruple sinks so there's plenty of room).

I cry as—okay, I sob—wait, what the fuck? Why am I in the bathroom? How'd I get here? Why is there drying come on my leg? Why—shut up!—what the fuck?!

Sitting down now (new pants fully on, by the way, so hopefully I don't forget) and—never mind, I at least slide them down so I can wipe off the come. I use the old pants to do this—ya know, one final mission? And where did I even (pun intended, I guess) come from?

Am I a rapist? I think so…sometimes, at least. But then isn't everyone a rapist? Cuz isn't masturbation just a form of rape? Like really…isn't it rape?!

Say I really like Jennifer Lawrence…okay, never mind—and I probably shouldn't use a living woman anyway…say I really like Shirley Temple and I…okay, that's a substantially worse example…say I—we'll call her "Emily Clayborn"—and one day maybe I see her in a cute cheongsam and I don't care that it may or may not be cultural appropriation and it really gets me going and/or I just had a general bad day and needed to let off some steam and decide to do a little wanking at the banking and resident cutie Emily Clayborn just happens to float into my mind. One thing leads to another—I'm eating her pussy—kissing her, cuddling her (cuz I'm not a total monster), as well as a laundry list of other potential activities we may have lined up depending on the day I've been having. Well, we do that and, cuz it's all my fantasy, it's goes off without a hitch with no resistance (unless of course I've had a REALLY bad day) and it—well—just all goes according to whatever plan I concoct at the given moment—but poor Emily Clayborn, though not physically present, though not even aware of what's going on inside this deranged man's brain, is still a sort of unwilling participant in my sexual deviancy.

Like, isn't that bad?

[58]

And then I'm gonna see her at school the next day. We're gonna take math quizzes. We're gonna run into each other in the lunchroom and make faces during parent teacher conferences...and all the while, I live with the knowledge that I've had sex with her (albeit in my personal Realm of the Unreal (Henry Darger eat your heart out, how's this for Outsider Art?)) and also the knowledge that she DOESN'T live with said knowledge.

What would she do if she knew? Why is jerking off not a federal crime? What would—wait, I—jumpin' Christ—has she masturbated to me?!

Have I been raped? (Thought-raped? Psycho-raped?) What girls have imagined having sex with me? Do we take math quizzes, too? Do they copy my answers while I'm not looking and glance down at my bulge and think, "Gee golly gee, if only Jhaegar would pull out his throbbing horse cock and—" —no no no! They can't, not for me at least, maybe for others—but the idea—the IDEA!—that's just mind-blowing. Someone's had mind sex with me and I have no clue.

Unless...

What if I've masturbated to them?

What does that mean?!

If I've fantasized about having sex with Emily Rath—Clayburn (whatever, who cares if I get her name right, she isn't real) and Emily Clayburn fantasizes about having sex with me...does that mean we've had sex? Even if we have no idea about it?! What does that count as?! And did the second person masturbate cuz they had some sort of telepathic message to do so, some sort of uncontrollable impulse to react to another's powerful—so powerful it's mentally invasive—libido? And—oh my—are you—?

—NO! NOOOOO!

[59]

It'd be so convenient if we all just knew about it! I have a crush on Emily + Emily has a crush on me + two teenagers being self-conscious and insecure about their sexuality = Jhaegar and Emily never having real sex. Conversely (inversely?)! I have a crush on Emily + Emily has a crush on me + each of us knowing our mutual faux nocturnal sex-capades = "Gee golly wow, Jhaegar, I never knew you felt the same way. What do you say you come back to my place after school, we watch a few episodes of *Cowboy Bebop,* and then you eat my pussy?"

Jumpin' Christ, this really IS a crime to think about. If only I—actually no, why do I have to feel bad about it? Does anyone else? Does anyone else even CONSIDER this kind of stuff? Here I am, having a panic attack after a possibly amnesiac masturbatory episode that was somehow necessary in order for me to even think straight and I'm sure every other guy's just like, "Oh? Jennifer Lawrence? Bam. Jennifer Lopez? Boom. Jennifer Hudson? Wham Bam Kablooey," and I'm—piss, how haven't I killed myself for this? I may as well be a serial rapist and I have the audacity to think I deserve to live?

And then they'll say, "Well, Jhaegar, it's just pretend," cuz just—just cuz everyone else is a degenerate, doesn't mean I have to be one, too! That's it. I'm done. I'm going clean. No more waxing the carrot ever again, it's the sober life for me. Celibacy or bust...well, maybe that's not the best word...but I'm going sober. Masturbation being a "fantasy" isn't an excuse.

But yeah, really interesting movie about rape I've seen—*Irreversible* (2002)—I've seen it a few times cuz I—okay, "like" is the wrong word—I "appreciate" it's artistic value, but nobody ever wants to experience real art so I'll just explain (and some say watching the movie itself— it's not French New Wave, but something called Extremist French New Wave—or New French Extremism, I think—is an irreversible act in and of itself so I wonder if talking about it is the same?). I don't know. Oh, well.

[60]

IRREVERSIBLE

by Gaspar Noé

(review by Jhaegar Holdburn)

And it's not even about rape, that's just what people (sickos, ya know?) focus on—and really it's an anti-rape movie if you watch it. So many people walk out (and not in a viewer-is-non-complicit-like-in-a-Michael-Haneke-film-so-hats-off-to-you-for-leaving way, but a this-movie's-just-gross way) during the rape scene and never actually get to see the rest of the movie which (if you ask me) is substantially harder to watch cuz the film's not about rape...it's about destiny!

First things first (again), we need to establish this movie isn't porn. Porn works up to a climax, right? Not this movie. This movie starts with the climax and flips in in reverse (irreverse?) and builds up to what is, chronologically, the beginning of the day—the beginning of the story—and it's not even like that nutcase Christopher Nolan movie Memento (19-who-cares) that just happens to be told backwards. Memento's "told" backwards, but the narrative still moves forwards. Irreversible moves backwards, AS WELL AS having a reversed narrative—which is why everything after the rape is so crazy—cuz it's not like a regular movie where we live in the present and have knowledge of the characters' pasts (backstories, flashbacks) to contextualize that present; we end up living in the characters' past (that is, chronological past) with knowledge of their future which then contextualizes their NEW present.

[61]

Anyone who's actually watched the movie (and when I say that I don't mean "watched," I mean like actually WATCHED) will know the scene way worse than the rape is the one a few scenes after (or before timewise) where the girl talks to her gay ex-boyfriend about how men worry too much in bed about pleasing women and how she feels the best when her man takes his desires into his own hands and does what he wants…what?!?! Oh my jumpin' Christ on a Cross! That's nuts!!

And really, it's not even her getting raped —it's us, the VIEWER, getting raped by the emotional trauma that is experiencing this film. It shows us how we have no control over our own lives and we're all just—like an immutable chain of chemical reactions continuing into an infinity from which we can never escape. Ya know—just nothing mattering at all—cuz everything you do is also an irreversible action that cannot be undone—even watching the movie itself (or I think I said that?) or reading this nifty review and having the now un-washable insight etched into your mind as a sort of psychological scar.

But yeah, is the rape destiny, as well as the violence the men face as the result of their revenge? Is this all a manifestation of a sort of punishment for arrogance? Karma? Is this film just some nihilistic vision to show how happiness (cuz her and her current straight boyfriend are actually super cute (at least in the end/beginning)) how true happiness hangs by a thread? What is time and does it indeed reveal all things? It's just a movie you watch that cancels all sleep cuz you can't stop thinking about how terrible life is. But

[62]

also pretty nifty, too—and all the stroboscopic and weird hallucinogenic stuff Noé does—ya know, it's that mise en scène stuff—you'll hear about that every once in a while—and watching it makes you wanna vomit up blood.

Four Stars (out of Four, not this Five nonsense)

I've been thinking about rape for so long that I'm just sitting outside the school on the grass. I guess it's time to break in and steal the janitor uniform.

But I can't just waltz on in and grab that disguise, I need another disguise (hopefully an easier one to acquire) to prove I belong here this late—I check the Three Beggars constellation (cuz it's night, right?) and by my—

—Oh piss...I just thought about women again. So imagine it's Christmas—and everybody's wearing jeans or some kind of soft pants and a cute Christmas sweater—like one that's really warm and fuzzy and nice to cuddle and watch non-French films on the couch (Japanese films are pretty good for—well, no—Kurosawa's pretty—I mean I wouldn't wanna watch an Ozu film like that—not that I'm against Ozu, I just think he's not very Christmas-y) and I'll wear a sweater and it'll just be normal, but a really cute girl'll wear a sweater and it won't be normal (even though it should be, hence the rather depressing issue here) cuz I see her in a sweater and instead of thinking, "Gee golly gee, she sure is Christmas-y," I instead think, "Gee jumpin' Christ, I sure wanna cuddle on the couch and watch *Lady Snowblood* (1973) with you cuz underneath that warm sweater material are two nice rosy nipple materials and between your thigh materials is an even warmer than usual—" —ya know? Like, why? Why?! Why can't

[63]

we just watch *Lady Snowblood*? Why do I constantly have to think about her va—constantly and just—imagine how she feels! She probably likes wearing her sweater except she knows I'm psycho French raping her or something and she's like, "Gee man, why can't it just be Labor Day?"

Sigh. I hope a woman kills me.

So yeah, I need a first disguise to get a disguise first (first?) I need a disguise. Hey! Disguise. Dis guy's. This guy's. "Hey, willya looky 'ere? Dis guy's trynna getta disguise," I say in my New Jersey accent. I'm getting better. Bettah, I mean. Aum gettin' bettah.

There's two nerds walking towards (or just—just for the sake of progression, yeah, there's two nerds who show up) and if Kiryu never killed anybody then I certainly never did either, so I put on their clothes (ya know, button-up shirt and pocket protector and shin guards and stuff) so now I have my perfect nerd this guy's to sneak into the school and "study" (I'm not a nerd regularly, more goth really) which I indeed do!

This all reminds me of a song actually. "The Angel and the Fool" by this pissy yup band, Broken Bells—the song begins to hum in that weird static-y in-between from the intercom. Sigh life. This thoroughly irritates me—not the poor audio quality, the song itself—the band really, the song just had the word "Fool" in it and I happened to—it's the band I don't like—well, not the band, I used to love the band, but I shared the band with a guy who I used to be friends with and we're not friends anymore (he's a nutcase and I hope he gets locked in a porta potty) and he really ended up liking them so now every time I think about the band I'm forced to think about him (which is a great example why you should never share anything with anyone cuz they'll just ruin it) and how much I wanna—I don't know—tell him he should feel bad and apologize already for how he screwed me and my other friend over—was that other friend Buggins? Wait,

[64]

did he know Buggins? Or was that Buggins? Who cares—it was a long time ago, the real irritation comes from the fact that I have a sort of playlist of my life, right? Where songs that either lyrically mean something to me or I just happened to discover at a pivotal moment in my life and a different song by them, "The Ghost Inside" (their best song), represents the time I was visiting colleges and the college I actually ended up going to was where I discovered Broken Bells—so now I'm like, "Whoa what a crazy song," but then, "Oh wait, I wanna beat that guy with a socket wrench," and it's just—

—Wait, I haven't gone to college yet.

Have I?

I stop in the hallway.

I haven't discovered Broken Bells. I've never heard this pissing song before. Ever.

"The Ghost Inside" plays now. I've never heard this song either. How do I recognize it?

Shut up

Shut up—you're not here.

I keep walking. No time for this nonsense, gotta find the jacket—uniform. Janitor uniform costume disguise.

Right when "The Ghost Inside" is supposed to hit the bridge section that I don't know about, the intercom abruptly switches to "After the Disco," another song by them that I don't know about. Yet, I know in my heart I somehow asked for this.

I twist my hips to the music and I slam my back into the lockers and mouth the lyrics and snap my fingers with the beat like the pissing nerd I've become and slide down the walls like

[65]

Bully Maguire and the second chorus hits and as it does the other nerds here this late at night burst forth from the lockers from which they've been jammed and we all dance through the ages in perfect sync: we Emperor Waltz, we Jive, we Thriller, we Single Ladies, we dance every move that's ever been danced and we're all crazy gorgeous while our muscles (now sweaty muscles) soak our pocket protectors, soften them up, and then eviscerate them with their piercing beauty cuz while pocket protectors can protect from a lot of things they're no match against the supreme power of white men who've learned to dance.

My Nerd Legion forms one of those big you-run-under-them-while-they-form-a-tunnel-with-their-arms-to-get-you-hyped tunnels that get you hyped and I fucking sprint through them as they jazz their jazz hands and get me hyped and the tunnel leads to a door—but a special door—a door that I know leads into the Realm of the Sanitation Engineer and one from which I know I'll never return the same.

I go through that door.

Turns out my knee's bleeding. I must've scraped it during one of my dives. The school floor is rather solid—and dirty—I probably have tetanus now.

It also turns out—aw piss, my head—I fall to my knees and say "Ouch" and probably scrape my scraped knee once more. The ochre tactical jumpsuit of the School Janitor consumes me—fuses with me (I do save my pocket protector, I mean you never know) and as I—oh, piss, what's going on? What's—?

—I feel a sort of Divine Truth flow into my mind, as if this uniform possesses the knowledge of all janitors who have come before and, dare I say, all janitors who are yet to be. I am one of those janitors. My arms and legs vibrate with power. Warming sensation thrums throughout my body. I know the number of each room in this school. I know which students

[66]

have slept with Winston Shorngoer (zero). I know not only how to clean a toilet, but how to restore a toilet. I know how to eat a vending machine sandwich.

And I also know Snowelda Roach's about to undergo a back-alley abortion behind the school. What? She's pregnant? My clothes tell me to look at her clothes, her double layer of thick clothes. My clothes tell me to look past her clothes at what was there all along. My clothes tell me I'm a fool. They say clothes are the key to everything. They say that underneath my clothes, I'm just a naked boy. I tell them I don't identify as a boy. They tell me to go to hell and that they won't help me kill myself if I give them too much lip.

So yeah, I go outside to find Snowelda and lo and behold there she is with some sort of "doctor" and—actually it's a real x-ray machine thingy. Weird. How does that work out here?

"Don you vish to know if it be boy or girl?" the "doctor" asks her. I guess they don't see me yet. Maybe I'm in stealth mode?

"No, just get rid of it, I can't let my girls know."

"Okey-dokey," the "doctor" says as they glance towards the x-ray. They do a spit take (no drink, though, just actual spit) and peer harder at the screen. I peer as well.

Snow's baby appears to have wings and a tail…and horns, I think.

"Holdburn, you're here?!" she yells.

Oh piss, guess I'm not in stealth mode.

"How'd you get pregnant, Snowelda?" I ask. "What's the Puritan Club been up to nowadays?"

"Holdburn, I will burn you at the stake!"

"Would that really be setting a good example for your baby? Also, have you checked out this x-ray? What the literal—?"

[67]

—Snow's hands ball into very punchy looking fists. Rivulets of liquid hate gush from her mouth.

"That's it, you get your wish! We're aborting you, too!"

"I just wanted to be a janitor!"

Snow lets out a scream of battle rage...

Then lets out a scream of extreme pain as her torso explodes and some demon vampire baby thing latches itself onto my face. I scream myself as it claws my skin.

"Ah, yes," the "doctor" interjects, "dis just like vone uv my vavorite shows. You know da vone?"

EATING OUT

coming to PornWorld Plus this Valentine's Day

EXT. CAFÉ PATIO - NIGHT

Leaves drift over VAMPIRE and GIRLFRIEND drinking wine.

Blood drips down Girlfriend's neck and is smeared over Vampire's mouth and fangs.

>   **GIRLFRIEND**
>   Honey, there's really something I
>   have to tell you.

>   **VAMPIRE**
>   Not now, dearest, I would prefer
>   we sit here and enjoy the air.

>   **GIRLFRIEND**
>   But it's, like, super important.

>   **VAMPIRE**
>   Silence, my dove. Drink more wine.

[68]

                    GIRLFIEND
         It's just—it's just—I don't know
         how to—I feel so guilty—

                    VAMPIRE
         —Fine! What is it? What is it you
         believe to be so "important?"

Girlfriend leans over and grabs one of Vampire's hands.

                    GIRLFRIEND
         Baby, I have H.I.V.

Vampire puts his other hand on top of hers.

                    VAMPIRE
         I know...

"Who'd watch that nonsense!?" I shout as I endeavor to keep my quite bitable face intact. "And by the way, it's more like one of MY favorite shows."

(So yeah, this is where I (I write screenplays in my free time, not sure I've notated that yet) where I'd insert a section from one of MY shows that I wrote—but I know nobody cares and everyone'll just say, "Oh, it's amazing," ya know? "Exceptional pacing, fantastic structure, likeable and empathetic characters," but nothing'll ever come out of it like usual. A competition comment once said my script was, "Solid finalist material," and it didn't even make it to the second round! How?! Doesn't that reader/reviewer know THEY are the ones who advance it? A simple yes or no from THEM? That's all it would've taken. Why did they make that glowing comment and then be like, "So yeah, this is definitely a fail," cuz THEY would've been the ones to turn it down?!)

I manage to grab Snowelda's monster baby and use my super jacked arms to throw it into a dumpster. I—I don't know—I even went out of my way to make it super woke—no cis whites allowed, ya know? People don't care about how genuinely well-crafted something may be, they

[69]

just wanna see themselves. If you're a half Cambodian half Jamaican transgender Buddhist then you don't wanna watch a white Frodo Baggins go to Mordor (though he's a hobbit and shouldn't that be woke enough?) No! You wanna see a half Cambodian half Jamaican transgender Buddhist Frieda Baggins go to Mordor! Who gives a shit if that doesn't pertain, or even RUINS, the story? Forget best. Now it's *most eligible*—ya know, and it only ever pertains to skin color— sexuality if you're lucky. They'll say, "Gee golly, look at Jhaegar's Mexican hero, I bet he doesn't have any so-called-Mental-Illnesses cuz only white people have so-called-Mental-Illnesses! Joker! The guy from *The Machinist* (2004)! Doomers! If anything, this man right here is only mentally handicapped—or no he's not, he's mentally handi-capable!"

Sorry, George (Carlin again). I rub my cheeks and contemplate how oppressed I am, how worthy I am cuz of it. How I deserve my own T.V. show and how the lady from the Progressive commercials should be replaced with someone like me. Who needs insurance? Not white people, they've stolen so much money from us working class colored folks that insurance isn't necessary for them. Who cares if they get into a car crash? They'll just buy another car! They'll just—

—Head splitting gunfire reverberates throughout the school. I check my surroundings. Yeah, I'm at school (as in regular daytime) and alarms and screams and—whatever. I got into my representation rant, didn't I? Oh well, I appear to be standing in the midst of a school shooti—

"—Hello, Jhaegar, how do you do?" someone asks.

I turn to find Rooz facing me with an AR-15 pointed at my chest…and a tactical shotgun strapped to his back…and two bandoliers of ammo…and an armored vest…yeah…

"Uh, h-h-hi, Rooz."

[70]

"Oh, do not be afraid, Jhaegar. I am not here for you. I just happened to overhear your postulating about race and thought we could continue our conversation from before. But first, would you step to the side?"

"Sure."

So I step to the side. Rooz raises his AR and mows down those stereotypical Black teens still debating hoochie mamas. I guess they'll never have their answer...

"So, uh, yeah, Rooz. What're you...what're you doing?"

"I am killing people, Jhaegar. Here. Walk with me."

I join him on his stroll down the hall. He unloads a clip against a row of lockers. After a beat, the doors swing open and four Nerds fall to the ground dead.

"It is just as you said earlier," Rooz explains. "Representation is the key. We want to see ourselves represented in our art in order to feel seen, important, et cetera. What people often times lack, though, is a sort of 'true' representation, that is, people only desire to be seen as measured by how the culture already sees them. Take those Black students I just killed. They desire to be seen, correct? But why do they want to be seen in such a way? Baggy pants? Poor grasp of the English language? Most likely misogynistic? It is how the culture as a whole already sees a young Black male, and yet, they do not seem to desire to be anything different."

Just then a teacher rushes Rooz from behind. Rooz spins, drops his AR, then pulls out a stiletto from apparently somewhere and drives it straight through the teacher's neck. He lowers their dying body to the floor and picks up his AR.

We continue our stroll.

"Anywho. Black people say they want representation, but what really is 'representation' when the films they desire to be represented by are about street thugs, hip-hop, barbershops,

[71]

hoochie mamas, and any other item on the long list of Black stereotypes? If they want to be represented so badly, then why do they limit themselves to their own clichés? Is it so impossible for a Black man to speak such as I am speaking? Is it so impossible for a Black man to dress as I am dressing? Is it so impossible for a Black man to become a school shooter? Well, Jhaegar, these are the questions I am exploring today."

Rooz stops me to put a hand on my chest. Whispers:

"And please do not misunderstand me here, it is not just Black. It is anything, really. Name a fictional Asian character where their name does not represent some sort of inherent attribute in their native language. Name a Middle Eastern character who is not either a terrorist, lampooned as a terrorist, or struggling in a maudlin television drama because their community views them as a terrorist. Name an indigenous character—if you can find one, that is—who does not appear on the screen and five minutes later spout some mystical, magical jargon or try to generate sympathy from both the protagonist and the audience for how the White man took his culture. Have you ever considered that maybe minorities took their own culture?"

We continue our walk. He holds out his shotgun to me.

"Would you like to try?"

"Uh, not today."

"Alright."

I hear sirens in the distance. Rooz doesn't seem perturbed.

"Are you familiar with Duane Jones, Jhaegar?"

"Nope."

"He was the hero of George Romero's classic horror film, *Night of the Living Dead* (1968). He was also a Black man, one of the first Black men in a leading role in such a film. It

[72]

was progressive. It was historic. People viewed *Night of the Living Dead* as a civil rights accomplishment. Some still remember it today as such. Jordan Peele—"

"—Oh Jesus—"

"—Yes. Yes, I feel your frustration. Even Jordan Peele hails it as a pivotal film in his childhood that impacted him forever. Why? Because it was a film about a Black man who was a hero, a star, an icon, and you know something?"

"What?"

"It was all a mistake. It is not some sort of hokey civil rights anthem. Duane Jones was not chosen to lead some sort of Black cinematic movement. Duane Jones was picked because Romero was broke, had open auditions for the lead, and decided that he was the best actor. It does not matter that he was Black. History only thinks it matters because it refuses to acknowledge a minority who does not conform to the cliché of what a minority is supposed to be. Culture has to make something of everything and will not allow whatever it is to BE what it is. So he is Black: who cares? Why does it matter? Why does he have to be a Black hero? Why do so many prevent him from being what he truly was: a Cinema Hero?"

As much as I find Rooz's ideas interesting, I can't help but focus on all the dead teenagers around me. Even more interesting: there's Black, White, Asian, Hispanic—wait, I— are they being killed in even numbers? One, two, three, four—one, two, three, four—

—Three Asian boys run past us down the hallway. Rooz doesn't even flinch.

"Why are you letting those Asians live?" I ask. "You need to kill some Hispanics first?"

"First things first, Jhaegar," Rooz says, slightly mocking, "those students are Hmong. There is more than just 'Asian' or 'Hispanic.' How ignorant can you be? Would you tolerate me calling you Southern?"

[73]

"I mean, you'd be wrong. I'm Midwes—oh, I see."

"Very good. And yes, you were correct in one assumption. I have already reached my current limit on Hmong students. I need to even it out with Argentinians and Ethiopians then I should be able to increase my numbers once again."

"Better watch out, Ethiopia."

"Better watch out, indeed. Regardless, do you know why Duane Jones is a Cinema Hero?"

"You know I don't."

"Also correct. He is a Cinema Hero because his part was not written for a Black man. It was simply written for a man. Now, is that to say it was written for a White man?"

"I'm not sure what you mean."

"Duane's part never alludes to him being Black, it never gives in to Black stereotypes: rap music, Black swagger, name calling, White women screaming, what have you. One could say it is a 'normal' role. But, and this is where a rather fascinating 'but' comes in: does that necessarily mean Duane's role was a 'White' role? Are there 'White' roles? Is a 'White' role a classic action hero like James Bond or Rambo? Or are they 'normal' roles written for anyone that coincidently were played by White men because, at the time, White men had more access to such a role? Because, really, what would make them a 'White' role? They are an action hero? They save the day? They are a general movie star? Well, why may not a Black man fit the same bill? Or anyone for that matter? Jhaegar, pray tell me some 'Black' movies."

"Uh, the *Madea* movies, *The Color Purple* (1985), *Black Panther* (2018)?

"Excellent. Now name some 'White' movies."

Oh, piss.

[74]

"I, uh, I'm not really sure."

Rooz pats my chest. Seems quite exuberant.

"That is because there are none, Jhaegar. Is *Citizen Kane* (1941) a 'White' movie? Why? Why can a Black man not be successful? Is, what, is *Blade Runner* (pick your year) a 'White' movie? I guarantee you, these students I am killing today? They would grow up exponentially more insane than the adults here now already are! They will in all likelihood BAN *Blade Runner* and why should they not? After all, it is the, uh, metaphorical coming of age journey of a Klansman...or something."

"What?"

"Exactly! And that is why I am here, Jhaegar. I am going to be the first Black school shooter. I am breaking the mold of White-Only school shooters so that I, in fact, will not even be referred to as a Black school shooter but simply, *A* school shooter. I am not an Incel, I have plenty of healthy relationships, and I have yet to write even a single page of a social reform driven manifesto."

Rooz stops me to put his hands on my shoulders. He gazes deep into my eyes. I get the impression he's about to kiss me.

"If we are truly going to fight for an egalitarian civilization, how about we get serious?"

The sirens I heard earlier stop. Heavy footsteps come towards us. Like, booted footsteps. Large man boots.

"Finally, Jhaegar. They say Black people—supposing 'Black' even means anything—cannot kill themselves because, as I am sure you know, only 'dem White folks' like you have Mental Illnesses."

Rooz pulls out a 9mm. Giggles. Sardonic (I think).

[75]

He points the 9mm at his head (above the eye connector thingies, he must've researched this beforehand) and winks.

"'Rest in Power', right?"

Rooz blows his head off in front of me.

Just then, a S.W.A.T. team emerges from a side door. They train their rifles on me.

"FREEZE SCUMBAG! WE GOT YA SURROUNDED!"

"What? Are you kidding—it wasn't me, it was—Rooz has like three guns strapped to his back!"

"CAN IT, SICKO! YOU'RE A DEAD GIVEAWAY! HANDS UP!"

I raise my hands. How in Christ's name am I a—wait, I glance down.

A copy of *The Catcher in the Rye* sticks out of my front pocket.

Sigh…

***

So yeah, I guess I'm in prison now?

Definitely in prison—not as good as you'd think. Ya know, in Sweden and stuff, they have like flat screens and tennis courts and edible food and everything. The whole idea there is rehabilitation. I don't know what the idea is here.

Maybe the idea is dogs? Cuz guess what nonsense has been painted (assumedly in blood) on the wall? Presumably.

Dog City Never Sleeps

[76]

I know my life is a total waste, but I really don't understand this aspect. Where even is Dog City? I feel like it's in New Jersey, but I dismiss that thought as just my fetish talking—and why does it never sleep? Never Sleep, I mean. Does it need medication? Do I—haha—do I need medication?

I lean against the wall below the writing and think about dogs. I think about dogs the way Rooz would think about them, free from stereotypes and clichés. Do you think dogs know that they're dogs? I enjoy watching dogs walk, ya know? Cuz if they're walking, that means they have some sort of destination. Dogs have destinations! That's such a human thing, I feel. Guess not. Dogs are basically humans in that aspect. Could you imagine if humans had tails?

"Dog is coming!" someone in the cell next to me shouts.

"Like from Dog City!?" I shout back.

"Dog is coming!"

"Yes, I'm aware, what I

Dog is coming

Just shut up.

"What do you want from me?"

"Dogs!" my cell neighbor yells.

"Not you!"

Dog is coming

[77]

All this ambiguous stuff really gets me sometimes. I mean, I like it in a movie or something—we don't get enough of it in movies, to be honest—but not in real life. Real life's bad enough. Movies, though, movies are fine. Being that I'm in jail and'll most likely be here for a while (they have to fingerprint *Catcher in the Rye*) I suppose all I have is time. May as well dig into Radical Cinema!

Well—no, I don't really wanna talk right now. Plus, I wanna die. Horny of course. The title of my next book should be, "Horny and Wants to Die." That'd be accurate. Whatever. Nobody likes my ideas anyway, too transgressive. I still don't wanna get into it but—piss, my head, man—what's happening? I can't even think. Am I being dragged somewhere? I see all these other cells. *Dog City Never Sleeps* appears in all of them. Who the fuck is Dog City—no, where the—what? Where are they taking me? This isn't a Swedish prison.

I'll just—I'll just leave this here. It's called *She Bled from her Eyes.* It's kinda—oh just forget it, nobody likes it anyway. Everyone thought it was "great." I bet. What a fucking waste of time—honestly, they probably would've loved if Godzilla just randomly showed up. "Oh, Jhaegar, you're so talented. The Godzilla choice really matched your mise en scène—"—and ya know what? They probably don't even know what mise en scène is. Fucking creeps. Telling me how to write. I'm a school shooter now, I guess, wait 'til they get to school.

Sigh. I'll never write movies—write movies as in, "Get movies I've written produced." Paid writing. I can write movies all day, I'm nuts about movies, but it's useless writing them— that is, showing them. Sharing. Sharing's fucking stupid. People just get on your ass about it. I once had a comment (allegedly critical) about a character I had kicking a rock down the street. The comment was: "What if it was a piece of trash?" Are you kidding me? What if YOU were a piece of trash? What piss shitting difference does it make if it's a rock or trash? If it was a piece

[78]

of trash you would've read it and been like, "Hmm, good work, what a talented writer," like what? Why? And don't tell me I'm just too defensive and can't take a hit cuz I WANT A HIT. I WANT a critical comment. This "what-if-it-was-a-piece-of-trash" shit is mind numbing! Who cares, is that the best you can do? Is that the main critique people honestly have about my work? My inanimate object selection!? No wonder nobody accepts my stuff, look at the morons I have test reading!

How am I ever supposed to get better if I can't get any help?!?!?

That was...never mind...I don't need help...writing. I just need hel—DON'T NEED HELP, especially in writing is what I meant, ya know? It's my preference, I think—I just enjoy different sorts of movies—films. I enjoy different sorts of films. "Radical Cinema," right? Jumpin' Christ...

Here's a film I enjoy. The kind of film I try to write, something with real meaning and—and *oompf,* ya know? It's called *Sátántangó* (1994) and it's by this total nutcase Hungarian guy. Béla Tarr (Bay-luh, kind of like Bailey, but not a cute white girl) and his work? Jumpin'...it's, uh, something. But I love it. He makes Robert Bresson (Rob-air Brace-on) look like a party animal. *Pickpocket* (1959) is basically just Italian *Animal House* (1978), right? And *Sátántangó* is basically just, uh, it's actually a lot like slitting your wrists.

Sátántangó

by Béla Tarr

(review by Jhaegar Holdburn)

Jean-Luc Godard once said some pretentious nonsense like, "Films have a beginning, middle, and end, but not necessarily in that

[79]

order." Well, Béla Tarr must've said (at some point), "Fuck that, my films only have middle," cuz that's what Sátántangó is: a film with constant middle. For the record, it's only seven and a half hours (about) and like 156 shots (like 'takes,' ya know?) which means the average shot length is two and a half minutes…the average Hollywood shot is two and a half seconds! But don't tell Béla Tarr, he don't give a damn.

Yet, the film isn't slow. It's mind numbing. It's soul sucking. It's staring into the void. You just sit there and watch and watch and watch and wait with the characters as their world ends—it's like this neo-Biblical nightmare of the slow self-destruction of humankind and the inevitable immolation of intellectualism—and you just wait next to them, pretty much in real time, while capital M Madness courses through their brains—and there's no real development, well, no REAL development. There's setups with no payoffs. Characters introduced here and never used again. Narrative threads that spiral out into nothing. And that's, like, the point! It's just emptiness!

Every once in a while I love to scream, "The Turks are coming! The Turks are coming!" (Sátántangó joke) just to freak people out— or hopefully inspire them to look it up—but what I also kinda interpret this film to mean is more centered around the spiders. There are these spiders that come creeping in the bar after that big drunken bang shebang and they spin their webs over the drinks and chairs and faces of those passed out. I think that's just so pivotal (pivotal?) and really representative of the

[80]

film as a whole—it's also like halfway through so a good pseudo-midpoint—pseudo cuz there's no real structure—cuz spiders are the best symbol out there for so-called-Mental-Illness. They're there, but not really there. Quiet and subtle, existing in the background and only visible when no one's watching—and when they come, they drape their power over everything in sight. So, I—I mean, other people—would see this and really get it, ya know? And where are the spiders that we don't see? Are their webs inside our minds?

Whatever. The ending's really nuts, too. There's this guy called the Doctor. He's a drunk nutcase, but he's also like the town intellectual—the man of culture. But, when the false prophet guy comes to town and tricks everybody and leads them away to their own dooms, the Doctor doesn't go. He stays in town by himself—that's cuz he won't give in, he decides to stay true—and what he does is, he, uh, when he's in his house, he nails boards and shit over his one window. Yeah, he nails BOARDS OVER HIS WINDOW and when I saw this I was like, "What? That's pretty cool," cuz, ya know, it shows that the reward for independence is quite literally locking yourself away from the world to live a life where nobody wants you and they think you're an idiot even though they're the real idiots unknowingly following some sociopath to their deaths. And really, that's not even it!

It's not even it cuz years later—it was while I was at work—the pandemic? We had to work from home and stuff so I could listen to music all day, it was pretty nice at least—but I was listening to some DSBM

[81]

again and this crazy song I worship, "Life is my Coffin," came on and I was jamming out. Well, fans of any kind of thing always make unofficial videos to share and such and I glanced over at the screen and saw the fan made video and was like, "Is that fucking Sátántangó?" cuz playing on the screen was that final moment! And then I realized: the Doctor is nailing shut his own coffin!

Like...sigh LIFE. And while he's doing so, he's just muttering away unintelligible madness about the ringing bell that's somehow ringing even though the bell tower's empty and his mutters match those at the beginning of the film—showing this to be a sort of endless cycle that repeats and repeats as we the audience wait and wait. And ya know what else? This one free thinking hero can't even kill himself and get out of it and—

—shut up. Just fucking—go away.

Four Stars out of Four

I don't know. Suicide's fun to research (I have a lot of free time) and discover lots of cute little facts—or historical facts/opinions? Not sure. They're pretty old. Emile Durkheim wrote *Suicide* before 1900 I think. Is his work still factual? Is there a certain amount of time that has to pass once a fact is accepted for it to no longer be a fact?

Whatever. So. There's basically three types of suicide. There's (am I really gonna try to explain this?) Egoistic, Altruistic, and Anomic. Those of course are divided somewhat afterwards into cute little subtypes depending on differing cultural situations (and they can even blend together into Egoistic-Altruistic or Anomic-Egoistic) but there's basically—wait...

[82]

GRANDPA J'S PARTY TIDBIT NO. 3

Egoistic Suicide: This has more to do with the "self," the "I." It's not to say Egoistic suicide goes hand in hand with selfish people, it's just that this form of suicide results from situations when the individual commands more focus than the collective. It's for people who are isolated, people who don't have social groups like religion or family or after school activities to fall back on for support...a person lives a solitary life, they spend less time in groups and more time alone, the self or "ego" is disproportionally strengthened, thus the person finds themselves estranged from civilization as a whole and allegedly depressed with no other option but down. Boohoo, right?*

Altruistic Suicide: Altruistic is the reverse. It's not to say these people are selfless altruists, philanthropists, Do-Gooders—it's to say that these suicides result when the livelihood of the collective is placed higher than the livelihood of the individual: so really nutcase religions and families and (hopefully) after school activities! My husband's dead and I'm an oppressed Indian woman? Guess I have to throw myself on his burning funeral pyre! My general/lord/boss is dead and I'm an oppressed Japanese/Chinese/Korean solider? I guess I better stick this sword in my guts and disembowel myself before my friends!** These entertainers live in cultures that put far too much value on other people and demand that you should be ready to give up your life whenever the need (or desire, sometimes it's just for laughs) arises.

Anomic Suicide: Now this one's kind of weird and to be honest, I didn't understand it much. These suicides result from anomy—some kind of social phenomenon about class difference. Well, not 'class difference,' but more like...more like...like, difference in life. It's one of the reasons there's more suicide in places like America than third world countries like

[83]

Yemen (Christ, now I'm sure I have all the Yemenites mad at me. "We're from Yemen! Yemen's so nice! You don't know an—") —cuz America has more variety in regards to how someone could live their life than somewhere like that where it's more limited. There's more stations here. There's more social classes and they're all jumbled up—which is anomy, social anomy—some kind of entropic tendency for things to shift around. We may be a richer country sure, but cuz of that there are devastating mental consequences when a rich person suddenly plummets into poverty and no longer knows how to handle themselves and when a poor person shoots up to international super pop singer stardom and overdoses on Tylenol cuz every fat dad with a camcorder is trying to film them take a shit. It's a lot like Egoistic—and Durkheim (the bastard) even warns that they're often confused (like I'm sure I've confused them), but Egoistic has its roots in a more collective activity—like less opportunities as a whole—while Anomic lacks that activity in the more individual aspects of life—giving people too much freedom to bounce up and down and all around the social spectrum and—yeah, I don't really know.

*Tidbiter's note: I think Durkheim's full of shit.

**Also: Asians are the hypest people to ever live.

All this nonsense is honestly pretty easy to fix. As a great man once said, "Social activity must never and on no account be directed toward philanthropic flim-flam, but rather toward the elimination in the basic deficiencies in the organization in our economic and cultural life that must—or at all events can—lead to the degeneration of the individual." First off, I'd like to point out that we both use dashes to organize our thoughts—I admire that in a man. I'm not telling you I'm gay (though I know you'd prefer it), I'm just saying I have a lot of thoughts and need to uses parenthesis and dashes to organize them. I just try to stay organizized (got 'em) and not kill a

[84]

presidential—or wait, he wasn't a presidential candidate, wasn't it just like mayor or something? Whatever. Parenthesis and dashes don't really help much—I mean, to be honest. There's just so many ("Earth certainly is full of Things"), ya know? I also have to stop saying, "ya know" (ya know? Winky face). Someone once got really mad at me and told me, "No, Jhaegar, I DON'T know," like piss off, man. Who cares? Maybe I should drop the other stuff while I'm at it…I don't know. I need them to stay together, but even then I'm not really THAT together. Alas. Alack. In vain. Something. All just swimming in my noggin. Floggin'. Loggin'. Dr. Mantis Toboggan. Now I'm just rhyming. Just wanna feel clever. Also, am I the only one who has to spell "rhyme" like thirty times before they come up with the proper way? Who made that fokkin' word?

Jhaegar gets out of his car

What the hell, I was driving? Yeah…yeah, I'm in the street now. I was in prison! And now I'm in the street! And everything's tinted to BLACK AND WHITE!

I head off into the night (think it's night) and notice that it's a "same ol' street" kind of thing—but not really, cuz it's like a street from the 1950s, ya know? Like I went back in time seventy years? Snow flitters down around me and I realize I'm shuffling through heavy slush on a thin layer of ice.

Everything's cold here. Though I can't immediately touch them, I feel the cold of the surrounding buildings with my mind—uh, my memory of how they should feel—the bricks and their dry chill and deadly little bump thingies all around them and I say "deadly" cuz the cold somehow makes those bumps even harder and sharper. I know that if I touch a stop sign then a

[85]

ripcord of frozen tension will stab into my hand and plunge deep within my body. I know that if I so much as flick a finger at a shop window it'd shatter and the warmth from inside would be wrenched into the night.

Also...

There are dead bodies. On the ground. Slumped over in silent cars. Hanging from light poles. Each one wears a black and white shirt. I glance down. I'm wearing a black and white shirt. Everyone's wearing the same clothes! I attempt to study the faces of the dead, but they seem to be sort of scraped off—there's just, uh, just like a slab of blurry, frozen flesh.

I continue past the Jhaegar Holdburrrs (ahh?) until I spot a fire up ahead. I stop and think for a moment as I believe caution's important in situations like these. It's a big fire—like a huge fire, like a mound of flame almost two stories high. I figure I'm probably just jacked up on some sort of turmeric cocktail my jailors surely injected me with and approach—not like I can get hurt any more than I already am.

But yeah, I'm getting closer and it's not looking good. The burning mound is just more bodies—more Jhaegar bodies by the way (pretty sure). Nifty. A man's here working. He takes from a small stack of fresh (fresh?) Jhaegars and hurls them onto the conflagration. I watch one burn. As a matter of fact, I think I watch it glance up at me (somehow from the frozen slab face) and send out a silent plea for help. Speaking of silent...

"Am I in Silent Hill?" I vocalize.

The man pauses and cranes his neck around to see me (the RE4 way, though (someone got their signals crossed)). He seems surprised to see a living Jhaegar, grunts and gets back to it.

"So, uh," I continue, "am I in Silent Hill?"

"I thought you were all dead," he responds without looking.

[86]

"Uh, what?"

"The Doggening. The new world was born once Dog City Awoke. These are simply the Afterbirth."

"Okay."

"It killed them all. When it arrived. It killed them."

"Well, it didn't kill me."

The man grunts again. Kind of a cheeky shit.

"Doesn't the, uh, burning body smell bother you?"

"I am the custodian of this town. I have to take care of it. If I did not burn these bodies, then I would have to throw them into the lake and the water would go bad. I cannot allow that for this town."

"I've never even seen you before."

"I do not live here."

I think he forgets about me. I stand there and watch him for an hour. The stack of fresh Jhaegars never runs out. That's a perk, I guess.

"Do you need help?" I ask.

"Do you?"

What a nutcase.

"I—"

"—It's all your fault," he sneers (signals double crossed). "You chose this life. Just because you brought them into a new age of enlightenment, it does not mean that they simply go up and vanish."

"Somebody turmeric-ed me, didn't they? And jumpin' Christ, this really—wait, what?"

[87]

My arms are melting.

I'm on fire. I am fire. I glance up to see the man throw another body on top of me.

***

If I don't know why

I'm a fucking ghost

And I don't know what to say

All I do is cry

So I'll eat some toast

And I swear I am not gay

One day I wasn't

The next day I was

And some God damn Dog appeared

So cry I mustn't

Just do what Chuck does

And I'll grow a manly beard

***

This museum's pretty nifty. I wish Buggins existed to see this.

[88]

Oh, well. I'm used to wandering around alone anyway. Of course (just to spite me, I believe) I see the usual ladies hanging out with their friends: Snowelda and the Puritans, Viviiviana and some, it looks like rats? Gwynevere with dolphin shaped manifestations of turmeric. That's the one that throws me for a loop. Wouldn't security see them as basically monsters—not cuz they're dolphins but, ya know—and say, "Hey maybe you, uh, you should take those outside or something," and she'd be like, "Yeah, no." I don't know.

Some of my classmates snicker as I stroll by. Stupid young people. They always give you *The Look*, the *So-Called-Mental-Illness Look*. They give you *The Look* and then tell their girlfriends to hide their wives or something. Sigh—it's when they can't run away with their bodies so they sort of run away with their eyes, not a physical but a mental withdrawal? Bunch of nonsense. Frankly, I'm probably healthier than they are. They're just arrogant. Think they're better than anyone else—well—think that their life is the base blueprint of all life and that everyone is different from them, not that someone else may be the base blueprint and that it is THEY who are in fact different.

No matter. I find the guillotine and remember I was gonna kill myself.

It rises above me. So noble (OH MY FUCK ME IN MY—

—I head to the nearest bathroom (restroom, my brother says restroom and it's like jumpin Christ, we're at Mom's place, not Buckingham Palace). Once inside, I head to the nearest stall...closest stall, I mean. I try not to reuse words that quickly. I really am a failu—I start changing into my stolen janitor uniform. Divine Truth (and truth about Divine (crazy that was REAL dog shit)) flows into my mind once more—I see Winston Shorngoer is now at negative one. I ponder how that's possible and come to the conclusion that I don't care. I march out of the bath—res—it's a bathroom. I'm ready.

[89]

But anyway, the guillotine. I approach. Ah yes, noble (FUCK ME MOTHERFUCKER MOTHERFUCKER MOTHERFUCIreachformy suicide checklist and realize I didn't bring it. I suppose it doesn't matter now, though! I swing my legs over the dividing rope. Tears come to my eyes—Christ, I'm so happy—

"—Hey! Asshole!" someone rather upset yells.

I glance over.

A man—a janitor!—glares at me from across the exhibit.

Why should he be mad at me? I'm just a janitor as well, you'd think he'd greet me with—oh, piss…

My uniform is an ochre cotton blend…

His is clearly violet cashmere…

Viviiviana appears behind my right shoulder and whispers into my ear:

"Indeed. School janitors and museum janitors, while similar, are not the same. It was known, but you did not listen."

"Vivi, not now." I raise my arms as gregariously as I can towards my janitorial friend. "What ails you, my companion? It is I, a sanitation engineer, such as yourself! It appears I have committed a social blunder, a faux pas, by bringing my—my stained uniform—you know what eating—drinking—consuming chili can be like, eh?"

"Stained, my ass. You're a SCHOOL janitor!" he roars as he draws his mop.

"Oh, piss."

"Did you bring your mop, Creepy?" Vivi asks.

"Leave my territory or else I'll have at ye!" the apparently-clearly-designated museum janitor roars (albeit louder and more frightening) again.

[90]

Vivi pulls out a record player from—whatever, Vivi's probably not real either—she pulls out a record player and sets the needle.

Prince's "When Doves Cry" starts. Jumpin' Christ, can anyone even afford to use this?

With a leonine roar (he roars a lot) the enemy janitor leaps towards me, mop raised for a downward smash. I'm concerned.

Health bars also rise above our heads. Double concerned.

And whilst concerned, he lands his downward smash on my skull and my health bar depletes by sixty percent. What a bunch of nonsense, he's OP!

He barrages me with a flurry of mop cross chops. I block with my wrists and feel my health bar steadily diminishing. I assume his downward smash used up most of his EX Meter and proceed to Tornado Punch his chest.

He must not have an EX Meter cuz he blocks—piss shit, he parries—my punch and leaps into the air again for another smash. I counter with a Burrito Blast—by MY pissing EX Meter is empty so I—ya know, this is my problem with fighting games. Whenever you get to a boss character, it's just fucking unfair. I roll backwards instead, narrowly escaping his clutches.

The janitor flips his mop over and raises it above his head like a javelin. Vivi also takes a few steps back. Have I even hit him once yet? I forget that I don't know what a javelin is and prepare to counter his "obviously" incoming charge with a Hurricane Kick (which is actually a real jujitsu move, by the way).

So yeah, he throws his mop and it impales me through my stomach.

My health bar drops to zero. I drop to the floor bleeding. The janitor raises his arms in victory as Prince abruptly yells "Purple Rain" in 8-bit victory.

I'm somehow still alive. Typical. While the janitor's absorbed in his victory, I turn myself and crawl towards the guillotine. Almost there. Just a few more feet and—

—Everyone laughs at me. They're all laughing. They surround me. Mock me. Block my path to freedom. They're giving me *The Look*. It's always *The Look*.

Why are they even—how are they even here? Aren't all these kids dead? Yeah, Rooz killed like all of these kids. I went to prison for killing these kids! Snowelda—I don't know if she actually died in our fight, but I'm sure Rooz got—oh wait, her baby killed her. But she's not pregnant anymore? And Gwynevere got killed by the water, right?

They're all laughing laughing laughing—I didn't ask to be like this. I flip over on my back and they lean over and utterly fill my view. Somebody wrenches the mop out of my body. I scream and they laugh harder. Giggle. Chortle. Guffaw, whatever the hell they do. Just make it—it's not my fault, I didn't ask to—I can't even hear my own—

—Vivi stares down at me. Melancholy. Almost seems afraid. Why? She holds my hand.

"Hey Creepy, we have to break up."

I stare back at her. A canopy of hanging bulbs bathes her in comforting light. But—but I'm so cold. I—

"—Jhaegar?"

"What?"

"You need to be done now. You've been here for eight years."

"What?"

We're at a carnival—or a mall—jumpin' FUCKIN' Christ! It's like that dream I—but she was blonde, Vivi's black—black hair! Some guy keeps asking if we want falafels, like, leave us alone, can't you see we're—"But they're two for one"—I don't give a—

[92]

—I look down at my hand as Vivi leaves it. It's old—not *old* old—but old. Older, at least.

"I still love you," she says.

"So why are you leaving?"

"Because you can't love yours—

this fucking shit shit again huh this fucking shit shit shit oh my fucking god whatever

doesn't even matter nope nope no doesn't even I don't care what's it even matter the mall the

mall so many lights and vaporwave Marissa Nadler playing like I don't care don't care about

your sad fucking sad person sitting looking sad in a sad picture I don't fucking

shut up shut wannabe singing songwriter discount   Lana del Rey but then again she's really

discount Marissa Nadler fuck her fuck her she sucks

NO

NO

Shut up Jhaegar you fucking retard motherfucker shut up with the
fucking rants Vivi doesn't care she's gone now I can't see her
I'm on the bench alone and the falafel guy's telling me that I
look like a big strong guy who could eat two falafels and I
don't just tell him he's a asshole and he ll go away they'll all
jus t go away once you tell them to fuck off I've been here for
eight years   eight   fucking
I've been here for eight years where did th   e time go I
 don't   have a   fucking
              problem you just don't like the way I think
 Vivi please don't   what
        I'm sorry I'm
You're fine   I
   don't go   bitch
                    whore bitch fucking
   fucking shut up   she's nice   she's nice
kill   wants to kill you change you   bitch bitch
     not her fault   die Jhaegar   you're the
        you're fine   it's   shut up
should've left   carnival fucking
          I'm gonna   kill you   I'm

[93]

you're the bitch   get over it J   it's you
    maybe you should see somebody
                                          what
        I was the one   I can't
          ya know, a doctor   just see a   it'll be
        jumpin' fuckin' Jesus fuckin'   it's all
            you're the loser   it's not my   look
    all gonna die   watching you   it's
        I'm just concerned for you honey   please die
                favor   from you to me to you to me
        not   right   not   right   not
                    it's all your fault
        all the bodies here   everyone was dead
altogether there   here and   ya know?
            new being   stop lying   stop it's hey
            you ruined her life
        help me   me
          can't think   shut up shut   I need
        look   why do you think they all look like her
            her
                                    you're the fucking bitch
            you lying   her
ants your rants your rants your rants your rants your rants your
        ruined her life   the villain   just
    just fuckin' stupid like a stupid fuckin' you're stupid fuckin'
            why won't you get over yourself
it's her   isn't it   bothofthem
            and forgive you   just
    you're gonna have to die   its fine
    you deserve it   youre fine   earned it
            asked for   eight years
                                        just die
        gotta piss   piss   I need to
                    Prince lived in Minnesota kinda of where
open and close   Prince was a   rained when he
    Durkheim posits   forgive
            nobody can   drink something feel better
    I met a kid in college who went to Prince's house and he gave
        Vivi says I still love you"
    just chemical just man just chemical reaction
                        who cares   who
        altruistic   had this spiritual s u b d i v
    do it loser no balls   meet her at
    I meet her at the ice rink
guess I have   now I think
I mean what a deal free dinner   diner   dinner   piss
                                    smiles like her

[94]

```
        acute                      like a s u b d i v i s i o n
      knife in my hands now                        in
                    Snowelda laughs at me         her baby
weird fucking terms                nonsense    waste    my terms
        ascending your morality
      acute altruistic              Im a waste
that look               pointing ascending morality
     theyre all here too          laughing
greater than your                    not         no no no
        Snows fucking baby thing laughs at        flying around
   I hope I look as metal as that guy from The Thing 1712
           always laughing at me         museum or the mall
cant her out of my                            your cute
      this piss shitting mall            a cute acute
      slit my wrists                  blood
      wait it was mortality              just go away shut up
        because real life happens af                    where
   across the wrist for attention
              should have bought the falafels Jhaegar
Hmong kids                    really                    Rooz
        who cares wont die              die       your fault
ud feel pretty bad if I was dead youd feel pretty bad if I was d
              Duane Jones is a fucking      I dont care
                    down the river for results
  , ya know   better there because        killed them Buggins
ead youd feel pretty bad if I was dead youd feel pretty bad if I
              never do              wont die by this anyway
    Vivi'i''s dead           I wish I was shot
   I dont care Rooz it doesn't pertain to
because mortal chains hold me back from my true potential and I
      around the lake for fun                I slit my
                          dead Cambodians everywhere
        I open up my whole arm                not laugh
  Cambodians        dead Cambodians
                should have bought them
        lots of         drying and caking   Mary cake patty
        they dont laugh now do they     those fucking
was dead you' fee pretty bad i I was de d you d fee pre
     killed them             how long
its really                          I cant
        Godhood    cake we all fall down when doves cry
 d    as       dead y   f       if I       ad          yo
cant feel my          oh piss
    ee         this what it feels like          Doghood
              I killed everybody            lot of blo
     I m bleeding        my head
Dog sees goD          good musical              jumpin
```

[95]

```
       its real this time                    I cant
         typical              Im      sh       its f i n e
                  now I'll never let you leave
       theyre shutting up               finally          finally
still ringing but                Ergo-Anomic          fuck me
    changed  my           dont wanna anymo
             how do I                       stop
 oh piss            piss              Im in the    I    shut
      too confusing too                      what
         I definitely              so yeah      riders on the st
             where I    Ergo er-go I
```

II. Hell

Fuck me in my ass, I'm alive.

I'm also in a hospital—hospital room. Rather strange, I pretty much ripped my veins out and shouldn't be—

"—Jumpin' Christ!" I yell.

My arms...my arms...my piss shitting—

"—We apologize, sir, we didn't have any white arms on hand."

I glance over. Some nurse grins at me from the doorway. Her grin widens as she attempts to cover it with a palm.

"Or should I say: on *arm*."

She snickers and vanishes into the hall.

I seem to be recovering from some sort of arm transplant surgery—though all they fucking seemed to have were black guy arms and for some reason they decided to (without my consent which they doubtlessly need (or I guess fucking not!)) proceed with the procedure (proceed-ure) and—I mean, uh—no, it's fine cuz I'm black. I mean, Black. I'm Black. And they gave me the exact colored arms I needed and already had.

"We're glad you see it that way, mister," some doctor—I'm glad they let anyone wander in here—now apparently in my room says.

I rub my new arms. Bulging stitch marks form an interesting border between Black and I-swear-not-White.

"We had to dispose of your last arms," the doctor continues for some reason. "They were done for. But trading up? That's always fun, too, eh?"

[97]

"Why did you save me?" I ask. "Why did you have to save me? Also, how did you find me at that carnival mall? Where even was that?"

"Oh no, we didn't save you. You're dead."

Sigh, I wish.

"Well," he adds, "in a loose sense. As you'll come to find out, someone like you can never REALLY die. It's just a matter of—"

—But I stop listening as it appears my heart's ceased beating.

never **REALLY** die

I swing myself out of bed.

The "doctor" (cuz he's probably just this lab coat renting armchair psychologist freak) rushes me.

"Oh, no, no no no no no, you can't do that, you have to—"

—I must investigate this worl—wait, what happened to the doctor? I step into the hallway. Normal hallway décor greets me. Maybe this is the regular world? Other "doctors" mill about, do their duties and whatnot…but none of them harass me and say, "You have a problem that we need to get checked out, Jhaegar, cuz your life will—" —so I flip back to the belief that this is an alternate reality, "Alt-Real" as they say. I—

—Wait, what? There's this little orange pill on the floor. And it rests on a mound of matching orange powder. Smells vaguely Eastern (in a non-racist way, of course) and I feel like I would assume dishes made with this are rather troublesome and time consuming but would be surprised to find them in actuality being quite simple, fun, and delicious.

[98]

One of the "doctors" seems glad I've discovered this floor powder. Not sure why as the "doctor" doesn't seem to have feet to touch the floor in the first place, so I doubt any sort of floor-like connection. But this "doctor" does float menacingly in the air. I enjoy that. It's the little things. This "doctor"—I don't know, it's really glossy or—glassy or something, glassy and phallic (though I think everything's phallic), I don't know—but it's holding up a newspaper like it doesn't see me…but I see it, so it has to see me, right?

Whatever. The powder seems kinda cool—kinda chill—and I think I hear police sirens in the distance. I also think my mind—my multiple minds—Multi-Minds—MMs—I don't know, I forget things regarding bodily health cuz we hate ourselves. I bend over the pile and take a

***

I'm a dauuuhog I'm a dauuuhog we know Major M's a Frauuuhaud

One for the money
Two for the show
On three we get ready
And on four come with me and

It's no gaaaaaaaaame

(Japanese Japanese Japanese)

A bodybuilder, she's like a body builder now

What? Why? And how? She didn't do anything
She bodybuilt

But she was a bad worker
That doesn't matter

She should've cried and suffered

[99]

Oh, so like you?

                                                      Yeah but

but you enjoy it

              (Thin metal metal metal metal metal)

                        splits

Everyone was going on here and I said to myself what the fuck
but it didn't matter you see because if you actually see you see
then nothing ever happens because that's just how it works right
you see everyone just everyone and that time after work in the
in the lobby just showered and her hair smelled like lilacs or s

INSERT DOG MEME

                                          INSERT DOG MEME

              WE KNOW MAJOR J'S A HUNKIE

                        GWYNEVERE
                  Last name's *Hunking* now.

                        JHAEGAR
                   What the fuck, why?

                        GWYNEVERE
              You don't even know. And why do you care?

                        JHAEGAR
                 Because you're my girlfriend.

                        GWYNEVERE
                 No, that Vivivi…whatever narc is.

                        JHAEGAR
                 Vivi? I haven't even dated her yet.

                        GWYNEVERE
                    Yeah okay, Jhaegar.

                        JHAEGAR
                        Gwyn—

                        [100]

                    GWYNEVERE
              —Yeah okay Jhaegar—

                     JHAEGAR
              —I didn't do anything—

                    GWYNEVERE
               —YeahokayJhaegar

Gwynevere glances at the CAMERA. She looks PISSED because she
knows she's not living in proper screenplay format.

Jhaegar grabs his skin and rips it off to reveal VIVIIVIANA
inside who then rips off her skin to reveal dddddddddddddddddddd
dddddddddddddddddddddddddddddddddddddddddddddddddddddddddddddddddd
dddddddddddd   dddddddddddddd

                smoke fills the apartment
            and the smell will linger for five days
               lavender will help (kinda) (maybe)
                but it wont cover it all the way

        she tries to hide her teeth but it doesn't work too hot
                        too hot
                        huh?
                  It cant be that bad tho
                 so they add five more days

                    nows the ketchup
                   on mustard, on Prego
         on Marzetti on Cuervo on Wong's House Original
                    forget the juices
                      they sure did
                    theres a mess now
           but they wore their "dumpster pants"
               wait, where's the trash can?

                   its not very good
                  you're not very good
                        aww
                 don't make me hug you
                      (nothing)
                    well say it back

              she gets out the phone book
           so she can reach her charging cord
                 whats the name again

                        [101]

I don't know
cool place
she dials
they didn't even have to kiss

well what now
lets mess around
what
yeah
no
come on
dude Jhaegar
please
hey whats that
huh?

STUNNER! HOLY SHIT!

his nostrils turn black
the smoke sank into the carpet
everything's quick here I guess
her socks are mismatched
one green
the other perfect

and then when the pizza boy finally comes they tip him fifty dollars
not because he was really good
or really cute
or really clever
it was because who cares?

("Weeping Wall" Noises)

***

But yeah, definitely hate ourselves.

"Ya betchya do, assholes," some—New Jersey accent! Woman New Jersey accent!

A girl my age (a real New Jersey (actually probably hateful stereotype) NEW JERSEY GIRL!) grimaces at me. She rolls her eyes and lets me go. Apparently she was holding me by my medical robe shirt collar thing.

[102]

I fall back to the ground (dirt? I'm outside?) and notice New Jersey wears a Devil Halloween costume. Pitchfork and horns and tight leggings and…

Whoa.

Though she's no longer looking at me, I sense her roll her eyes again. She glances around the forest we're evidently in. I gotta stop taking drug—

"—Nah, ya gotta stop huffin' fuckin' turmeric," New Jersey says. Aw man, her voice…

"Sorry, I, uh," I mumble. Damnit, Jhaegar! Stop being a loser all the time! "So, uh," I cough a few manly coughs, "where are we?"

"We're in Hell, jackoff, ya killed yaself, where else would ya be?"

She turns to examine me. She rolls her—okay, maybe I don't like the eye roll thing.

"An' YOU just happened ta fuck yaself so fuckin' bad ya woke up in dat fuckin' Him awful infirmary. An' did ya learn ya lesson? No. Bettah ways ta do dat stuff. I mean, I heard ya was stupid, but not dis stupid."

"But you just said we're in Hell?"

Now her eyebrows arch. She puts a hand on her hips and drums her fingers along her now rippling costume. Ya know? That kind of ripple thing when someone's wearing tight clothing and it's so tight that it—like—rises up from the skin like a tripwire?

"Fuck, he was right 'bout da thinkin' out loud ting, too," she continues. "But correct, we're in Hell."

"Yeah sure, I know—but Hell looks just like real life?"

"Oh, I'm aware."

"But, uh, Miss, I—"

[103]

"—Mothafuck! Shut up! Just shut up, okay? I heard ya was comin', we've all been hearin' 'bout ya fuh years, so I, being da evah so gracious host dat I am, came ovah ta dat fuckin' shithole 'hospital,' as if we needed one, as if it really fuckin' mattahed, ta come pick your sorry ass an' bring ya back home. Just as a—as a common courtesy cuz you're—ah, you're you!"

"What?"

New Jersey bends her knees and throws her arms out in exaggerated importance. Trying to express importance? She's theatrical. I love her.

"You're 'you!' Da one who's coming or somethin'. If ya ask me, though, you're rather, uh, rather…"

She glances down at her palm as if something's written there. Mouths a word to herself as if practicing.

"You're a mi-as-ma!"

I feel like I need to roll my eyes now, but if I did she'd hurt me. And while I know I'd enjoy that, I—shut up, you don't want her to hear you—I stand up and brush myself off.

"So we're just gonna stay in the woods?" I ask.

She grunts. Does a (cute little) spin and starts off through the trees. I know I need to follow her. I indeed do.

"Nature is Satan's church," she muses.

"Ah, I see." What?

"Kinda like dat forest in Japan, yeah? Forests are populah places. Anyway, like I already said, I'm just doin' dis ting fuh, uh…"

Is she blushing? I can't even—

"—Mothafuck, nevah mind," she groans. Yeah, I must've said that out loud, too.

[104]

I decide to be quiet…and to try to still my thoughts as well. You never know, ya know? It's hard not to stare at h—shut up, Jhaegar!—it's hard not to—Jhaegar! Stop!

I start repeating the same word over and over in my head, kind of like TM (Transcendental Meditation, you plebes) cuz if it's good enough for David Lynch, it's good enough for me—but the word I come up with is "fish eggs." Fish eggs fish eggs fish eggs. Fish eggs fish eggs fish eggs fish eggs fish eggs fish eggs. Fish eggs. Funny thing about David Lynch, though, I can't stand any of his movies. I don't know why! And people always tell me my writing reminds them of David Lynch, that I have a very Lynchian sense that likes to create dynamic and bizarre worlds—and it bothers me that I can't stand his movies cuz I adore him as a person (not that I've met him—just interviews and—ya know?) cuz he seems so genuine and exciting and he's one of the few unique thinkers we're blessed to—

—I hear New Jersey groan again.

"So, whadya think a Hell so far?" she manages.

"Oh, I, uh—I think it's alright."

She shakes her head. Whispers:

"Shit."

"What's that?"

"So, uh, ya don't like David Lynch?"

"I mean, he's alright."

We keep walking.

"Alright," she says.

Wait, was she trying to have a conversation with me? Oh piss, I have to get back in this.

"So yeah, I'm in Hell?" I ask.

[105]

"Yup…can't escape ya troubles dat easy."

"Ahhh…cool…and what's your name?"

New Jersey stops.

Bursts of palpable rage flow through every fiber of her body. She spins around (still cute) and gestures to herself.

"Are ya fuckin' serious?"

"Huh?"

"Who da fuck ya think I am?"

"You're a girl?"

She arches an eye brow. Rolls her hand at me like she wants me to keep guessing.

I mean, I kinda knew but…you know me, I didn't wanna assume…no wait, presume! Cuz I have evidence!

"You're Satan?"

"There ya go, gee, aren't ya so fuckin' smart?"

"But, isn't that kind of stereotypical?"

"I don't see dat. Maybe fuh Halloween, but certainly not real life now. Wouldn't ya agree?"

"Well, sure, but that's just what people want you to be—"

"—First off: exactly," she nods at me for half a second and I don't know quite— "—second off: you two really are friends. Like pitches on a fork, huh?"

"No?"

We keep walking.

"So, uh, 'Satan,' I guess. Why are we walking?"

[106]

"Gotta get back ta camp."

"Camp? You're the kin—Queen of Hell and all you have is a camp?"

"I have an office, too, but mostly just da big camp. Alleged 'civilization' is da plight a God. We don't take dat shit here. Here we live close ta nature an' da natural order a tings."

Don't crucify me, but I'm starting to like this Satan girl. She's sick. And I also feel I'm about to overcome a common misconception (or several common even!) on religion.

"People aren't too bright, I mean," she continues (jumpin' Christ, here it comes!), "dey always try ta see it as some sort a ultimate dichotomy. It's a load a shit. It's not one bad an' one good, just two alternative ways a lookin' at tings. Hell ain't bad, it's just fuh people who prioritize temporary worldly pleasures ovah a false promise a piety in exchange fuh an eternal, an' boring as shit, life. Ya know? We just got different interests. Kinda like *Da Last Jedi* (2017)? Da one people were just too fuckin' stupid ta undahstand? 'Dark' ain't synonymous with 'Bad,' da Dark Side just has an alternative viewpoint on da Force. But no, fuckin' God? He's a real shit, ya don't wanna—*God* forbid we bring intellect ta *Star Wars*."

I stare at her as we walk. Not at her, uh, but at her hair. The back of her head, the back of her MIND! She's so—!

"—Soooo," I flounder, "you were able to realize what that movie was about, too…"

I sense her blush. Mostly cuz she catches her foot on a fallen branch and stumbles.

"Nah, I mean, I don't, uh, nah, we don't watch a lotta movies down here. Da woods?"

"Didn't you say you have an office?" I ask. Hopefully not too boldly.

"Yeah. Yeah!" Aggressive now. Yes. "A woods office! Just—look ovah there or somethin'!"

She points to the right side of our path. I guess I follow her finger, it's not that I—

[107]

—Holy fuckin' piss!

Dog City Never Sleeps

Letters have been spray painted against tree trunks and seem to line up only from certain vantage points. It's not just this, though, I glance around and see the same letters all over the woods, all different colors and fonts and—what the—what the HELL?

"Dey started appearin' 'bout a few days ago. Yeah," suddenly gloomy, "den we heard 'bout you."

"I thought you heard about me years ago? And what'd you hear?"

"*Dog is comin'.*"

Dog is coming

"Shut up," says I.

"Huh?" says she.

"Nothing. Am I the dog?"

"Maybe. Could be. We'll have ta see."

"When'll we find out?"

Satan thinks this over. Or at least stalls for time.

She raises her arm again and points straight ahead.

"Oh hey, here we are."

[108]

Indeed we is and "camp" it are! Thatched huts and fires (comforting fires, not scary Hell fires) stretch for what I assume to be several blocks in each direction. I check skyward and find treehouses, treebridges, and tree-everything-else-s disappearing into the clouds. Shame on me, I was in the woods and never thought to glance up before—the trees here seem to go on forever. Considering Hell, they probably do.

It's like—wow, it's actually just like the Ewok village from *Return of the Jedi* (1983). Like a thoughtful, heartfelt, and incredibly accurate recreation.

"No, it's not," Satan interjects. Insists, even.

Whatever. Don't care. I adore it anyway.

"Young White Male!" someone shouts. Wait, I recognize—

—ROOZ! Leaning over a railing from a treehouse above. He grabs a rope and swings down to meet us. It's—okay, he's probably had practice from living here, I'm not saying Black people are good at swinging from ropes or being in the jung—

"—And I'm not White, Rooz."

"Oh?" he says in exaggerated curiosity, "you must be an Ally then?"

We both erupt in good natured (or hateful depending upon one's perspective) laughter. Even Satan cracks a smile. I knew I lov—liked her!

"It's just—it's just nuts you're down here, Rooz, I never thought I'd see you again."

"Is that so, Jhaegar? Really? Even after I committed suicide right before your eyes? You never thought you would...?"

"Join you?"

"Success! I believe your lack of supposing you would see me again is a positive sign."

[109]

"I mean, I thought I'd kill myself, I just didn't think Hell was real...or this nice, like jumpin' Christ—"

—Satan holds up a hand:

"Can we not?"

"Ohh, sorry." Then to Rooz, "Did, uh, did you know before you, uh...?"

"Well, no one can know for sure," he responds. "But wishful thinking prevailed, did it not?"

"I just thought you'd be more, ya know, grounded in logic or something."

"Jhaegar, please. Were I permanently gone, your plot would be unable to advance."

Wait, what?

"Wait, what?"

Satan nudges Rooz. Circles a finger around one of her ears:

"Comin' down from dat turmeric."

Amused disappointment spoils Rooz's face as he grins at me.

"Do you not remember? Inhaling Indian powders does not serve your senses well. What have you been seeing this time?"

Satan nudges him again:

"He's been seein' da dogs."

Rooz shakes his head in even more, uh, amused disappointment.

"Jhaegar."

"See!?" I point at Satan. "Dogs! You said 'Dogs!' You DO know about Dog City! That's why you came to get me!"

"Nevah said I didn't know anything. An' dis is Hell, asshole, I get everybody."

[110]

Rooz grabs my shoulders and leans in close. I'm not sure if this is a thing that friends do, but I'll just take it at face val—

—I said "friend." Rooz is my friend!

"I know this must certainly be a lot to take in at once," Rooz says, "and I know this is likely not the outcome you were hoping for, but it is my most ardent belief that—"

"—Rooz, can we hurry it up?" Oh, Satan. My kind of girl. "Let's just do da tour already, I got three Belgian Doomers an' Thundercat droppin' in any minute here."

My jaw widens in horror.

"Thundercat kills himself?"

"Yeah, gets drunk and injects himself with cat litter. Ya know? Dat counts. Poor guy's still upset 'bout Mac…"

"Is Mac Miller here, too?!"

Satan nods to herself in approval.

"He was a good catch. Recorded a new album down here, we're pretty proud."

Rooz reins me back in. Ah, so this IS what friendship is like. He's better than Buggins already.

"A lot of your—what I presume to be your heroes—are down here, Jhaegar. Maybe we shall come across a few. Only one way to know for certain. Shall we?"

Rooz puts his hand on the small of my back (sure, I guess, I'm still new here) and guides me through camp. Ha. Camp. Like I'm at summer camp. Hell camp in the—

"—Wait," I must know, "is this the Woods of the Suicides?!"

Oh piss, she's mad…

[111]

"No, ya fuckin' asshole, it's not! I already said what it was, okay? Dat's a made up fuckin' book an' a made up fuckin'—shit—are ya fuckin'—are ya literally fuckin' stu—argh!"

Rooz gives me a clear 'shut-the-fuck-up' hand signal.

Satan plunges her pitchfork into the ground several times. It's fine, though, she cools off after a while. Rooz waits, accustomed to these outbursts apparently. How long has he been down here? Or rather, how long was I in prison? Was I in prison?

It's fine. Satan pats her hair back into place. Cute enough: her horns are actually a swanky headband.

The tour continues!

Rooz guides me through the trees. I don't remember how I got up here, but the bridges are pretty neat to walk on. Satan kind of trails behind us—I hope she's not embarrassed—I wouldn't be. I mean, her place, her rules, right?

Rooz (I haven't used parenthesis for a while) cocks his head back towards me.

"By the by, Jhaegar, I apologize for the whole *Catcher in the Rye* business, though of course I had nothing to do with it as framing you for my 'experiment,' so to speak, runs contrary TO said 'experiment.' I simply desire to assure you it was not me. Does this sufficiently clear things up for you?"

"Not really, but it's okay."

"Swell."

"So, Rooz, what do we, uh, what do you guys do down here? We are 'down' right?"

"Of that, I am unsure. As to what we do: many things. Dance practice. Intellectual discourse. Raids on Heaven. Those are the main three I would say."

"You guys 'raid' Heaven?"

[112]

"Yes." He gestures with his right hand. "These are the tree homes, Jhaegar. Being blunt, I have doubts as to the efficacy of this tour. To me it all seems quite self-explanatory…but yes, we raid Heaven. As I am confident you have noticed by now, you and I do not seem to be burning in eternal damnation?

"Yeah, sure."

"And 'why is this?' you may ask? Well, as it would happen, the idea of 'bad' people being tortured in Hell is in actuality quite ludicrous once one gives it a few moments of thought. After all, if all the 'bad' people were sent to Hell—a place made for 'bad' people ruled by the ultimate 'baddie' herself—why would they be tortured?"

"Listen up, asshole," Satan adds from behind. "I'd nevah hurt one a my own."

"And therein lies the point," Rooz continues. "If anything, Satan would be pleased to have 'bad' people sent to her. Why would she not? And when they are sent to her, for what reason would she torture them? They are like her, think like her, some even worship her. Often times you will hear the phrase, 'Oh, that man will burn in Hell for all eternity,' in the case of a Ted Bundy or a Charles Manson. Well…why? Would not Satan be utterly pleased to have cretins such as them join her following? Why would she subject Charles Manson to pain and suffering when it is in fact the pain and suffering Charles Manson caused others on earth that so caught her admiration in the first place? If anything, the ones being tortured in Hell would be the 'good' people."

"Hence da raids!" shouts Satan.

"What? Is this pissing World of Warcraft?" I ask. "You guys really raid Heaven?"

"Dey started raidin' us first, da pricks, but yeah…dey like ta capture us an' teach us 'moral lessons' an' other shit. So we drag their yuppy asses back here an' have a little fun."

[113]

"That's amazing."

"I know," Satan and Rooz say in tandem.

"An' buildin' on dat shit 'bout Charlie," Satan adds, "he's like a celebrity down here—an' yeah, we're *down*—people love 'em. An' I'm always happy ta bring in a celebrity, adds ta our *prestige*, ya could say."

"Do you guys have, like, an end goal here?"

"Well, God's pretty fuckin' irritatin' an' he hardcore cheats—so we nevah make much headway, but, ya know, it's somethin' ta do. Otherwise ya just get sad an' ya don't wanna get sad down here. Dat's a whole can a shit."

Piss, this is interesting. I'll have to sit down and explain this to myself later—just to work out the kinks. As much as I can tell: Hell bad place for good people, good place for bad people. Heaven good place for good people (probably boring, though), bad place for bad people. Raids sound kinda neat, too. I'll—

—So yeah, I tend to "explain myself" a lot. It mostly comes off as me ranting or raving—and I know it's a total waste, but just let me explain…myself. I have to explain things to myself, that way I can better understand them—and not just like things I don't know that I'm learning for the first time, but any kind of thing, things I've already explained to myself dozens of times. Explaining something to myself helps me contextualize (right?) the information and cement it into my brain. What's actually better, is sometimes I just explain things to somebody else (in my head, that is) cuz then I really get cemented. I guess it makes me feel important, too. Not sure, I, uh—yeah, ya know? Everyone wants to feel needed, so if I explain German Expressionism to someone in my head then that head person is like, "Gee wow, Jhaegar sure knows a lot about

[114]

German Expressionism, he must be really cool," and then I think to myself, "Gee, ya know what? I AM pretty cool," ya know? It's like telling someone something makes it all real.

Wait. I feel I've abandoned my prerogative.

"So Rooz," I begin, "how do you get out of here? What if you actually wanna *die* die?"

Rooz just grins and shakes his head.

"Why are you still so focused on that, Jhaegar? You are with us in Hell now, the best place to be. Why do you not instead focus on learning to be happy?"

I can't look at Rooz anymore. I don't know why. I just have to look somewhere else (I don't hate him, just can't look right now). I don't know. I can't. I don't. Typical me.

Rooz seems okay with it, though. He grins that grin of his—that one that tells you he knows too much? Rooz is a chill guy (Mentally Ill? More like Mentally Chill ("Yo, I'm afflicted with dat Mental Chillness")). I like him.

"Got some people ya'd like ta meet. Why don't ya step inta da dance hall?" pipes up Satan.

I need to pay attention more. One: we're on the ground again. Two: we're stood in front of some jumbo dance hall. Well, more like an event center or something—I feel like it's not just a single room inside, ya know? Like wings and stuff, too. But it's really big. Made of trees and logs, I guess.

Whatever. We go inside. My suspicion (hey, a new word I can use instead of presume!) was correct. It's a foyer or grand entryway or reception thing first. What I presume (back at it!) to be the true dance hall waits behind a set of gilded double doors. I glance around. Nice plac—

—Oh my jumpin' fucking shit!

Two people—two GODS—smile before me.

[115]

Satan—actually, Rooz, I just wish it was Satan—claps his hand on my back.

"So, Jhaegar? What do you make of this? Satan was correct about celebrities, yes?"

Standing—towering—probably levitating before my eyes are Christine Chubbuck and the one and only Bud Dwyer (pretty sure I've mentioned Christine, not so sure about Bud. Rest assured, he killed himself, too (and for a greater cause! (and shut up with the "Die for a greater cause or live for a humble one" shit)))))(fuck, how many parenthesis?).

I raise my hands in reverence.

"Christine! Bud!"

"Hello, young man," says Bud. Just like I imagined he'd say!

"Satan told us you were something of a fan," says Christine. Of course!

"Don't say I nevah did nothin' nice fuh ya," Satan grumbles.

I'm just so happy right now I think I could hug them both. Actually, I think I did. Do. Wait, what time is this? Then I wring my hands. In…disappointment? What's wrong?

"Not to sound disappointed," I say. I say? Why am I saying this? "But is Thich Quang Duc here? It's just that you three are like my Holy Trinity."

"Ah, no," Bud starts, "that pansy assed prick made it up to Heaven."

"Buddhist," Christine clears up.

I raise my hands in, uh, when you had an idea but you didn't know if it was true or not and just found out it was true.

"So it doesn't matter what religion you are, they all just blend into one afterlife?"

Satan snickers.

"In a mannah a speakin', yeah."

Rooz snickers.

[116]

I stare at him.

He snickers more. What a—

"—Oh, Jhaegar."

"Why don't you guys tell me anything?"

"Cuz dat would," Satan starts but then pauses. She glances down at her palm and reads something. "Dat would put us in a in-vid-i-ous situation."

"*An* invidious situation," Rooz corrects.

"Both a ya fuck off. Lemme get my word a da day in."

"You have a word of the day calendar?" I ask. Puppy dog eyes no doubtly (doubtedly? how do you say that?) forming on my face.

"Well, yeah. Sure. I wanna be a bettah leadah so I gotta work on myself. Ya know? Takin' accountability fuh your own—?"

"—Awwwww," I sigh. But not at the accountability—I tuned out at that. She has a word of the day calendar! So cute!

"I have one, too!"

Satan pulls slightly at her Halloween costume and sighs.

"Yeah, an' dat's kinda da point...Jhaegar, ya really need ta get past dis—"

"—But you've had like three words of the day so far and it's been like two hours."

She seems mad again. Tehe. "I already said before, time goes different down here! Don't ya listen ta nothin'? You're really being," as she checks her palm again, "uh," and again, "uh, eff-er-vesc-ent."

Rooz raises his eyebrows at her.

Satan shakes her head.

[117]

"Sorry, geez, *an* effervescent."

Rooz raises his eyebrows at me.

"What?" I ask. "What do you want me to say?"

"So," Satan interjects. Trying to dodge cancel (it's a Smash term. Don't much care for that game, though (Miyamoto's a saint, though) fuck I said "though" twice) our conversation, "are ya both excited fuh ya first raid? An' aww, ya'll getta do it togethuh!"

"I mean, yeah whatever. Sounds kinda fun—wait, where'd Christine and Bud go?"

"They was like a one-time deal. He figured ya liked 'em too much an' couldn't exploit their lives fuh low comedy anymore. Ya'll see easiah targets from now on."

"*He?*"

Satan snorts.

"Yeah, whichevah one."

"Introspection," Rooz adds.

"What's that?" Satan asks. And not, "What's that?" as in, "What's that object?" but like, "What's that?" as in, "What did you say?" Cuz, uh, New Jersey. Probably. Sure.

"Introspection. Their suicides fail to correlate to Jhaegar's hopeful suicide as others may, for example Thich Quang Duc's. We shall definitely see more of him, or so I would predict. Christine and Bud? Social reform and honor bound altruism? Alas, no."

"Hey, I read that book," I tell him. "What are you trying to say, Rooz?"

"*Dog is coming.*"

"Uh? Miss Satan?" a new voice asks. Jumpin' Christ, who now?

A man (I'm going on the record for not pointing out he's Middle Eastern) taps Satan on the shoulder. Three other...men wait behind him.

[118]

"When you say you need us?" he continues.

"Ah, Mr. Jarrah. Glad ya showed up, these two boys here were da ones I was hopin' ya could take undah ya wing."

Satan grins at the men and then at us.

"Gentleman, meet Jhaegar Holdburn an' Tiresias Tyrone Tyreke Washington Lincoln Roosevelt III. Jhaegar and Rooz, meet da gentleman. Dis guy's Ziad Jarrah an' his, uh, coworkers here are da three Als: Ahmed al-Nami, Ahmed al-Haznawi, an' Saeed al-Ghamdi."

The leader, Ziad I guess, nods at us.

"How you boys d...?" he trails off. His eyes bore inquisitive holes into my face.

"You," nodding at just me now, I guess? "We meet before?"

"Uhhh, I mean, I, uh, I don't think so."

Rooz nudges me and nods in return for the both of us: "I am confident you shall meet him again—before—eventually. But we are splendidly well, sir, thank you for asking. And how do you fare?"

Now I nudge Rooz.

"Hey," whispering—hopefully whispering, "I think I've seen—well, maybe not personally—do you recognize these guys from somewhere?"

"Jhaegar, your white elitism is showing," Rooz says before he hits me with a wicked wink. Wicked wink, huh? I like that.

Satan sighs. "No, ya didn't whispah, an yeah, ya're probably racist, but also yeah, I'm sure ya've seen pictures a these guys. Unsurprisingly, dey're really good at da raids."

"I'm still not following."

[119]

One of the three Als (sorry, I already forgot their names) holds up his hands and makes an exploding gesture.

"Boom!" he cheers.

"Oh, *those* Middle Easterners…"

Ziad claps a hand on my shoulder.

"Yes, friend Jhaegar. We here? Best in world—now best in un-world. You two boys catch up no time."

"Well, Mr. Jarrah," Rooz says, "consider me quite intrigued. I eagerly await your instruction."

"I'm sure you do, Rooz," I mutter. "But yeah, were you guys the first plane or the second plane then? Not, uh—I mean, just curious."

Ziad shakes his head. Seems earnest enough, though.

"No. No, no. We not tower plane. Our plane one crash in field." He balls his hand into a fist. "Damn Americans."

"You'll get 'em next time."

"Oh," he laughs, "we make up for it here."

"Yeah. Well, I suppose that still counts as a suicide so that makes you a hero in my book."

Satan and Rooz trade puzzled faces.

"Yeah, yeah, I guess dat would count," she says. "I nevah really thought a it like dat."

"Wait, what? You didn't introduce me to these guys cuz they killed themselves?"

"Nah, I introduced dem ta ya cuz dey're fuckin' crazy an' I thought ya could use a helpin' hand."

[120]

"And Satan," Rooz now, "these men would fall more into the acute altruistic spectrum, would they not?"

Satan mulls it over.

"Well shit, I really DID nevah think a dat—hey no! If dey really was, den dey wouldn't be in Hell." After more mulling, "But dat may be a technicality…I don't know. I didn't plan dis parallel."

"How could you not have? Did you not plan any of this?"

Satan, mad (oh baby), "Well, I—ya know—I can still fuckin' get it all organized at least! Don't mattah if I don't do it direct, dat's his fuckin' fault if he wants to throw 'em in here."

"God's?" I ask.

"Fuckin' YOU, dumb shit!"

"What?"

"Jhaegar? Jhaegar?" Rooz patting my shoulder. What's with everyone and the touching? Why do people need to touch each other when they talk? Like, touch your fucking self instead.

Rooz takes his hand away from me.

"Jhaegar? I will have you know that I was alluding to dogs earlier, not these men."

"Thanks. All clear now."

Rooz beams: "Swell."

Ziad holds up his hand.

"Miss Satan, lady, when raid start? How long we have train them? Big mission tonight."

Irritation. I know I get irritated a lot (I anger easily), but I swear I…what was I mad about? Ya know, that is one small perk to being like me. At least I forget that stuff, too.

So yeah, I just kind of twiddle my thumbs—

[121]

"—eah, yeah, it has ta be tonight," Satan apparently continues.

"But would it not be better for Jhaegar and myself to gain experience and first practice?"

"Oh Rooz, honey, I'm sure ya've had enough practice."

"Well, what of Jhaegar, then?"

"He'll be fine, too. Listen. Dis is BIG. Like real big. Like fuckin' huge. We lost one a ours last time—we lose a lot generally but not like dis guy—an' tonight's da night we get him back."

"And who might this 'guy' be?"

"A fuckin' hero we all know an' love, dat's who! What? I gotta tell ya more?"

Sigh sigh sigh, please just yell forever—I don't care what it's about, just yell.

One of the Als nudges one of the other Als. I hear him whisper, "Simp."

Satan rolls her eyes. It only makes her—

"—All ya gotta know is dat he's no doubt being brutally fuckin' tortured as we speak. Dem cocksucka fuckin' angels a pack a shit horned bastard mothafuckaz but hey, once a yup always a yup, dat's why we gotta do it tonight."

"What's tonight?" I ask. "Sorry, you know me. Dumb asshole Jhaegar with no sense of time and a general—"

"—We get it. But tonight's Eid al-Fitr. Angels all gonna be busy harassing brown people."

Ziad and the Als grit their teeth.

"Yeah. See why we need dem?"

"I see, but...uh..." I don't really know what to say here. "The raid sounds cool and all and, uh..." But I...I don't wanna hurt others.

[122]

"If I go on the raid, can I just watch?"

Ziad and the Als look to Satan for an answer. Rooz awaits her as well. I don't—I mean, and what if Gwyn or Vivi are up there? They died (I think?) and I wouldn't wanna run into them and—they'd see I'm a total shitbird now and "with the wrong crowd" or some nonsense thing people always tell me.

"Are ya fuckin' serious?!" Satan exclaims after the few moments she took to calm down. "It's da RAID, what else ya wanna do down here? What? An' I mean really?! Just play with yaself fuh all eternity?!"

She takes a threatening step towards me. People always pull that shit. Why? I can tell you're upset, you don't need to rub it—

"—And dis ain't a rhetorical question, I wanna know. Ya just plan ta play with yaself fuh all eternity?" She gestures to herself, pulling at her costume. "Cuz dat's what it's fuckin' lookin' like ta me so far ya fucki—!"

—I...I don't know. I probably take a step back or hunch my shoulders trying to get away like I always do, but everyone is looking me, giving me *The Look* of course now cuz she brought up sex—masturbation, I guess—whatever, still a hateful stereotype, still a—shit fuck! See Rooz and everyone else? Stereotypes aren't just skin color, they can be—

—She takes another step forward. I just wanna go home. I'm scared. I tell myself I like strong angry (dominant) women but I—I don't know—I can't handle them. I can't handle anyone. I don't care, I'll just play PS4, that's fine, that's—it's not wasting my life if I don't know what I'm missing and—and it's still better than dying, right?! Fuck you! Fuck you! See? Aren't I doing what everyone wants?! At least I'm alive—

—I want her to slap me. I don't—cuz I—yeah, I deserve it. Just fucking hit me already. Keep hitting me so eventually I'll be—just—just slap me and tell me I suck.

I'm being held. What? And then let go. I find that I backed away from Satan and into Rooz and he set me back straight again. He pats my back as he does it. I even think I hear him whisper, "It's okay, man." Did Rooz just use a contraction? And say *man*? Is he my friend? Why couldn't he just push me instead, I fucking hate it when—

—No, just stop. Stop it—oh fuck. Jumpin' Christ, I'm—I'm having an attack or something, I'm like bent over I think and everything's just—I don't know, it's fucking something and I think Rooz talks again but I can't understand English right now and I keep— fucking, ya know? Like song lyrics just appear sometimes when I'm woozing out. All I hear is, *ain't nothin' but a nothin' but a,* and it's like, "Really? Are you serious? Now's not the time," and I—I'm on the ground.

"Miss Satan," that, uh…I forgot his name, too. The not Al one. "How say we just go dance practice, hmm? To loosen boy man up?"

Dance practice? Jumpin' Christ…

"Ya wanna ruin my fuckin' show, do ya? He ain't even been on his first raid an'—?"

"—No, Miss Satan. Not for show, just for practice. Calm his nerve. Maybe get him hobby?"

"What's going on even?" I mumble. "I don't understand."

Satan glares down at me. Then points down at me. Pretty…pretty hot honestl—no! Shut up, no it's not!

[124]

"Listen here: ya fuck up my numbah, I fuck up ya life. Ya undahstand dat?"

"Huh?"

Then she grabs my hand and pulls me up.

And I'm there.

WE'RE there. In the dance hall, the REAL dance hall.

I glance down to see my body popping and bouncing to big band jazz from the 40s…no, no, imitation big band jazz from the 50s made new again in the 90s. Least I look good. I wish someone took a picture actually, like that picture of Kurt by the billboard or whatever? That, like, Kris Noveselic said was the only picture he liked of himself? Still makes me cry. Me and him are like the same person. Kurt, not Kris. Kurt. "Kurdt."

But yeah, I guess I'm dancing now. Thank God (or the Devil) that Satan appears to have changed clothes as well…or uhhh, she just wears her jazz dancer costume thing over her devil costume. Wait, does that mean she was naked before? I don't really get it to be honest, but legs are legs. Jumpin' Christ, I'm a creep. I just wanna die.

That—his name's Ziad! Ziad nudges me cuz wishful thinking distracted me and I must've missed my mark. I didn't know I had marks. I—wait, things are coming in now. Rooz taught me how to dance earlier, but how would he know if we got here together? He probably took dance lessons before…ya know, being Rooz and all?

Also, why are we dancing in Hell? I mean, not like the evil, "We're gonna torture you" dance, but a, "Hot dawg, let's swing!" dance? I just really (by the way, I wasn't saying Rooz is gay, I just meant he's the kind of guy who would know how to dance cuz he's all into representation or something) and I—sigh, fuck me in my ass.

Oh well. Satan's got a bangin' voice…ah, New Jersey…

[125]

SATAN
I don't believe ya've eva seen a lady
with dis bag a tricks!

An' I don't believe ya evah
wanna fuck with 6-6-6!

So I'm tellin' ya, right here,
right now, get out, run!

Cuz ya're about ta find out
what makes Hell so much fun, ow!

CHORUS
Welcome to the Jazz Inferno, baby!
Welcome to the—

—What the—hey, even I'm singing! The band behind (there's a band behind us?) behind

us picks up—drummer's going nuts—and then there's like a brass solo. I—Christ on a Cross, is

that Tom Waits? Must've got that frontal lobotomy.

Huh?

I don't understand the things I think someti—oh no, new song!

SATAN
Hey Mac,
I know what ya're thinkin'!

Some good lil' thoughts,
ya'll end up just like Lincoln!

CHORUS
Hey Satan!

SATAN
What now?

CHORUS
What'll we do instead?

[126]

SATAN
We're goin' up ta Heaven
ta take God's fuckin' head!

EVERYONE NOW
Gotta get hyped, gotta be tonight, (gotta get)
gotta get ready for the big ol' Raid!

Makin' wrong from right, set the clouds alight (clouds alight)
gonna make those Angels scream for days!

Got our friends all together, got our buddies in tow,
we're gonna show 'em all what we've got!

Their ol' pals from the Nether, 'bout to be in the know,
and see that Hell is HOT, OWWW!

Hey, how old is she? Maybe she's just seventeen (or—or twenty-five? I really don't—)

—cuz I'll go toe to toe with anyone to argue that life begins when one's life begins—I mean, if

you weren't there, how can it be proved to be real? Anything pre 90s is suspect to me—very *sus*

as they'd say. Ya know, is it solipsistic in here or is it just me? Sorry, I stole that joke…but yeah,

everyone and everything was created to suit my needs to live whi—

—Piss, that's bleak. Everything in existence created just for me and I still can't win?

Imagine that.

Hey, I'm in the bathroom. I find myself here quite often (not *here* here, just *bathroom*

here). I can't remember if I—oh, I did. I'll wipe my ass, too, just in—

—Oh, also: May I please take a moment here to apologize to all women (not that I'm

necessarily a man, I—) —cuz women's underwear? What? How do you eat at Taco Bell? If I

have so much as a bite there, I'm having diarrhea for the next thirty days and thirty nights. BUT!

I'm a man (I mean, uh—) —I wear men's underwear which is loose and flowing and—so

afterwards I can just stand up and air out and whatever and it's all fine…but women?! You really

just grab your panties and ZOINK! Pull them up right into your bits? HOW?! Are you all just

[127]

eternally screaming on the inside?! HOW DO YOU DO THAT?! Notwithstanding that your—deal is right next to your asshole and bound to get obliterated come the hour of fast food reckoning, how do you wear those tight (not that I've ever personally slipped once and bought women's und—) —and just walk around like that? Hell, if I'm walking out of McDonald's, I'm walking out of there a level three biohazard!

And that's just like regular panties, sometimes you wear lingerie! Like...NO MAN is worth that, let me tell you this right here, NO MAN is worth that. Let your body breathe, gurl. You don't need to destroy yourself on our (their) behalf. It's just like...UGH, I just can't. I just—I would just never eat! Maybe that's why women are always trying to eat less or healthier or whatever: they don't give a shit how thin they become, they give a shit that they don't have to TAKE a shit.

I don't know—you'd really think underwear would be reversed. If anything, women need to air out and men need to be reined in. But I'm just a fucking loser who doesn't know or do anything and I've wasted my life yada yada I should've stayed in college yada yada gotta stop living in fantasy yada yada who cares? It genuinely seems that I'm the only one who does. Why do only I give anything any legitimate thought?!

Sigh.

I wish I could wear panti(shut up shut up shut up shut up shpust usuptu suput shup up upu

I notice the toilet paper whatever thing is almost out. Can't forget Grandpa J's Party Tidbit No. 2 (tehehe, *number two*).

***

[128]

I slap Rooz's (cuz it's my turn for slapping backs) back. I guess we're by the water cooler? We're definitely in a place.

"Hey, Rooz," I start. "Before we get back to dancing, don't you think you should empty the pipes?"

Rooz's jaw drops. Appalled (appalled for Rooz).

"Excuse me, Jhaegar, but you wish me to masturbate?"

"Whoa, no, no, I—"

"—And in a public restroom at that?"

"No, don't you have to take a shit?"

"Why do you suppose physical activity would be analogous to me having to relieve myself? If anything, would it not be—?"

"—Go to the bathroom, Rooz!"

He gives in and walks off.

Ziad and the Als (that's halfway, right?) watch me from down the water cooler room. They nod approvingly at my demonstration of authority. Got 'em.

Someone taps my shoulder.

It's Rooz! Jumpin' Christ, why? He doesn't even look traumatized.

"Rooz, why aren't you traumatized?"

"Is that another one of your demands?"

"But you used the bathroom?"

"Indeed."

"But, I…I…"

I glance over.

[129]

Ziad and the Als now shake their heads in disapproval. What have I done? I've already lost their respect.

I decide to punch Rooz in the jaw.

I'm just—

—I'm just fucking hitting him now. What? Why? Stop it—just—I'm sorry, Rooz. I'm—I keep punching and punching I think his nose breaks yeah it definitely breaks now Ziad is pulling me off. He's pulling me his nod is in approval again I think I don't know people like it when I do this stuff I guess. Rooz bleeds on the floor—bleeds a LOT and what sucks is that I don't really care. It's not that I don't care from some malevolent "fuck Rooz I hate that guy" viewpoint I just don't care he could live or die or be my friend or not and it's just like whatever why does it ma— I wish it was different I don't know how to care I don't know what went wrong I used to be so good.

Rooz is saying something now. I don't know if he's mad or—STOP SAYING I DON'T KNOW FUCK ME IN MY—shut up, just shut up, go away. It's like there's other people who make me don't care, I don't—no, don't blame them you asshole—I'm just not knowledgeable about it. There. It's like I'm just watching my life happen sometimes. Buggins'll text me and I don't wanna respond. He shouldn't bother, he knows I'm gonna die soon and just cause him more pain when I'm gone. Satan's here, I—just shut—I can't even think some—shut up. Fuck! Piss!

She's saying something and I can't understand English anymore. Again. Does that ever happen to you? Whoever you are? Are you enjoying this? Sorry it's taken me this long to notice you, there's just so many of you in my fucking head anymore that I can't tell. I just—ever since that one time I ran away and that guy stared at me through my car while I was sleeping? Ya

[130]

know? It wasn't like he was staring at me, it was like he was staring INSIDE me. That's the only way I can really describe the feeling. Ever since then it's just gotten—it's just gotten worse, I don't know.

I can't form a coherent fucking thought. Rooz is being wheeled away. Did I hurt him that bad? What did I even do? I only hit him a few times. Satan's grinning at me grinning so fucking big you'd think I was—I—now she's patting me on the—I hate when people FUCKING TOUCH ME jumpin' fucking Christ, I—shut up shut up sfhfukeshuf

Just calm down.

They're not here. Just calm down. You're still in your room, J. You're back in your room and no one here can touch you. They can't touch you and can't see you.

You're listening to The Sleepy Jackson and everything is fine. You're in control I'm in control my name is Jhaegar Holdburn and I own my life I can live or die as I please and today I choose to—it's fine. I kick my legs to the beat. I do this thing where I like gyrate my torso. I don't know, I don't know how to describe dancing. I love it, though. Maybe I should dance more.

So like…your lower body is stationary and instead of like bobbing your head imagine bobbing your torso. As a matter of fact my head stays rather stationary. Like someone has grabbed me by my legs and head and are just playing with me.

That's a thought. Some celestial being X dominatrix X South Korean transfer student just doing whatever she wants with me. That'd be fun…and I mean, someone has to take revenge, right? Might as well be—no, I probably shouldn't be allowed to enjoy it. How do you hurt someone who enjoys suffering?

[131]

I guess you could give them something they *want* cuz whatever they *want* would force them to take the lead or charge or something and they rather just sit back and be shit on…but then they get what they *want*…what if you just *want* to get things you don't *want*—I don't know. I feel like it's a win-win but also not really. And you'd think I'd enjoy my life more then, so really what the fuck?

But now that I think about it my head does kind of bop around—but not like my external head that everyone sees but more of an internal bop that I feel ya know? I love that part when they just do that "nananana nyaaa yayaya nananana nyaa yayaya" I just imagine all this crazy stuff going on and everyone singing and dancing in this churning storm of movement like whoa now THAT'D be a movie.

***

"See? I know man boy good killer from start," Ziad (I think) says to the Als.

"Toldya," Satan now. "He's a real fuckin' berserker. Don't give a shit 'bout nothin' or nobody. He'll be great on ya team."

Wait, did I KILL Rooz?

Satan turns to me: "Nah, he'll be fine."

Piss. This again.

Ziad and the Als laugh at m—laugh WITH me, I guess. They like me now—or at least, FOR now.

But I feel guilty about Rooz. Great. Just another one to add to the list, right? I feel worse cuz earlier (pretty sure) he told me to try to be happy here. Is this "Happy?" Am I just supposed

[132]

to slaughter Angels the rest of my life or whatever this is? I can't just cause others pain, I only wanna hurt

myself

and besides, I feel like it'd get old—get old real quick. Like, "What'd you do today, dear?" "Oh nothing honey, just brutalized a bunch of Biblically accurate Angels." "Aw, that's nice." But yeah, I sure hope they're Biblically accurate Angels—just shapes and shit. Maybe then I wouldn't mind.

I don't know. I'll give it a try. And apologize to Rooz. Maybe we can tag team.

***

That was a short section. I'm not used to dividing my life into nice little bits like that. Oh well, I'm sure this one'll spin out forever.

I think Durkheim mentioned one of the counters to suicide (not that I, uh, care) is something like military comradery—or just general comradery (and wasn't that spelled camaderie?) cuz not only does it give you a purpose (aw, so cute, a purpose), but it also strips you of your individuality by making you part of a sort of social machine. Something like that, I don't know. Maybe I can befriend my fellow Hellions? I guess I'm vicious as shit now.

Whatever. Better track down Rooz and apologize for beating the quite-possibly-literal-Hell out of him. That's not really something you do to people—unless you're me, I guess. But then again, I'm—what's really stupid, though, is—I'm *Mentally Ill*, right? Don't you love it how

[133]

people always play that *so-called-Mental-Illness* card—like ALL THE TIME—like, "Gee golly gee, sorry I cheated on you, stole your credit card, and killed your dog, I'm *Mentally Ill*," like calm down, no you're not, cuz nobody i—

—We find Rooz in the Healing Hut healing himself up (eating a green herb or something). Rooz glances up at me and says, "Been expecting you," in his best Donald Sutherland voice.

"Wow, Rooz, I'd expect *Metal Gear* to be too mainstream for you."

"I am not a total contrarian. I do find joy in some aspects of life accepted by the common man. In fact, Werner Herzog once said—"

"—Oh, my—yeah yeah yeah, I know what he said—I came here to say…"

I trail off. I feel like it's against my will, but I know I'm just playing the *so-called-Mental-Illness* card. Ha! What a waste.

"I'm…uh…"

Rooz tilts his head. Curious and expectant. Are those—those two aren't mutually exclusive, are they?

"I'm…sorry." Piss, that really IS the hardest word to say. There's another joke in there, but…eh, I won't go for it.

"Oh Jhaegar," he says as he eats another green herb. His body flashes with bright light and he appears fully himself again. "There is nothing to worry yourself over. I am aware you are given to instability and that sometimes your actions may not be your own."

See?

"Gee, thanks, Rooz, that's really cool. But yeah, so…that Raid tonight?"

"Yes, indeed. I am rather excited myself—"

[134]

"—think you're doing?!" A woman yells outside. "You told me you learned your lesson!"

A man's voice replies: "Things've changed and now I gotta do this thing. Eddie's up there, honey, I gotta bring 'em back!"

Rooz and I trade glances. We shrug and head outside to investigate.

I should really be surprised, but—and I don't know if I'm already jaded or just too sad to—but Chris Benoit and Kate Spade (who are apparently a thing?) argue over what appears to be an AR15 in Chris's hands.

"God, you know," Chris says as he looks down at his weapon, "I shouldn't even be here. I should be up there wrestling with the Angels."

"Chris, come on, man," I murmur under my breath. Wouldn't want him to hear me. "You felt her tap out."

Kate (who honestly flew under my radar, but I'm suddenly gaining new appreciation for her and jumpin' Christ! People were right—her handbags ARE just the right thing!) slaps Chris across—well, Ric Flair chops Chris across the chest.

"Wooooo," I murmur-shout. Doesn't look like I'd want her to hear, either.

Satan (apparently next to Rooz and I) nudges me. "Wow, ya listened ta what Werner Herzog said, too?"

I turn to peer into her (I believe to be deceiving) seemingly genuine eyes.

"You know who Werner Herzog is? What, is he also down here?"

"Nah. What? I can't just know who da guy is?"

[135]

"You think you know, Kate," continues Chris. In Hell—just like Earth—everything is somehow the woman's fault. He says once again, albeit quieter and more defeated, "God, I shouldn't even be down here. I didn't mean to kill myself."

I think you might be here for a different reason, Chris. "Or wait, what supersedes the other down here?" I turn to Satan. "Does it—?"

—Satan shakes her head. "Ya eithah here or ya ain't. I like ta think I don't discriminate, but I really just don't care."

Some new guy—I can't make a joke cuz I don't recognize him—gets in between Kate and Chris. I—actually, Rooz tenses up. Does he—wait, who is this guy?

"Yo guys—GUYS! We're not the enemy. It's those a-holes up in Heaven we're after. Chris, dude, I like your enthusiasm, but cool it a bit, okay? Kate, it's alright, you just gotta give him some space. You sure you don't wanna Raid tonight?"

"Yes, I'm very sure."

"But it's way better than just sitting around doin' nothin' down he—"

"—Oh, shut up, Eric," Chris pipes in. "How 'bout you go jerk off with Dylan?"

"Hey, man, that's not cool," says apparently Eric.

Chris—oh piss, men never change, do they?—gets up in Eric's face and pushes him and Eric (of course) pushes back and Kate (of course) rolls her eyes and the men keep (of course!) going on like they're piss shitting kids until Chris has enough, takes a few steps back, then unloads his clip into Eric's chest.

Eric collapses as everyone watches in more or less shock. Actually...no one's in shock. What? Why does nobody—?

—And as quick as he died (he did "die," right?), Eric's body dissolves into dust.

[136]

Satan grunts. Smiles to herself.

"Hey Satan?" I ask.

"Yeah?"

"Did he *die*?"

"Yup."

"So where does *he* go?"

"Didn't I already tell ya? He'll just end up somewhere else. Maybe find his way back here someday, hopefully not."

"When'd you say that? And wait, if suicides on Earth go to Hell, where do suicides in Hell go to?"

Satan grunts again. She turns away and cocks her head.

"Come on, step inta my office."

I step into her office.

"Take a seat, asshole," she says as she plops down in a sweet leather chair behind her desk. She puts her feet up—yeah, she puts her FEET up on the desk cuz she somehow like— kicks her costume shoe/footsie part off? What? Her bare feet glow from across the room and they're just like—

—Oh piss, am I becoming Quentin Tarrantino? Please no, anything but that. I'd rather become Uwe Boll.

But yeah, she's, uh…she's…

"Shit, Jhaegar! Take a fuckin' seat already!"

I take a fuckin' seat.

[137]

Satan clears her throat. Waves her hands as if giving me the "down low" (whatever that is).

"Alright listen, man: I'm gonna drop da tough dyke bitch act fuh a sec, I—"

—I point at the wall behind her. Her eyebrows furrow and she swivels around to follow my finger.

Mounted above her waits a red flamethrower engraved *Bitch Burner*.

Satan swivels back to me.

"Ya just got a problem with fuckin' everythin', don't ya?"

"Huh? No, I'm just—"

"—'No, I just,' fuck you! I don't—grrr—look, can ya forget 'bout killin' yaself fuh five minutes here? I'm tryin' ta connect with ya, ya fuckin' asshole, an' every time ANYBODY reaches out ta YOU, den YOU always have some fuckin' ting ta say 'bout it. Am I right?"

"I don't know, I guess."

Satan slams her hands down on the desk, shoots to her feet, and fucking slaps me across the face. Like...HARD.

I stare up at her.

"I love you."

She slaps me again. Blood gushes out from behind my bandaged ear.

"Please, I—"

—She picks me up and Rock Bottom's me (ya know? That thing The Rock does? Hopefully he's president by now (actually, he's a Face and he sucks)) through the desk. I stare up at her from the debris and try to catch her eyes in hopes she doesn't notice my erection.

[138]

Satan grabs me by the throat (not the scruff of my shirt mind you, my throat) and pulls me in close.

"Ya need ta stop with dis dominatrix-I'm-a-bad-an'-guilty-little-boy-so-I-just-want-women-ta-hurt-me-cuz-I-deserve-it-from-a-ting-I-did-years-ago-dat-I-barely-remembah shit. Okay? Okay."

She throws me and I land perfectly back in my chair.

I close my eyes and try to process what just (try to shove away all the memories I now have to battle against cuz she brought up that nifty old bit and) and it's just, uh—what what what? What, huh? Okay—shut up—okay, okay fine.

I open my eyes again. Fine. Fine now. All good. Yes. Very good.

Satan studies me from across her (now either back or just remade or maybe never unmade) desk. Hands folded, swanky horned headband just a tad droopy with end of day exhaustion.

"What I wanted ta fuckin' say, Jhaegar, is...well..."

She glances down at her hands as they rap against the desk. Satan seems unsure. Nervous. Nervous as a seventeen-year-old girl in a Devil Halloween costume should (dreamed) be.

"...Is...I'm kinda a fan a yours. I actually HAVE been lookin' up at ya fuh decades now—"

"—Decades—?"

"—Shut da fuck up. I've been studyin' ya an' I really enjoy ya mind—as much as it, uh, pains me ta admit," she sighs. "In an Underworld a sameness, Jhaegar, you are a sort a shining light a true individuality."

"And you wanted to tell me this...alone in your office—?"

[139]

"—No, no, I don't wanna fuck you—an' now I'm sure ya think ya gotta blow up a doctor's office cuz I said dat—but your joy ain't my responsibility an' let's face it, ya've done enough damage ta me an' mine as it is. Now what—"

"—I really don't—"

"—WAS TRYIN' TA SAY WAS—ah, fuckin' nevah mind!"

Satan pulls out a notebook from a drawer and slaps it down in front of me.

I grab it and leaf through. Jumpin' Christ, it's a book of—

"—It's a book a movie reviews," Satan finishes for me. "Ya know? I saw dat ya liked 'em a lot. I…like 'em a lot as well…an' ya did dis shit all da time so I figured, hey, I could do it, too."

I continue flipping through her notebook. There's hundreds of reviews in here! Who knew?! But…I don't know. I don't really want a girl who knows about movies—not cuz I'm an Incel like Satan thinks and then thinks again that I just wanna assert some kind of primitive dominance over the girl (1. Cuz she needs to dominate me and—) —cuz, uh, uh, if you have two people who know the same stuff, then you can't really learn anything from each other. It's only when you have two different people who are together and have the capacity to share their lives that one can truly grow. See!? I can be "healthy!"

"I really, uh," Satan continues, nervous again. "I really liked ya review a dat *Sátántangó* movie. I haven't gotten a chance ta watch it yet—"

"—Heh, no one has—"

"—But it's fuh sure on my watch list."

[140]

Well she has this movie review book so she can't be all bad—not that I ever thought she was bad—or that her liking cinema elevates her in any way, cuz like I said, I—wait, I—oh piss, I don't know. I'll just open up a page in the middle and see what kind of film she fancies.

MORTAL KOMBAT

by Paul (not Thomas but W. S.) Anderson

(review by Satan)

Heya its me.

Nah ya eyes aint mistaken Paul Anderson——(da greata a da two if ya ask me)——took on one a da most solemnest tasks a da modern era Bringin ta da Big Screen da best franchize a all time An ges what assholes He sucseeds.

Lets begin wit da basics an mention dat dis movie is cheesy but in da perfect cheesy but fun ratio ya no Da guy dey got playin Johnny Cage is super fuckin hot an dont wory boys da girl playin Sonyas pretty sexy two Dey even fight realy good Ya can realy tell dey trained a bunch fuh der roles an whateva Real professionals ya no Not fake Hollywood superhero shit dey try ta jam down ya throats Oh an Lui Kang two Hes realy good.

I ges da movie is bout like his journey Hes all sad an whateva cuz ~~Shang Soon~~ Shang Tsung kils his brotha an he has ta get revenj but den Raiden hoos like a fuckin chainsmoka but I ges dats open ta interp retation in dese kinds a things so dats okay tells him he has ta find da power witin himself an be best frends with Johnny an Sonya Its really good ya no an all dat Your

[141]

Soul is Mine shit just really kracks me up two.

Peeple are gonna narc on da special efects but narcs are gonna narc am I right cuz ya no—(fuh da time)—dey were super neat an ya just gotta reallyze dat its not realy bout da special efects Da musics really good two It reminds me a lot a da game My favorite karacta in da game is Noob Saibot Hes not in dis one I dont think wit kinda makes me sad but I can just play da game istead an like I I I Johnny Cage is if ya ask me pretty hot.

Jumpin' Christ, I can barely read this. I skip ta da—piss!—to the bottom to see what she rated it.

Five Stars out a Five

Oh, my—are you kidding me? Better to just straight up not rate it than use *out of Five*. I feel a tension in my throat and glance up to see Satan peering at me with great intent. Happy sigh, she's just so—fine, I'll let it slide.

Back to the book:

MORTAL KOMBAT: ANNIHILATION

NOT by Paul (not even W. S.) Anderson

(review still by Satan)

Heya its me.

[142]

An okay what da fuck was dis one.

Rememba how da last one was cheesy but fun? Well dis one is cheesy but fuckin stupid I wanna say dis hapened cuz dey threw Paul away but I ges I dont no much bout da Biz ta say fuh suh Dis ~~one was just~~

Okay dey kil fuckin Johnny Cage in like da first seen Why Why Hes like da most important karacta Like I can see how ya can kil like Lui Kang or Kung Lao or da othas ya no but not even da games kil Johnny Like hes da one guy ya dont kil an dey fuckin kiled em Dis is an important leson I think in how ya cant insult da fanbase.

So ya got a fanbase right Well ya cant piss em of Ya can do like tryin shit out an what not but dis was like a total betrayal Kinda like Transformers 3 where dey got a new girl wit out tellin any one Like what Hoo asked fuh dis My frend—(cuz ya no I have a few frends dat kind a no dis stuff)—told me dat da executives or whateva make a lot a dese decisions well are dey fuckin stupid.

An da rest a da movie Fuckin shit it just makes me wanna peel my fuckin skin of Dey make Sindel like da main villain an nobody likes her Like actualy nobody Da guy dey got playin Show Kong looks like a fuckin twerp Like whered dey find him koodnt dey get anybody else Hoo da fuck else is even in it Shit I dont even no its one a dose movies ya just gotta turn of half way throo.

Bad Just fuckin Bad.

Rub Sawdust on my Clit out of Five

[143]

Not sure what this rating means, but I take back what I said about the *out of Five* scale.

"So, what'd ya think?" she asks.

Vivi looks at me from across the—no, Vivi? Satan looks at me from across the desk. She does kind of look like Vivi. Which one was she? Wait, does Satan look like her or more like Gwyn? Actually, they're all kind of similar looking.

"Do you have any sisters?" I ask her.

"What da fuck? No!"

"Oh sorry—I just, uh—"

"—Why da fuck would I have a—?"

"—Sorry. It's great. The reviews are great, you're quite perceptive."

Satan reaches over and snatches her review book out of my grubby hands. She grimaces and tucks it away again.

"Yeah, whatevah. I heard what ya thought 'bout it. I guess I just have ta be stupid like everybody else, huh?"

"No, hey, no! No, it was great, really. You'll just, uh—you're on your way."

"Just drop it. Ya know what? I bet if dat GIRL wrote dat shit den ya would've loved it."

"Vivi? No, she's just a friend I—that I may not have met yet. I've met her and—you just look similar."

She slaps a hand down on the desk and stares me down.

"I look similar ta ALL a 'em ya fuckin' asshole!"

I consider her for a moment. Slightly taken aback, I guess—or whatever people are in situations like these.

Satan rolls her eyes.

[144]

I open my mouth to speak, reconsider (lots of considering going on), and close my mouth.

She shakes her head. Speaks as if incredulous (I think that's how it's spelled. I also think that's the right word):

"An' why do ya think I talk like dis? What? Ya think dat's a cute coincidence, too?"

"What? Sorry—again—I just really—"

"—Shit, I don't get it. Why don't ya like my reviews—dey ain't even really mine! How can ya be upset 'bout somethin' YOU created?"

Rooz takes a seat next to me (apparently there's an open seat) and (also, apparently he's in here) pats me (again with the patting!) on the shoulder.

"Rooz? Now what?"

"Oh Jhaegar, there is no need for irritation. It is alright to be confused."

"Jumpin' Christ, I'm not confused, I'm just…"

I glance over at Satan and—sigh piss. Gwyn stares back at me from across the desk. I blink and then it's Vivi. Blink. Gwyn. Blink. Wait—it's not either separately: it's like they're both there, but just in or out of focus depending on how I look. What?

The Devil woman focuses back into Satan.

She groans and pinches the bridge of her nose.

I look to Rooz for an answer (though I know I won't find one).

"Well, Jhaegar," Rooz says in answer, "you are not in 'Hell' per se. You are in YOUR Hell."

Now I get to consider him.

"So then why are you here?"

[145]

All he does is wink at me. What a nutcase.

"No, asshole," Satan/Vivi/Gwyn interrupts, "YOU'RE da fuckin' nutcase. It was yaself—all yaselves—dat created dis place an' ya still ain't satisfied."

Satan takes off her swanky horned headband and massages her temples.

"And he never will be," Rooz adds.

"Guys, I really don't get it."

"Jhaegar, do you not know that is a cliché? The protagonist saying they do not 'understand' something?"

"Yeah." I point at him. For drama, I guess. I also stand for even more drama. "And I hate clichés so this definitely isn't some world I made."

"Yes, I am aware, but you also LOVE to point out that you hate them and further educate your internal audience against the pitfalls of literary platitudes."

I open my mouth to say something, then reconsider (fuck me) and close it.

"I apologize, Jhaegar. I have been too busy enlightening you through social and racial theories to the point where I have neglected to enlighten you regarding religious ones. Have you ever heard the term, *Chain of Infinite Regress?*"

Satan says something, but I don't (can't? was it English?) understand it.

Rooz tilts his head towards her:

"Pardon me, Satan, but with the accent please?" He also twitches a finger and indicates her horned headband.

Satan groans, puts on her headband, and clears her throat:

"I said, can ya just fuck off outta my office fuh now so I can getta break fr

[146]

OOOOOOOOOOOOOOOOOOOOOMMMMMMmmmmmmmmmmmmmmOOO

7764   exi   ”

I glance over at Satan and hand over her review book.

"That was amazing," I tell her. "Are you sure you didn't possess Roger Ebert in a past life?"

"Gee," Satan blushes, "thanks a lot, Jhaegar, I really know it's somethin' when it's comin' from you."

I hear a knock on the door. It's Rooz.

"Young White Male, the time for preparation is upon us. How about you leave this fine woman alone and we become 'all Raided up' as our new compatriots would say?"

"Yeah, sure. Sounds good."

I get up. Nod at Satan.

"So, yeah. See you later?"

She blushes more. Christ on a Cross is she spectacular.

"S-sure—hehe—don't use up too much a ya energy now."

"Oh, I won't," I wink as I leave with Rooz.

Satan waves by just grinning and wiggling a few of her fingers. What a Queen.

Outside, Rooz pats my back. What a friendly guy.

"So Jhaegar, back there I noticed that—"

—I forget what he says. There's a crack running through the forest floor—but it's like a ravine? Is that what they call it? A crag or a ravine or just like, uh, an underground pathway kind of thing that I can see through fractures in the world surface.

[147]

People are—uh, well not "people" but—piss, clarity didn't last long, did it? They're definitely humanoid but I can't tell if they're people cuz their heads are all wrapped in thick balls of bandages. Like, totally.

My hand rises to feel the ear bandage on my own head. A spooky little shiver runs up my most likely scoliosis ridden spine: the bandage seems like it's grown.

I feel like I wanna yell something at the pilgrimage down below—cuz that's what they appear to be: a pilgrimage...though I know not where they're pilgriming. They just drift down the crag/ravine/whatever until they travel too deep that they're out of sight, like frail ghosts dissipating into the air.

"Look away, Jhaegar," Rooz warns.

Warns? Piss, why's he sound so mad.

I look over at him, my eyebrow raised.

"They are not meant to be watched."

I'm confused. I glance back at them and—and Rooz grabs me and spins me around. He pulls me close.

"The Invisible are not meant to be watched," he reiterates.

"Nifty. Who are they?"

"The Invisible are those who do not win the AFI Young Filmmakers Grant when someone like David Lynch does. The Invisible are the ones who never get the call or receive the letter. They watch game shows and read Dan Brown novels and work in customer service centers."

"So they're Untouchables? Does Satan have a Hindu tick she tries to hide?"

[148]

"No, Jhaegar. Would that it were so simple. Satan would not see them, even were she able."

"Why?"

"They are—"

"—They're Invisible, okay, fine, sure—so what's with the bandages?"

"They have gone blind themselves. And good that they have."

"Uh huh. And why's that?"

"There are those yet Invisible to them…" Rooz whispers.

I purse my lips (interesting phrase) and study him. He looks to be real serious. Ah, whatever.

"So, uh…did you bring me out here then to tell me I can't go on the raid…and that I have to go join them or something?"

Rooz chuckles. Gradually grows into a full blown cackle. I think I take a step back.

"You are not an Invisible, Jhaegar."

"Jumpin' Christ, what? So what's the poi—why would you—but I 'don't get the letter or the call' either and my life sucks."

Rooz settles down. Stops laughing and just grins at me.

"Does it?"

"But I—I'm—" —I just start bumbling shit out. I speak incoherently as it is and I only get worse when I'm challenged emotionally. Not that I'm acknowledging I'm, uh…I guess I…well, Rooz needs to just…um…

"But I'm," ~~I struggle to say~~, "I'm so lonely."

Rooz's grin deepens.

[149]

"Do you believe yourself to be the loneliest person on earth?"

I don't say anything for a while. I ~~finally manage~~ say:

"I...then who is?"

"I do not know."

I stare at my feet and feel my bandage. It's wet again. I cross my legs. Apparently I'm sitting on the floor in my room. Apparently I have a room. Rooz is gone. Typical. Piss, is he Invisible?

No. Sigh. No, he's not.

But yeah, I guess I'm here to "meditate" or some shit. That's what I was told (or at least I have the feeling Rooz told me that before he left and I forgot the whole

...

...

Am I meditating or brooding? I never know anymore. Who cares, not like it'll—it's fine. I'm sure it's working. I'm calming—I'll just do some pushups. Have to retain my big strong man ar—

—Ya know? What the fuck? I drink whole milk, eat like a chicken a day, and am always doing these stupid fucking pushups and curl ups and squats and nothing ever fucking changes—how do big people—they're not even fucking BIG they're MEDIUM!!! How do they get to that size?! They don't do anything, all they do is play Call of Duty and touch themselves—is THAT the piss shitting fucking fucking—

—I'll just do some pushups and hold my tongue (my thoughts) my thought tongue. One. Two—jumpin' Christ, do you count when you go up or down? Three. And four. Five. Six.

[150]

I stop and claw my nails down my face. Why am I such a freak? Why do I (sometimes when I do pushups, like, a naked woman appears in my mind beneath me and I'm just—what? Doing pushups on top of her? Or is this what's it's like in real life? What the fuck is—do other people think this shit?).

Sigh, I just wanna be fucking shot. I really should go on this Raid. But—I don't know—I'll probably die and go to some worse fucking realm. Die and have to play Call of Duty and jerk off for the rest of eternity. I don't get how people enjoy jerking o—well, I get how they *enjoy* it, but how do they not feel like utter trash afterwards? I just wanna chop my hands off—and my dick—chop off my dick first and then use that to chop off my hands, I don't know…

GRANDPA J'S PARTY TIDBIT NO. 3 (or was it 8?)

I'm sure nobody gives a shit, but when you see someone in a movie or T.V. show and they've slit their wrists? Fake. Can't happen. Key word is *wrists*. Plural. You can only slit one wrist cuz damaging the wrist to the point of lethality actually destroys functionality in that hand. You could slit your left wrist with your right hand, sure, but then your left hand wouldn't work to slit your right wrist: you'd have to do some Cirque du Solei shit to slit your right wrist with your right hand which'll never happen…or bite out your veins with your fucking teeth or something…uh…yeah.

"That is quite interesting, Jhaegar," Rooz says.

I guess he really is here. He meditates (full on Buddhist) on the floor next to me. Wait, so is this OUR room then?

"Rooz, how do you tolerate me?"

[151]

"What do you mean by that?"

"You're doing your thing and I'm just over here doing pushups and crying."

"That is no matter. Everyone meditates in their own way."

Jumpin' Christ, here comes another one of these—I just gotta—I'll just escape here where I'm not vulnerable.

GRANDPA J'S PARTY TIDBIT NO. 4

I met Vivi when—wait, is this even a Tidbit? Who cares…so I met Vivi in college, yeah? And yes, I know I'm in…I'm in, uh…so when I get to coll—there's a woman and her name is Vivi, okay? She was pretty hardcore. Not like "smoke meth" hardcore, but she went her own way and didn't give a shit. It was amazing.

We'd go to Goth rock concerts and eat ciabatta. It was nice. No one ever brought up stupid nonsense so it was a real, uh, I don't know, like a matured and developed relationship I guess. It was always other people who—she wore this black lipstick all the time and stuff and other girls would make fun of her. I'm not saying I kicked the shit out of some girl over it, but I definitely said something and she was like, "I'm gonna tell Professor Whatever-da-Fuck," and I'm like, "Okay?" but I ended up losing my credit for the class. I don't know. Vivi and I just laughed about it so I didn't really care.

She was sick. Kind of like (sick as in *cool* by the way) like a Heel, ya know? Like a huge punk, but super cool and genuine in real life. Like, she was CM Punk and I was AJ Lee. But…was AJ Lee a Face? Well, not a Face, but—okay, I guess we're just two Heels.

[152]

Whatever. She was Punk and I was AJ and it was just the best ever but she told me I'd never love myself and I didn't know what that meant. It really hit me cuz I thought I was doing so good this time…I don't know. It doesn't matter.

Rooz stares at me—his stupid grin again. But I guess it's a bit different now—just a tinge. More *awwww* instead of *uhhhh* if you know what I mean.

He pats my (AGAIN WITH THE) back.

"That was pleasant to hear, Jhaegar. But no matter now. Off to war."

We load up the U-Boats. Not sure if they are U-Boats cuz they're like mini airship things (Heaven, right?), but they're still in that boat-like shape.

I sit down next to Rooz and Ziad. The three AIs sit across from us. They're all decked out like you'd think. I'm wearing some pretty sexy (I mean, cool) combat fatigues with a cute little beret. Rooz wears…the same clothes he wore when he shot up the school…that's ominous. He passes me one of two AR15s he has resting between his legs.

"Did you retain the lessons I taught you?" he asks.

"Sure." Hope I did.

I poke my head above the modest walls of the U-Boat/mini airship and see we're one of dozens of similar airships rising from the trees of Hell towards glimmering stars above—which I can only assume means Heaven. Satan poses (less JoJo, more Washington crossing that river thing) in the front airship, leading our ascent. She spins around (with some splendid flair, actually) to face her army.

"Listen up, assholes!" Satan yells into a megaphone. "Tonight, we have one mission an' one mission only: bring Our Man back alive!"

[153]

Shouts of—dare I say *Satanic*—glee explode from the airships. Fellow Hellions stand up and cheer. Some (looking at you, Als) discharge their weapons into the air.

"Believe me when I say dat I don't give a fuck about ya! Ya are all expendable in my eyes!"

More cheers. Wait, what?

"Dey who finds Our Man or become vital parts a his rescue will be rewarded all handsome-like back in Hell! So be on ya fuckin' toes!"

More cheers. More gunfire. Piss, some of the gunfire catches another airship and it goes down.

"Oh, an' one more ting!"

Silence falls upon the army.

"LET'S FUCK DOSE YUPPIES!!!"

The army erupts in utter madness. Even Roo—shit, even Rooz shoots to his feet and swings his AR through the air. What the—?

—The gate at the end of the airship swings open and clamps down on a cloud (a somehow very thick, very dense cloud) and the Kingdom of Heaven lies before me.

"Yes, big man! You bet it lie!" screams Ziad.

He and his Als charge ahead onto the clouds towards the Kingdom (by the way, it's like a bunch of—I guess Satan's right—a bunch of yuppie looking gold and silver buildings. Piss, this place is lame) and as Hell's army charges, mortar shells explode, landmines blast off, and merciless streams of chain gun fire eviscerate all who invoke the Biblically accurate Angels' ire.

And when I mean Biblically accurate, I mean *Biblically accurate!*

[154]

Just—like—fucking SHAPES float through the air and cast down beams of searing light and fire. And it's not just them! As the Hellions advance closer towards the Kingdom, more "traditional" Angels (just these yuppie Do-Gooders in white and yellow clothing) burst from fox holes with their flaming swords and free ranged assault rifles and organic frag grenades or whatever the fuck. I see—oh baby…

I see Satan just impaling assholes left and fucking right! The Yuppies shoot at her, but her costume just…deflects bullets? This really is World of Warcraft, what'd she level that thing up to? One of the Biblically accurate Angels targets her with some Evangelion ray and she evidently doesn't give a fuck cuz she just jumps up, drives her pitchfork straight through it's, uh, central sphere thing (something), and rips it out in a stream of deafening sound.

Rooz rubs the drool off my chin and pulls me off the airship.

"Jhaegar, come," he orders. "Do you not want to find Our Man?"

"I…I'm really not sure. Why again?"

Rooz raises his eyebrows.

"You would receive a reward from *her*."

I lock eyes with him. He locks eyes with me.

We bang our ARs together (probably not safe) and charge after Ziad and the Als.

Bullets fly, grenades explode mere feet from (by the way, I hear nothing at this point. Like, people don't realize that literally one gunshot from even a pistol'll destroy your ears—and that's just if you're outside! All those crime movies about cops fighting robbers and having shootouts in hallways? Jumpin' Christ!) and, uh…we're outside a bunker kinda thing, I guess.

But yeah, all of us are here and Ziad (what a nifty leader) points at each man in turn.

[155]

At Al #1 and #2: "You two, you two provide cover fire bunker window." At Al #3: "You and me, we circle round back, infiltrate." At Rooz: "You, you follow make sure no one kill us."

"What about me, boss?" I say eagerly. I think I have an erection. What is it with men and war? Do they like being deaf? How can I hear Ziad's words?

I read Ziad's lips: "Oh yes, big man. You, uh, you stay here, uh, cover."

Suddenly, I feel word-formed vibrations in the air pulsing towards my ears. I focus on them and make out human speech:

"Hello Neighbors, what can I help you with today?"

A red armor plated Mr. Rogers glowers at us from atop the bunker. He flips two long daggers in each of his hands.

"It's him!" Ziad screams.

Ziad and the Als (and Rooz, he picks up quick) all point their guns at Mr. Rogers and unload—but he's too fast! Mr. Rogers *Chancellor Palpatines* (yeah, that's a verb), even makes the noise, and finds himself in the center of our Mötley Crüe. In the matter of two seconds:

"Goodbye, Neighbor," as slits Al #1's throat.

"Goodbye, Neighbor," as he plunges his daggers in Al #2's chest and rips them sideways, cutting him in half (guess he really is #2).

"Goodbye, Neighbor," as he drives a spiked boot through Al #3's face and wipes it aside.

Rogers now turns to us and grins that—frankly, I ALWAYS thought it was creepy—grin.

"It's such a beautiful day, isn't it?" he suggests.

Ziad, overcome by the death of his three Als, watches Rogers's deadly advance.

Rooz, overcome by the death of three potential converts, fires straight at Rogers's chest while charging ah—

[156]

—Rogers's armor deflects the bullets. He drops his daggers and grabs Rooz by his neck. Pulls him in close.

"You know, Neighbor," he purrs as he begins to strangle Rooz, "I used to have a friend a LOT like you."

I point my rifle at his head.

"Let 'em go, scumbag."

He pauses to consider me.

"Hey now, that's no way to talk to a Neighbor."

"Last chance."

Rogers chuckles. Then winks.

My rifle turns to ectoplasm right in my (now goopy) hands.

He chuckles harder (the creep) and prepares to kill Rooz...

...when a flaming pitchfork bursts through his chest!

Rooz falls to safety. Rogers sags on the pitchfork to reveal (my hopefully future wife) Satan.

"Gotchya, bitch!" she proclaims.

Satan plants a foot on his back and wrenches her pitchfork free.

Rogers bleeds for a moment on the ground (cloud, cloud/ground) before dissolving into particles and blowing away with the breeze (the Als are gone, too, by the way).

Satan pulls a very lucky Rooz to his feet.

"I've been waitin' years ta kill dat shitbird."

"Miss Lady Satan," Ziad says, wiping very manly moisture from his eyes, "you want help us take bunker."

[157]

"Nah, not fuckin' really. Come on, our eyes are on a biggah prize."

I find the Kingdom of Heaven burning (what have I missed?) and Satan leading us through the ruins of collapsed buildings. Rooz and Ziad happily mow down any Yuppie who tries a sneak attack. I wonder how stuff works up here—I only wonder cuz we're wandering through ruins and stuff, but I also look around and see fallen buildings just slip through the cloud floor and vanish from sight, plunging down to…Hell, I guess?

Where do those buildings go? Do they have to make more? Do construction workers still not get a break, even in Heaven? These are the

Dog City Never Sleeps

painted in blood on a wall. What?

Satan rolls her eyes and says, "Yeah."

"What do you mean, 'yeah'?"

"People up here are upset, too. Just don't worry 'bout it," she insists as the wall crumbles through the clouds.

The wall took a chunk of the regular floor away with it and a basement layer waits visible below (not sure how it didn't—what's the architecture of this place?) forget it, I guess forgetting things just helps. We're in a basement/dungeon thing now. It's all gold and Heavenly and there's labeled rooms on either side.

Satan leads our covert squad onward. She scans the names of the rooms as we go: Unwarranted Circumcision, Possession of a Vibrator, All White Movie Casts, ya know? Shit like that.

[158]

Satan bites her lip. None of these must be the one for Our Man. He must've done some pretty serious shit. By the way, are there really no guards down here? What's this place go on, the Golden Rule?

We find a stairwell and descend another floor. Satan pokes her head into the main dungeon hallway, shakes it a tinge (I like that word), then brings it back and leads us down another level.

"Shit," she says. "We're gonna have ta go furthah down. These are all da bitch floors."

We plunge into the Heavenly, cloudy, whatever depths of the dungeons. Satan doesn't even bother to check the floors anymore, I think she's probably assuming (cuz she doesn't have any evidence to presume (I don't think)) that this guy must be on the bott—oh, here we are.

The stairwell ends and the final floor awaits. Satan leads us into the hallway and a single door stands at the en—jumpin' Christ, not even guards in here? Who runs this place?

The label above the door simply reads *Big A*. I wonder if that stands for *Big Asshole*. Satan—opens it? What the—not even locked, does no one here care? We step inside.

Desks, chairs, recycling buckets full of dried gum. It's a fucking school classroom. What? Why? Windows on either side bring in fresh rays from the sunlit skies of lower Heaven. A man writes on a chalkboard with his back to us. Written over and over again across the board:

I Will Not Persecute the Nation of Israel

I Will Not Persecute the Nation of Israel

I Will Not Persecute the Nation of Israel

Satan drives the butt of her pitchfork into the floor and approaches the man.

[159]

"Well, gee fuckin' shit. What dey got ya doin', Big A?"

The man turns around and—oh my jumpin' Jesus, it's fucking Hitler!

His face lights up in joy and English subtitles appear over his chest as he speaks.

"Guys! I was wondering when you'd show up!"

Satan, Hitler, and Ziad (and Rooz, too, already) exchange warm embraces. Hitler locks eyes with Ziad and seems to silently ask after the three Als. Ziad shakes his head, tears of sorrow on the edge of release. Hitler pulls him into a tighter embrace.

"Let it out, my friend. It is alright to weep."

Ziad promptly sobs into Hitler's chest, knocking away his subtitles. They now appear over his head.

Hitler's gaze falls to me. He flashes an ever so quick and ever so subtle salute.

"Well met, Mr. Holdburn. I've heard so much about you."

"You have?"

"Everyone's heard of Jhaegar Holdburn. After all, Dog City Never Sleeps."

Jumpin' Christ...

"I...well, uh...pleasure to meet you as well, sir." Do I call him *sir*? Does he deserve common manners? I mean—hey, wait a second.

"Hey," I ask. "Didn't you kill yourself, too?"

Hitler frowns a frown that seems too complex for one as demonized as himself (I'm not a Neo-Nazi, by the way (and I know that's exactly what a Neo-Nazi would say to try to convince you they're not a Neo-Nazi, but I'm not a Neo-Nazi (also, these people who are like, "The Holocaust never happened," well if the Holocaust never happened, why would you even like Hitler in the first place?))) filled with mournful nostalgia, yet wistful glee.

[160]

"Yes, Mr. Holdburn. Indeed, I did. And most unfortunately so, as if I hadn't done that, then I would never have found myself in this mess and instead be found lounging in Van Gogh's Heavenly art studio."

"Van Gogh made it to Heaven?" I ask.

"You were not meant to go to Hell?" Rooz asks.

Hitler turns to Rooz with much fondness.

"Ah, I knew you would find this interesting. But yes, Mr. Roosevelt. After all, why would I have ended up in Hell if I hadn't taken my life? I did nothing else wrong."

Rooz licks his lips. Here we go. Satan raises her palms up as if to say, *preach brotha.*

"In fact," Hitler continues, "most of my life is subject to misunderstanding. History thinks I hated Jewish people. I didn't hate Jewish people, I hated the German Ruling Class. 'Didn't anyone read my book?' I constantly thought. 'Didn't anyone notice the numerous times I mentioned that the only way to back up a massive social movement is through religious zealotry?' I kept saying to myself. It was all a…all a…"

"A test!" Rooz helps.

Hitler smiles. "Yes! A sort of test. And as a matter of fact," he says as he points towards the blackboard, "Israel is a nation BECAUSE of me. If anything, I helped them: just as all forms of persecution help Judaism as that is what they rely upon to substantiate their belief that they are God's chosen people. Hurting them only makes their conviction grow. Frankly, the only way to truly eradicate Jewish culture—not that I care, mind you—is to accept them and love them and erase their identity by absorbing them into a globalized—"

—Sorry. Sorry. The subtitles are going too fast and I—I just can't keep up. I never understand how people do this shit, like, like, like, like let's slow it down, huh? Strangely

[161]

enough, I prefer films with subtitles cuz I so often can't hear what people say. How can people hear when their dumbass neighbor's going nuts or some dog's outside and—well, I guess I don't mind dogs. I know this one dog—his name's Irwin—and I always get the impression he's an animatronic. I guess that'd make his name IR-WON (if you know what I mean).

So Hitler's done talking. I somehow felt a lot of the stuff he was saying and I'm thinking I may be a Neo-Nazi after all. I really need—it's fine. I'm sure it'll all—I'll just—it's fine.

Satan leads us all out. Hitler and Rooz have a nice chat. That leaves—piss—that leaves Ziad to me.

"Big man, Jhaegar, what you think first raid?"

"Oh, it's, uh, pretty nifty."

"What 'nifty' mean?"

"Nifty mean, uh, means, uh, like 'cool.'"

"Ah. I see. You nifty, Jhaegar, man."

Aww, that's kind of sweet.

"Aww, that's kind of sweet," I tell him.

"What other word you know? I think Miss Lady Satan nifty. I need impress her."

Never mind.

"Do you know the term: 'minge biscuit'?"

"No," he says in childlike wonder. "What that?"

"You call someone a minge biscuit when you love them so much that there are no other words to say. It's like *I Love You* times a thousand."

Ziad grows nervous.

"I, uh…nifty Jhaegar, man. I don't know I can tell her that. She make fun of me."

[162]

"Aww, nooo. She won't do that. She's definitely in to you, man, just look how you helped save Hitler."

Ziad blushes. Piss, where do they get these people?

By this time, we reach the exit of the dungeon and step outside into sunlight. Fun Fact (not quite a Tantalizing Tidbit): I knew a girl who used to call dungeons "Don Johns." Was that Gwyn? I think it was Gwyn.

But yeah, a group of Yuppies jump out from behind hidden cover and point T-Shirt cannons at our heads. Why is this a thr—?

"—Freeze, bullies! Drop your weapons or the Nazi gets it!" the lead Yup shouts.

Satan throws down her pitchfork. Rooz and Ziad toss their guns to the ground. I guess I don't have a gun anymore so I just stand still and do nothing. Then I—

—The lead Yup points her cannon at me.

"I said, drop your weapons!"

"I—hehe—I don't have a weapon," I say, trying to hold back laughter as much as I can. Are they really—?

"—Drop that *attitude*, motherfucker!" the Yup yells.

"I, uh—hahaha—what?"

"Drop it!"

The rage of the Yuppies fires up. Rooz nudges me.

"Jhaegar, please, I would advise you drop—"

"—No!" I defy the Yuppies. "I don't have to do—"

—One of them points their cannon at Hitler and blasts!

A *The Patriarchy Kills my Vibe* T-Shirt wraps around Hitler's body and—

[163]

"—ARRRRGGHHHH! ARRRGHHHHHHHHH!" he screams as it burns into his skin.

"No! Big A!" Satan yells. The T-Shirt scalds her hands as she tries to pry it off him. She yanks them away in pain.

The Yuppies focus on me now.

"Any last words, Straight White Male?"

"Oh piss," I raise my hands. "I'm sorry. I didn't mean it, I'll drop the attitude!"

"Too late."

"Yoohoo, Yuppies!" Rooz yells.

They turn to him and find a big, fat, trademarked Rooz grin spread all over his face.

"He is not straight, that man is closeted Trans!"

The Yuppies gasp from the unexpected shock that they could be wrong about someone. A distraction! Now's my chance to strike back!

LITTLE WOMEN (20XX)

by Greta Gerwig (and whomever inevitably remakes it again)

(review by Jhaegar Holdburn)

Let's talk about fake feminism! And "fake feminism" you ask? Rooz? I'm looking at you, cuz films like Little Women *only serve to hinder, and not help, women's reform by in fact limiting them further and confining them to a sort of "separate but equal" social pocket.*

First things first: I don't have anything against Greta Gerwig. She's a great director…but you'll never hear people say

[164]

that cuz instead they'll say she's a great FEMALE director. Same goes for BLACK filmmaker or GAY writer. Why can't she just be a director? Why do we have to add FEMALE to her name? To remind us that she's a woman? Or to low-key say, "Hey Greta, you're great…for a woman, that is." You wouldn't say Masaki Kobayashi is a great MALE director, would you? By promoting yourself as a great female artist and by—we'll get to this soon—over feminizing the entire work, you basically open yourself up to the patronizing critique of, "Aww, aren't you a talented little lady/Black/Asian/Gay/whatever?"

And then these movies fail. This one did alright, but mostly these hyped up feminist movies crash and burn and people go, "Well, I guess filmgoers are just misogynists," when in actuality they should be going, "Well, it's unfortunate that traditionally female narratives star passive protagonists while traditionally male narratives star active protagonists which lead to more exciting movies, bigger blockbusters, more spectacular—" —ya know? People don't want four sisters sitting around all day gossiping about the neighbor boy, they want Hero Person going on Hero Journey from Points A to B to C. It's women gathering berries and chatting versus men going out on the hunt to kill the sabretooth tiger. People just refuse to see that. You try to write a screenplay—and no matter how great it is—you submit it to a writing competition and all the comments you'll get back'll be like: "Not enough car chases. Passive characters. Too much sitting and talking." Well, piss on me for trying, but

[165]

not everyone ever born is John McClane, now are they? Ya know—why are we discounting the lives of women just cuz they tend to be more idle and thought driven? What makes The Terminator's life more worthy?

And's this indicative of a sexist industry where male oriented scripts (and not talking who stars in it, you could have all women and it'd still be a male movie (looking at you All Female Remakes of heretofore All Male Films), we're talking structure here) male oriented scripts succeed and female ones are doomed to fail? Am I just sexist? The thing is, I don't know, cuz so many of these competitions and conferences and even fucking studios are run by women—and people of color, by the way! So what's the issue here? Why aren't they accepting their own work? Why do women hold back women more than men hold back women? Do men just succeed in life cuz, while toxic to women, at least men aren't toxic to themselves?

I know this review's going off the rails, but if you submitted this script—just literal copy and paste and changing all the names—to the Austin Film Festival or the Nicholl Academy Fellowship or just wherever: you'd get fucking laughed out of there! And then you—so what's even a male movie, too? And not just Predator *(1987) cuz it's about big beefy men hunting a monster in the jungle. What's a real MASCULINE movie exclusively about masculinity and its pitfalls and highs to compare to a feminine movie like* Little Women? *I'll wait while you think.*

[166]

LETTER TO THE EDITOR
by Tiresias "Rooz" Roosevelt

Fine work, Jhaegar, but let me add some "food for thought" as some would say. Does a film become "feminine" simply by adding women to it? Or, inversely, does a film become "feminine" based upon how the filmmaker chooses to USE those women?

I support the latter.

As I see we are wallowing in the rut of 1980s science fiction, let me add more work to the mix: Ridley Scott's *Alien* (1979) and James Cameron's *Aliens* (1986). Both follow the harrowing space adventures of Ellen Ripley and her encounters with the deadly, titular Alien.

In *Alien*, Ripley's survival instincts prevail while her spaceship crewmates succumb one by one to the Alien's predatory clutches. She proves to be the last human standing and drifts off into the end credits with her faithful cat. Does all that make this film necessarily feminine? Does just having a competent and capable filmic hero designate femininity just because that hero happens to be female?

And what of *Aliens*? Several hyper-sleep induced decades after the events of the first film, Ripley is once again dragged through the mire of science fiction horror...albeit now aware of the death of her only daughter. Where once she was a mother striving to make ends meet for her child, now she has no purpose but to care for herself. That is, until she meets Newt: a

[167]

girl newly orphaned by the recent Alien incursion. Ripley is a mother without a daughter. Newt is a daughter without a mother. They take each other in and fulfil the missing roles in either of their lives. This relationship builds to such intimacy that when Newt is taken by the Aliens into the center of their hive, under the nose of the Alien Queen herself, Ripley resolves to risk her life, and the lives of her companions, to save her new surrogate child.

And as the Alien Queen soon discovers: you would be better off not to dare Mama Bear. Ripley takes back her cub, obliterates the Queen's children in turn, and ultimately duels one on one with the Queen herself after the all-time greatest one liner in cinema: "Get away from her, you BITCH!" As much as that scene gives me chills, it also brings a wry smile to my face as it is reminiscent of a sort of "soccer mom" protecting her child from some hapless other parent foolish enough to trespass against their mother-daughter unit. Regardless: in *Alien,* Ripley is a hero who happens to be a woman. In *Aliens,* Ripley is a hero *because* she is a woman.

And you know what else, Jhaegar? All of that while maintaining a traditional male narrative of Points A to B to C to slay the beast and save the day.

Great takedown, Rooz.

Mad Max: Fury Road *(2015).* The Master *(2012 and shout-out to Paul THOMAS Anderson).* Jeanne Dielman, 23 quai du Commerce, 1080 Bruxelles *(1975 and I think I got it right this time). Now THOSE are feminist films.*

[168]

THOSE films show what it's like to be a woman, show their weaknesses and their supreme strengths, and demonstrate the future is indeed (hopefully) female.

...Uh, frankly, I don't know what to rate Little Women. Fine film, but "feminists" ruin it for themselves. Also, I basically just ranted about the industry. Wait...not sure I even saw this movie? Piss, I AM sexist.

Something out of Four

The Yuppies lie dead. Rooz and I's double review combo really did 'em in...not sure why as I think I'm getting more incoherent. Oh well, Satan walks over and shakes my hand.

"Gee fuckin' shit, Jhaegar, ya really are useful after all. Ziad was right."

I glance at Ziad (helping Hitler with the shirt thing) and he hits me with a quick wink.

But yeah, we just head back to the cloud/beaches/place/deal. I'd make a Thich Quang Duc joke at this point (we saw him as well), but I legitimately respect him enough to lay off. May you rest wherever your wondrous soul leads you, Thich.

The Raid seems about over now. The corpses of several dead Biblically accurate Angels litter the battlefield. Why are they still here, I thought you went to some new dimension when you died? Does God just take their cards to a Res Van (sorry)? Yeah, there's one getting up now and slithering away. Piss, God really does cheat.

Where are the Biblically inaccurate Angels we all know and love? Sigh. Not here. Life has a tendency to do that. You'd think there'd be—I don't know where I'm going with this—I just enjoy their flowy togas or whatever they wear—robes, I guess—and luscious hair and dreamy eyes and all that. Oh wait, I saw a few of them?

I don't know. I just wish I could be beautiful. Men are only allowed to be handsome (not saying I'm a man), but what if I wanna be pretty instead? I wanna be pretty instead…like, there was this time in preschool, right? Also! That load of shit about people choosing to be gay is a load of shit. You don't choose, why the fuck would you choose? Whatever—this time in preschool, right? Everyone has the dress-up playtime or whatever where the teacher gets out the big bin of clothes and everyone tries them on and has fun and there was this wedding dress. Oh man, this wedding dress! I still see it…it was long and flowy and white and pure and beautiful and I just wanted to wear it. But, even though I was literally like five and didn't know anything, I at least knew I wasn't allowed to wear that dress—that dress was for the girls and I was a stupid boy and had to deal with the cowboy outfit. Who the fuck wants to be some stupid fucking cowboy? Jumpin' Christ, they're not even real, just romanticized movie nonsense. What's really stupid, though, is people always get after me about how they think I pretend I live in a movie, but I'm the most realistic person I've ever met. I mean hey, you don't see me wandering around in a cowboy outfit. Piss…

But yeah! The dress! So good—and for years I think about it! How I'm stuck being a boy and have to wear all these coarse uncomfy (*comfy* is such an uncomfy looking word, you ever notice that?) and I just wanna wear skirts and blouses and—I don't know, I guess I'm—it really doesn't—so when I finally moved out after college, I—ya know—I figure, "Hey, well, nobody knows what I do in here or order from Amazon cuz I'm all by myself, ya know?" and I finally ordered some clothes…

Jumpin'. Fuckin'. Christ.

[170]

They're so much bette—shut up shut up shut up no no—and it just felt so right, I don't know. I (of course, it was like my prerogative after all) I put on "Venus as a Boy" by my queen—it's Bjork—and would just like dance around my—or really kinda drift and float— around my apartment. What sucks is how women's clothing's so (and unnecessarily, really) so tight. Why does having a vagina mean you have to fit in half as much fabric as men? I don't know, but fitting a penis in there was rough—and it wasn't even like—okay, maybe a bit erotic—but it just felt RIGHT more than anything. I used to even walk around in winter with my big ass winter coat over—

—Never mind. Doesn't matter. I just wish there were some nice Angels here. I just—I don't know—it's like white people listening to "Dancing Queen" on road trips, just a guilty pleasure harmless fun activity that doesn't hurt anybody. But as if that fucking mattered, I still always feel—always felt horrible about it, like I'm still somehow sexualizing women. Aren't I just sexualizing myself? What is that even called? Whatever it is, I'm sure it's just another nail in my coffin, just one more reason I'm fucked up and'll never find…I don't know, just never get anywhere!

And these fucking people again! These, "Why would you choose to be—?" —you think I CHOSE to be like this? Fucking see how—like—why the fuck would anyone choose that man Why? Its all fun and games wearing a bikini til you start cutting yourself in the bathtub and I just dont get it i just dont like i hope everyone just fuckin dies too you fuckin ass

Vivi's in front of me. Vivi and her Blue's Clues hoodie. Was that even her? She lifts it up for me and she's not wearing a bra. I look down and I'm wearing my bra instead. It was Calvin Kline and too expensive and I loss steam jerking off cuz now I'm thinking about how every woman on earth isn't just fucking broke

[171]

get her outta here, get her outta here. Gwyn's next. I think she had the Blue's Clues hoodie. I don't know—doesn't matter, she's not gonna wear it for long and—shit fuck piss! Blue's so innocent I don't wanna corrupt her mind too get outta here, Gwyn, or at least wear something different. She's—okay this is better now. I always loved that skirt—she wears it a lot better than me, but can't knock me for not trying. My penis would always fall—piss shut up shu up s

Snowelda. Sno—Snowelda? Why her? Whatever. Try new things, yeah? Doesn't matter, it'll just all be—just all be fine so Just clear my mind and everythi

"Everything alright in there, Jhaegar?" Rooz asks from the other room.

"Not now, Rooz!" I yell back. "Go play with social reform!"

Back to snowelda. This could work, this could work. She has, like, a strap-on—or maybe just a penis—but it's all fine. I don't mind, I'll try new things, I'm the girl tonight, anyway, I'm pretty, I'm, beautiful and swe,et and j,ust everything"s fine and back to Vivi God please just fucking stop I don't want this anymore I don't know how to stop I don't know how to make it go away otherwise I don't wanna wear this anymore and bloody water keeps getting in my mouth and it's salty and weird and I don't like it and (*All alone (All alone)*) piss, really? Everything's just coming in and out of my mind and it's just (*All Alone (AloneALLONE)*)) and and and and

Her the girl from the mall maze dream whatever and piss fuck no shes too nice im sorry i didnt wanna please just stop i wish (*No Love*) i was dead just go away please just die just die too die die die im sorry just okay fine well take two falafels now hell leave us alone now hell leave us alone now hell come here just come closer come cum jju st it doesnt matter itll be over im sorryi im

used as an object

[172]

Fuck me. Jumpin' fuckin' Christ, the sink, Jhaegar? The fucking SINK?

Sigh. Sob. Super sigh. Why can't I get over this? When did I even get here? Jumpin' fuck, man. I turn on the sink (I didn't even have it on, what the fuck) and try to wash everything down. Why is this Hell? Why can't I just be tortured? Or is this it? Is this right here the point?

I don't know. I walk (I really *storm*) out of the bathroom. Rooz glances up from his National Geographic and spouts some clever shit, but I just don't have time for it right now. I just fucking don't.

I get myself out of this village—this camp. Why does Satan even like Ewoks? Or did she imply I made this place and I'M the one who likes Ewoks? Fuck everything. I get out of here. I gotta find a better part of Hell.

I walk past Pasolini's *The Canterbury Tales* (1972) Hell.

I walk past Lars von Trier's *The House that Jack Built* (2018) Hell.

I RUN past Bergman's *Smiles of a Summer Night* (1955 and that's a thinker) Hell.

Now we have it: traditional, Biblically inaccurate, fiery burning pits of sulfur Hell. Comparable to the others, it's oddly comforting. But I have that piss fucking ringing in my ears so I guess it's kind of like *The House that Jack Built*...and Pasolini's Hell's actually pretty sick. Screw it all, I'm in regular vanilla Hell.

After some searching, I find some suitable bathtub looking things of lava. I undress and gently lower myself into one. Ya know, this actually isn't too bad. Is this maybe supposed to be the nice part of Hell? Is this, like, a day spa equivalent?

Sigh. I just wanted to be tortured. I sink lower into the tub so only my face pokes out above the flames.

[173]

"Ya fuckin'," I hear Satan start from behind me. Jumpin' Christ, now she's here? Um…but she doesn't say anything else, almost like she's— "—lug-ub-ri-ous asshole, Jhaegar."

Sigh. I sink lower.

"Don't fuckin' hide from me!"

The lava suddenly recedes and I'm staring up at Satan.

"That wasn't even a real word," I manage to say.

"Was to. Lugubrious. Means dismal as fuckin' shit. Fits ya perfect."

"Oh, very cute. Well, I—"

—Several things happen at once: lava fills the tub as if it was never gone, Satan lowers herself into the tub across from me…and now she's in a tight red bikini.

Satan glances down at her chest (seems surprised to find herself suddenly in a bikini, but also not really) and rolls her eyes.

"Fuck's sake," she murmurs under her breath.

She then reaches out of the tub, grabs an empty glass (like a malt glass?), dips and fills it with lava, and promptly begins drinking through a swirly straw.

"Alright, asshole. What's da problem?"

I usually hate this psychoanalytical nonsense, but a sassy teen in a flaming hot bikini speaking in a phony Jew Nersey (New Jersey! I meant Jew Nersey!) accent breaks down my barriers.

"I just don't get it," I tell her. Cue ten other clichés lying in wait.

"It's alright, ya at dat age where ya—well actually, who says ya ever gotta undahstand? Maybe tryin' ta undahstand is ya problem in da first place? Just let life happen."

"Alright…and?"

[174]

"Ya sure looked like ya had fun on da Raid last week," (last week?), "why don't ya just get used ta dat fuh a while, huh?"

"I don't wanna kill others, though."

"Why not?" she asks. Then tries for a deeper, gravelly voice, "Close your heart to their suffering, Jhaegar."

"Is that what God's supposed to sound like?"

"I—what—no! No, ya fuckin' idiot! Are ya kiddin' me, ya didn't get dat reference?!"

"No, what?"

"Shit, Jhaegar, buy a decent game once in a while! Can't touch yaself while playin' Bayonetta da rest a ya life."

I ponder this for a moment.

"I don't know. Like it matters…it doesn't make me happy anyway."

Satan takes a big sip of lava. Her eyes roll and I think my stomach does, too.

"Well why can't ya be satisfied with da dog ting?"

"Dog City?"

"What'd ya think?!"

"I don't get that either and you're implying you want me to be happy, so I—"

"—Don't ya fuckin' get it?!" she yells (nine more to go). "Ya not MEANT ta be happy. Dat is ta say, not happy in da traditional sense. Ya supposed ta be sad—an' I mean, really fuckin' sad—cuz YOU BEING SAD MAKES YOU HAPPY!"

She jabs her finger at me as she hits every word. I sink back into the lava (or is it called *magma* at this point?).

[175]

"Ya just have ta undahstand dat, Jhaegar. Then ya'll," Satan struggles with her words as she makes vague hand gestures in the air. "Ya'll ascend or somethin'."

"Dog City Never Sleeps…" I mutter.

"A supreme being is 'bout ta be born, Jhaegar, somethin' nevah before seen, biggah dan me or dat asshole up in Heaven…an' I mean…ultimately, it really don't mattah cuz ya only control da movements, not da destination, so just let it happen! Or somethin' like dat."

"So why am I a 'Dog City?'"

"I don't believe anybody evah fuckin' said ya was a 'Dog City,' now did dey? No. Dey just said, 'Dog City Nevah Sleeps,' an' dat's it an' dat's all we get."

Through Ascension and not Depression will I
Shatter the bars of this Mortal Prison

"What?" I say.

"Huh?" Satan say(s).

"Was that you or—?"

—Satan leans in close. So close I can see her—

"—I don't really fuckin'—an' stop dat—I don't really know. Unfortunately, I'm confined only ta what you yaself know, which as ya can tell ain't very much. I'm just a Comfort Charactah or some shit."

"But you're the Devil?"

"An' you're a masochist."

Satan kisses me—bites (aw fuck!)—me on the lips.

I pull away from her and wipe my mouth as we return to camp. I check myself to make sure I'm wearing clothes (then do a double check to make sure I'm wearing men's clothes—sometimes you just gotta be sure, ya know?) and everyone's pretending like me and Satan aren't a total thing like people do when they know you're totally a thing. But I don't think she and I are a thing. I don't think anything.

I hear Ziad call Satan a, "Nifty minge biscuit."

I hear Satan respond, "What da fuck does dat mean?"

I hear Ziad looking at—or I feel him being betrayed in my general direction.

I don't know what's going on. I'm heading back to my place. I had a place, right? Hitler comes up to me and asks if I know how to crochet. Not now, Hitler, I'm busy. I must've told him that cuz he runs away crying. I guess he really was a sensitive guy.

I put some petroleum jelly on my lips cuz they're cracked and bleeding and burnt and stuff. I feel like it looks weird and people think I've been like—I don't even know—just dipping myself in jelly? I've always felt bad for female violin players cuz everyone probably thinks they're whores (violin hickeys), but they're really not. What I'm trying to say here is that nobody ever believes me when I say I don't dip myself in jelly.

Rooz tries to ask me about this. I tell him to go crochet with Hitler. He seems hurt as well. I'm a fucking monster.

I enter the room it turns out I have. Viviiviviviviviana is here. Waiting for me. In our *special place* you could say. Satan thinks I don't know anything about good video games. Screw her and her nonsense.

But yeah, Gwyn holds me and asks how work was today and I don't know what I'm doing. I tell her what Satan said, that I'm unhappy and don't know how to enjoy my life. I can't

[177]

even remember what Satan said to be honest cuz all I remember was everything she said was true and something I already knew. I tell Gwyn my hands hurt from typing and that I just wanna die, that this exercise is pointless, that I'm gonna end up alone anyway and no one would care if I killed myself—at least in the abstract, I clarify. She tells me I think too much and I tell her lucky her. Lucky her that she doesn't and nobody else does either. Lucky fucky everybody, huh? Lucky fucky—she's telling me to calm down and that I—I just want her to go away so I tell her I just want her to go away and she says she can't cuz I won't let her. I say I'll just die here and we'll all go. She says that won't fix anything and I tell her bark woof sigh. She frowns and tells me I can't keep covering myself with dog humor. What does she know about dog humor? She asks me what happened today at work that I'm in this mood and I just stand there and she remembers that nothing specific has to happen, but that I just appear in this mood like a factory install or something.

"Maybe you're not meant to enjoy anything," she says. "But maybe you not enjoying anything is your way of enjoying something, and who is anyone to take that away from you?"

Gwyn never said that. Vivi didn't either. It doesn't make sense. It's not what I want. It's not what I think I want or what other people want me to think? To want to think? I can't think, I just can't think any fucking more, I think I fall down or something and she makes a Life Alert joke but I don't laugh cuz I don't laugh anymore. I just want an answer even though I know there isn't one. Where is he? Where's Glass Pipe? Turmeric Pill stares up at me but where's Glass Pipe? Is he gonna kill me again, is he even a *he*? *An* he? Fuck me. I reach for Turmeric Pill and I know I'm just coping. I know I'm just taking these cuz my hands fucking hurt and these don't fucking help but I have nothing else so I just wanna jam it in my fucking ass and and and I pull away cuz I know these are bad for me and I hate myself and oh my jumpin' Christ there he is.

[178]

There's Glass Pipe with his Glass Penis so I know in fact he is male—or at least a trans man. I wanna be a woman. I wanna be dead. Health bars appear above me and Vivi. Same for them. Sigh life, one of these again.

I punch to the left. I punch to the right. And that's how you do the Skarn—oh fuck me. Fuck me, not that, not that, get that outta here. A girl I knew—a different girl—a—honestly, who fucking knows—she liked that show and so did Buggins and it's like, "Buggins, you're fucking blind," and I don't get it. Maybe that was Fig Dunkis. Not the girl, my friend. He was Fig Dunkis. Yeah, definitely was. I forget her name. Dunkiss had two S's's's, though. And it turns out we won. Did we even fight? Glass Pipe rests forever in pieces and Turmeric Pill cloudizizes and puffs into the sky. We're outside? Do I have a skylight? I remember that girl's roommate, though (*they were roommates* (you know the voice)), and she like laid out broken glass (hey, glass!) on the floor—well, maybe not *laid* out, I think it was just an accident. But there was broken glass and she didn't do anything about it. I wish I got laid.

Ziad, Hitler, and I guess just everyone else, like—sigh—lift me up on their shoulders and do a little parade with me. This irritates (aggravates) me cuz I'm reminded of Jacque Tati's *Parade* (1974) and how it's just his old vaudeville material reworked into a movie and how it's like—jumpin' Christ, why bother—and how he really got lazy after *Playtime* (1967). Then again, that film like ruined his life and (of course) he cheated on his wife with one of the non-actor stars of the film and that ruined his image of me—no, his image inside of me—my image of him. Like, if you somehow managed to get a wife, why on earth would you cheat on her? And then (double of course) people have the gall to say I'M the nutcase. Whatever.

Oh piss, I'm—they're taking me—oh please just stop ("Willya Pleez Stahp!" (sorry, Sioux Falls reference)) fucking harem and I don't have—I don't want this. Can I just get some

[179]

tacos instead? Some (nononon NO NO NO STOP GIVING everyTHING a seXUaL CONnotaTIoN) they just set me down in front of some women and leave.

Great. Perfect. And as per pissing usual, they're these hyper sexualized ("Willya Pleez Stahp!") and I'm sure they think, "Wow, he's a big strong man let's do some things and have hot steamy sex together," and it's like, "I have ED so this literally won't happen."

At least they're cute when they giggle and hey, I'm a fan of anyone who thinks I'm funny until I realize they're not giggling at my joke but rather my exposed penis. I don't know if it was Ziad or Hitler, but one of those bastards must've stripped me. The women wink and giggle some more and say some nonsense about how they'll "fix me right up" and I get PTS—no, I actually get Future Traumatic Stress Disorder and I—ya know, maybe Satan or whoever was right? Maybe I do enjoy suffering and pain and humiliation...but then shouldn't I be pumped right now?

The girls' (women's, sorry) attitude flat lines as they discover that no amount of "fixing" (wow, that's not the best word to use) will get us anywhere. But NOWWWW! (comes the part I always like) we're all too involved and gone too far and can't really back out so we just kinda have to hang around and pretend everything's okay and that they don't wanna shoot themselves in the head and that I don't wanna shoot myself in the head and that they don't wish they were with some Chad (not an Incel, I swear (I know that's what an Incel would say, but I'm really not an Incel. I love women and their fun smells and soft voices and the way they don't judge (okay they judge me a lot))))but I) I don't care)) and that I wish I was with Jaelyn (I never figured out how to spell her name, but I do believe it's that—wait, her name wasn't that, it was—oh piss, who?) and it's—oh? Harem woman (woman not women?) is Gwyn?

[180]

Yeah, here she is…sad and disappointed…um…I try to hold her (well, not "try," I DO hold her, I just don't think it's very effective) hold her and settle down her crying.

"Hey, it's alright," trying to convince both her and myself, "it's not your fault. It's me."

"Yeahokay," she heaves out, somehow one word. Oh, no…

"I'm sorry," I say about ten more times, but I won't stress the po— "—I'm just not—good at this stuff. I'm sorry, it's not your fault."

"Okay," she says like ten more times, once again not to stress—

"—Do you want your panties back?" Oh piss, please just fucking kill me. I love how—I love how I'm already ingraining this into my mind so I'll never be able to forg—

—She kind of just—I don't know—without speaking acknowledges assent or something and I really (REALLY) sheepishly find them and hand them over. I make a mental note to cross off "Touching Panties" as a thing that turns me on and to add it to the "Things Ruined Forever" list instead.

Suddenly, Gwyn turns to me, braving a shy smile (which regrettably indicates this to be a fantasy, but hey, I'll take it, my probably Turmeric induced hallucination, I can do what I want) and says:

"Maybe, like, I could make it up for you?"

Oh piss. I can't stand when people are nice to me. Like, I don't need it, all it does is make me feel trashy and—you didn't even do anything wrong! Why do YOU have to make it up to ME—why does ANYONE have to do anything for me—just do whatever you want and I'll—I'll just take it, I don't know. It's like, why are you so fucking weak? No, shut up—they're not weak, they're nice. I'm weak. So I should be doing nice things for—shut up, just shut up and let someone be nice to you!

[181]

"I hear you're like a chef, man, and that you cook fancy stuff while bumpin' music and dancing?"

"I, uh, well…"

She holds tight to my arm. Tugs on it slightly and grins.

"What song'd you lose your virginity to?"

Panic mode, gotta think of something fast:

"*Threnody for the Victims of Hiroshima.* What about you?"

She doesn't answer (I guess I do like humiliation (and sigh, it's actually not even a song, it's a piece of music)) and puts on a shirt (no bra, just a big billowy shirt oh my oh my oh my women are so fabulous) and pulls me out of bed (I'm still naked, by the way).

Gwyn leads me to her kitchen where everything is already laid out and ready to go. A piece of paper waits by the ingredients. I glance at it.

COUSIN J'S WORLD INFAMOUS APPLE BOTTOMED CURRY

A chicken breast, or two I guess (there's no real recipe)

An onion

A Pink Lady (every time you use a different apple a puppy goes Mad to the Eldritch Horrors) apple

Some ginger

A ginger (lady (Pink) preferably)

And cinnamon

And garlic

And curry powder

[182]

And tomato paste

And flour

And chicken broth

And a little deal of vanilla Greek yogurt

And some cilantro

And the two SECRET INGREDIENTS

Step 1. Cry a bit. Decide to make curry cuz it might make you feel better.

Step 2. You chop that onion and then chop that apple. You add the onion to the pan once the olive oil's hot, but you're gonna wanna leave the apple on the cutting board and dust it with cinnamon. This way it'll like infuse (I think) while we cook the other stuff.

Step 3. So once the onion's looking good, you're gonna add the um, uh, uh, you're gonna add the spices. Only cook them that way for about 30 seconds otherwise they'll burn and it'll suck. Then add the flour (cuz that'll thicken up the curry) and cook it until it smells right.

Step 4. Add the broth. This'll prevent burn-age and help develop it into a more taste-able dish. Then you're gonna wanna add the apples, that way they can boil kinda in the broth and spices and get really soft and beautiful. Dust with more cinnamon.

Step 5. Alright, now you gotta add your trimmed, filleted, and salt 'n' peppered chicken breast. Add it right into the middle and kinda nestle it in there (you should also probably have started the rice at this point) and then cover the pan. In 5 minutes or so just flip the chicken so it'll cook evenly.

Step 6. Once the chicken's fine, take it out onto a plate and cut it up. Add back to the curry, then also add your yogurt deal with some cilantro spliced into it and mix.

[183]

Step 7. Add your first secret ingredient. You only need about one knifeful. You'll know you have enough cuz the curry'll look and smell just right. The thing is, while you add the first secret ingredient, you have to THINK about the second secret ingredient.

Step 8. And I know the whole, "The secret ingredient is love," nonsense is kinda nonsense, but it really works here...well it's not really *love* so much as it's like...happy memories? As you smell the finished product you just try to push out all the horrible times with her and think of the good times you still have locked somewhere in your memory. And it's not like Gwyn or Vivi or whatever, it's, uh...it's the...

Step 9. She was my first girlfriend, right? We were like, ya know, fourteen or fifteen—just really young—and we didn't know anything and I—being like really...just shitty, I guess, I kinda...took advantage of her and...I didn't rape her, but just about everything else and I think that might as well count. I don't know. I think I abused her.

Step Kill Yourself. I guess I didn't realize it until years later. I had broken up with her cuz she (rightfully so) was pushing me away when it came to anything sexual and I was like, "Oh, she's a prude, I can find a looser girl somewhere else." Ya know...cuz I'm scum? But it was only...it was only after that when I kept seeing her around school that I realized how it affected her and how terrible I was. She got into drinking and drugs and (I think she's since stopped, I really do) but I would think, "Did I ruin her life?" And of course years after that, the whole #MeToo movement started and it was even worse cuz I saw these monstrous men being taken down and these women finally getting justice and all I could think of—all I can still think of—is how I'm one of them. I'M one of the abusers. I'M the villain in everyone else's—the WORLD'S story. Despite the good

[184]

things I tried to do and the ways I felt like I improved myself in the years to come, I couldn't change the fact that I was—and still fucking am—a creep.

Make It Stop. And when I realized that, I couldn't talk to women anymore. Every time I looked at one, I saw her and all I could think about was how much I hated myself. A girl—even a stranger—could so much as glance at me in the grocery store and I just wanted to puke. When I went to bed at night, I would think that while I'm going to bed peacefully, she's going to bed an abuse victim. I just wanna make her okay again or—I don't know, I wish I could trade my life for hers or some—I awkwardly texted her in college, right? Weird small talk conversation. She eventually asked me why I texted her (probably knew I didn't have the balls to come out and say it) and I just told her how sorry I was and how I hoped she could move on and have a happy life. She told me, "That's very noble of you," and it just fucking killed me cuz she HAD to be sarcastic. I knew she didn't care. She told me she hoped I could be happy, too, and I told her the same again and that was it.

Just Die. It only got worse after that. I stopped…being places? I don't know. Like I'd be sitting at a restaurant with my friends looking at a menu to order and I wouldn't know how to read. I'd just stare at the menu and the waiter would come by and be like, "Y'all ready to order?" and they'd all look at me cuz I was the one they were waiting on and I'd just nod and glance back at the menu and order the first thing I saw. It's like I'd forget where I was, I'd forget how to do things. I had those weird deals where I'd…like…see myself from behind myself? I don't know. It was so bad that I started…umm…

It just felt good that way? Like if I hurt myself, it was making it up to her, ya know? Like I deserved it? And for some reason, it helped. It really did. It made me so happy, I couldn't

[185]

believe—it certainly loosened a few more screws in my head, but that was fine—I'd have to take breaks, though, cuz I...I guess I started getting burn scars or...whatever. I think I may have even gotten nerve damage or something cuz I began to lose feeling in—but that just—in a way—made me feel better. I don't know, I guess I'm...

Maybe I just need to find a Goth girl. Am I even Goth? And dating sites are so—just nonsense! I won't bother to explain, cuz I'm trying to make it seem like I'm not an Incel—that statement was wrong—I don't want people to confuse me for an Incel, so I'll strive to not fall for Incel tropes. Also! As far as I'm concerned, the word "Incel" should be treated as what it ACTUALLY is: a slur! A slur to demean and degrade lonely or lackluster men (while also being a misogynist term as it basically confines women to the role of qualifying a man's "Manhood" and that their only purpose is to have sex with men as to determine which one's are Incels or not). I don't know. I just wish there was, like...a gothpeoplemeet.com. Or realistically—a gothpeopleinstallthisappmakeaprofileskimfor2minutesdecidethisisstupidanddelete.com. That'd be more like it.

I wonder what Goth girls' names are—and if they use their given name or make a new one. Like, I don't know if I'd be able to take a "Sarah" seriously. A Goth "Jennifer?" It'd have to be like "Willow" or "Velvet" or "Screaming Vengeance," ya know? Why do people always give nonsense names to girls like "Faith" or "Hope?" Where's my "Torment" and "Retribution" at?

Funny thing about names: You can always kinda tell what someone looks like by their name—and vice versa. Ya know...Karen? Leslie? Brittany? You know what a Brittany looks like—and shame on you, parents! It's like you're just setting your child up for failure.

I wish I could meet a girl named "Edwina" (yeah, I know) cuz then everyone would call her "Ed," but I would be special and call her "Eddy." Oh Eddy, what a queen. Or "Bailey." Girls

[186]

named "Bailey" are just better. The name's reminiscent of a Horse Girl (ya know, she's not a "Jessica") so it's a slight negative, but she's also kind of a "Kami," so I find they meet in the middle. "Bailey" is the perfect Girl Next Door. Did I mention this before? Pretty sure. "Bailey" is just like a cute white girl (oh piss, NOT SAYING white girls are the only ones who can be cute, jumpin' Christ, get away from me. It's just a name and I'm just a person).

But yeah, I'm working on the chicken. I try to fillet the breast—I say "try" cuz I actually stab the knife into my stomach instead—part of a dream I get, I suppose. In it, I'm fine and decent and doing everything right and then I start bleeding. Like, from the stomach for some reason and a tinge from the mouth—but I start bleeding from the stomach and then my intestines spill out and my mouth bleeds more and then my eyes bleed and obscure my vision and no matter how much I try to stuff my intestines back inside myself they're just too squishy and gross and keep going everywhere. All the while I think to myself, "I did everything right today. Why is this happening to me? I did everything right."

I find myself in Satan's office (yeah, alone). I find myself there cuz I have to die here. Vivi was right—I mean, Gwyn—they were all right. I'm not meant to be happy, maybe some people just aren't. I'm someone who's meant to be sad and kill themselves…nothing wrong with it, it's just how it is. I'll die here and go to whatever other dimension and die there and die at the next place and just keep suffering like I'm meant to. And then, when I've finally suffered enough and paid my debt, I'll (hopefully) get to die for good.

Or maybe I'm not aligning with Gwyn's idea, maybe it was Satan's? I don't know, they were both simi—forget it, I don't know. I just wanna make sure no one is confused after I die: people have "happy" things and "sad" things entirely switched around (notwithstanding that there's also "dismal" and "melancholy" and "bleak" and—) —and I'm fixing it right here and

[187]

now. "Happy" things aren't actually happy cuz usually the happiness is unearned and, due to that, it comes off as dishonest. Take most movies. Most movies have a "happy" ending where the good guy beats the bad guy and saves the day and gets the girl—all the stuff—and it's supposed to make the audience feel good. Why, though? It's so…it's so contrived. That nonsense doesn't happen in real life and it doesn't serve anyone to keep lying to them—if anything, these sorts of endings only remind the audience how these sorts of—fuck it, I don't care. Nobody else does so why should I?

But *Silent Hill 2*, right? The (*In Water*, by the way) nightmarish world of Silent Hill is used to express—really, to reflect—James's deteriorating psyche. Everything from the monster design to all the bodies in town wearing his clothes to the ever changing town itself shows that James just wants to die. But this still lends it to having a "real" ending, despite several "unreal" components. The "real" aspects that are important here are the human aspects, the emotions James (and the player) feel. James ultimately kills himself cuz that's the only thing that'll bring him peace and the only true logical conclusion to his unamendable suffering. What's even better about this game: **it never punishes James for killing himself**. It never says he's a bad person for doing so—better yet, it doesn't reward James for moving past his trauma (leaving Silent Hill with Laura) and making a "healthy" decision when you get the *Leave* ending by accident. It's not a game that's indifferent per se, it's just a game that doesn't judge. It allows you to make of it what you will. It's honest. It's true. It reflects real life while splicing in a fantasy world of madness…and if we live in this world of madness, then who's to say anyone's really crazy?

I think it's better that I just kill myself—or at least keep killing myself where I end up— you'd think they'd run out of places eventually. Satan's *Bitch Burner* flamethrower seemed like a wise choice, so I guess that's why I'm here. If you're gonna die in Hell, might as well be in a

[188]

flaming conflagration. Does this turn me into Thich Quang Duc? Oh piss, what if I end up in Heaven?

"Jhaegar, stop. Ya really don't wanna do dat here," Satan says from behind.

I turn to see her standing in the doorway with Rooz and Ziad. They're giving me *The Look*, that fucking *Mental Illness* look. I glance down and see the *Bitch Burner* already in my hands. I glance up and see them take a cautious step towards me.

"The gun didn't work last time," I say. "Maybe fire's more efficient?" I unintentionally do a creepy little chuckle and their *Look* intensifies.

"There is no need for that, Jhaegar," says Rooz.

"Yes, Jhaegar, man. Come back together us. New Raid this weekend," says Ziad.

Satan holds up her hands to quiet them. For half a second, I think she's the girl I abused—just for half a second and then it's okay again.

"Listen, asshole, there are bettah ways ta do dis. I think ya misundahstood our last conversation…again."

"No, I understood just fine. This is how it's meant to be. This is Hell and this is my punishment."

"Jhaegar," she says low, "nobody here wants ta punish ya."

I lock eyes with her. Her…

"I do," I whisper.

I point the *Bitch Burner* at myself and hold the trigger. An immeasurably bright and searing flash o

[189]

III. Dog City

I am born.

What? How? I'm like…still twenty-five!

Yeah, my adult head pops out of my Mother's vagina.

I meet the gaze of the delivery doctor who promptly faints. The technicians in the room promptly scream. My Mother promptly scre—well, scream-dies.

I wiggle around. Oh piss, I'm trapped! What? Someone get me outta here!

"Someone get me outta here!" I yell, but everyone in the room has either fallen unconscious or ran away.

I gather my strength. Try to shoot one arm past my head so I can work my way out. What I do instead is drive my elbow out of my Mother's uterus and through her abdomen. Oh well.

Thankfully (thankfully?), this creates enough room for me to fall out of her onto the floor. I stand up and survey the scene: my Mother (younger, almost unfamiliar) lies dead on the table. I glance around at the (wow, actually somewhat retro?) hospital room. I glace at—

—The calendar says 2001! I DIED AND JUST FUCKING CAME BACK HERE?! I HAVE TO START MY LIFE OVER?! THEN WHY DO I STILL HAVE THE BODY OF A TWENTY-FIVE YEAR OLD?!?

At least it's not all bad: my arms are back to being white again (not that having Black arms was necessarily bad). My—wait, I'm fucking JACKED! Like ACTUALLY this time and not just lying to feel cool!

How did this happen?

[191]

I grab the hospital bed and lift it—I can lift it! I set it down, then pick it up again. And again. And again! Is this what it's like to be a man?! I feel a need to buy tight clothing. I feel a need to drive around in a Honda Accord listening to the Pop Top 40. I feel a need to…catcall women?

Okay, never mind. I wanna go back to being gay. I mean! I'm…uh…I'm not *gay* I just…like women's clothing…and wanna wear it and kill myself. Can I just go back to Hell?

But yeah, I find some clean "gender appropriate" clothing and sigh as I put it on. Well…I don't know—are male doctor scrubs necessarily "male" clothing or "gender fluid" or something? I certainly don't feel good wearing them like I do when I wear dresses and stuff, but I also don't feel bad like when I wear tank tops and gym shorts. Is this my solution, just wearing a bunch of "bleh" nonsense?

I don't know. I run my hands through my manly (unfortunately, no longer womanly (people said it was womanly, I don't know, I guess it changed)) hair and—hot piss, my bandages are gone—my ear's fine, too?! What? Why? Why did I get a new body and not a new mind? IS this a new body? But I killed myself? Is this cuz of that dog shit? Is this Dog City? Am I—hey! Is this what Never Sleeping is—?

No

Oh…well…that sucks…

May You Find Your Worth In The Waking World

[192]

Don't use that reference on me! I'll dog ya!

I Will Dog You

Why did I say that? What's "dogging" someone? Man, I'm really sick—

—My ear spurts blood.

My intestines throb and threaten to burst from my body.

I clutch my stomach with weak, skinny arms.

No, no, no, I'm not sick. I'm not sick. I'm not sick I'm not. sick. I.m no

It's all fine again. It's fine. My ear's fine. My stomach's fine. Everything's fine.

Dog's In His City

All's Right With The World

That reference, too? Whatever, it's fine. It's fine.

***

As I walk to a home I remember I don't have, I realize I need food and money from a family that no longer (doesn't yet? (oh wait, I killed her)) exists.

Well, this is a conundrum. Do I have credentials anymore, like, is my degree still good? Maybe my old (future?) job'll take me back? I don't—

—Also, where am I sleeping tonight?

[193]

It's times like these that my near constant disorientation seems like quite a boon to me. I'll just find a bench as it gets dark, pretend someone asks me about the Czech New Wave, and boom, it's morning.

But yeah, turns out I do get the job back at my old place. Fuck will have it (luck! luck! why did I say—?) —my old manager is now actually young enough to be my desk partner. And she's like—piss, I hate myself. Whatever. The new manager (old?) is like, "Yes, thank you, Jhaegar, you can start yesterday HaHAAAHaahHAHAhHAHA," ya know? That crazy nutcase fake laugh when they overdo it as if to convince themselves?

At least my desk's still here. What's really stupid, though, is that it's not like a bunch of individual offices? It's one huge, like, HUGE room and everyone's "office" is made up of moveable dividers, so you're there to work and basically hear everyone chat amongst themselves about what a better life they have and that you may as well kill yourself now otherwise you'll be chained to your desk for all eternity.

Timsheil (Timsheil Loranda, my manager-now-desk-buddy, sorry) smiles as I sit down.

"Hey," she says, "how are you?"

Jumpin' Christ, really? Timsheil *likes* me? Come on, I—

—No, shut the fuck up, Jhaegar—just cuz a woman looks at you, doesn't mean she wants to get in your—I mean, have you get in—no, no, piss fuck shit, it's the same—it's the—and shut up SHUT UP SHUT UP—she's gonna hear your thoughts/speech cuz you're a dumb fuck and you always—

—She keeps smiling, as if awaiting a response?

"I'm fine," I manage(r), "how're you?"

[194]

"Really good," she smiles and nods and kinda giggles (really selling the "nice coworker" act), "I'm Timsheil, but you can just call me Tim."

"Okay, 'Tim.'" I try to mimic her jovial giggle as best I can.

She giggles back.

I giggle back again.

She didn't hear my thoughts—or to be more precise, I don't seem to be unintentionally vocalizing my thoughts.

Let's try this: Hey Tim, just wanted to let you know to drop the flirting/not flirting act cuz I have severe and guilt-incurable erectile dysfunc—

"—So, where are you from? From around here?" she asks.

Well gee golly gee. She doesn't—and why would I have tested her with that? Maybe cuz—cuz I was so confident it would be fine!

"Yeah, Tim, I've lived here all my—"

—Our (current) manager steps into our office-cubicle-whatever-thing: "Hey, you two, so how are reports coming? Did you see my email? Check the file?"

Subtitles below him read: *What the fuck's your guys' problem? Get to work, I don't pay you guys shit cuz all I ever see you fucks do is fap around. Stop flirting with him, Tim, he's gay. Don't you—?*

—Timsheil spins back to her computer and starts typing away as if somehow it'll make our manager forget she was messing arou—no, she wasn't even mes—piss, now I see where she gets it from...

"Yes, sir. I'm proofreading it now, sir. It'll be on your desk by the time you get back, sir."

[195]

"Great. Thanks, Tim." Subtitles: *Fuck me, at least she has nice tits.*

Hey! You can't say that! This is why I hate—

"—So, were you able to get logged in?" He says to me. Subtitles: *Jesus, fairy boy wants to fuck her already.*

"Excuse me, I'm gay."

I mean, not *gay* but—

—Timsheil glances over her shoulder at me. Our manager raises an eyebrow.

"Uh, alright," he says. Subtitles: *Wow...uh...he's so...confident about it...no one's ever spoke to me like...I...shit, don't blush, asshole!*

He turns (blushing) and gets the fuck outta here.

Timsheil fully turns to me now. Subtitles: *No way. He definitely eats pussy.*

"Wow, Jhaegar, it's good to know my new partner is comfortable in their own skin. You and I'll have to catch lunch sometime and talk more about your ferocious sexuality."

Piss, I do wanna eat her—no SHUT UP SHUT UP you DON'T! You—fuck off, where's the bathroom, where's the—no SHUT UP piss fuck fuck fuck it doesn't matter just sit down and get to work sit down and get to work sit down and I'm sitting down and working and I can smell her pussy from no I can't FUCK OFF Jesus jumpin' motherfucking shit I can't I can't I can't I can't it's all fine she's just my coworkers she's a human being too with hopes and dreams and hopes and one of them is fucking me and NONONONONONONONO it's NOT she just works here man she just she—sigh, we could be like the twenty year office affair imagine that imagine me and her and everybody else knowing like super knowing cuz it's so SHUT UP SHUT UP just get to fucking worrrrrrRRRR

I get to fucking work. I turn on my computer. I'm already locked out.

[196]

FUCK! FUCK! FUCK! FUCK! Timsheil slides her panties off and gently, covertly tosses them my way. I can see the—NO NO she's not and there's no—she's just working, too! Not doing anything!

I hit the "Forgot My Password" button. I don't even have a password. I twiddle my thumbs, wait, try not to think about—actually (just to try), I type in "Fucking Kill Me#840" and it accepts. Shit fuck.

It appears I already have fourteen hundred emails. I go to the screen to clock on and find out I don't have access (a pop-up message tells me it'll auto-clock me on daily for six and a half hours) and I guess I get to work—

—and also glance out the window.

People are outside burning. Just burning—black and white people on black and white fire. Nobody screams, though, they're just walking around. Or—or maybe they're not burning, it's just everything else is and they're trapped in the middle. I'm reminded of a sort of Monotheistic Singularity and how it's forcing humanity to undergo some kind of—piss, I don't know—some kind of exponential, unstoppable psychological growth. They must be aware they're burning—yet also aware there is no God to save them, so why scream?

Timsheil asks me what I'm looking at.

I tell her about the fires.

"How can that be, Jhaegar? The Dogs never came."

"But what about all the signs? All that *Dog City Never Sleeps* nonsense?"

"Turns out it was just nonsense. Everything turned out fine, like it always does."

She does that thing that girls do? When they move their shoulders upwards, but not in a shrug, more in a don't-worry-about-it-everything'll-be-okay sort of gesture? I don't know.

[197]

There's a speaker deal—a lot of speaker deals—on the ceiling playing basically elevator music. The current song ends and "Time Heals Nothing" by Through the Pain—or "Through the Pain" by Time Heals Nothing—I can never remember—comes on. This is a bold choice for the workplace—but, if you ask me, DSBM is a rather fitting one.

I ask Timsheil if I've ranted to her about DSBM yet. She asks what that is. I grin. A little spark of—a spark always goes up in me when I have an opportunity to rant to—or really to elucidate some—that's a better word—to tell someone something they don't know.

"Well, it stands for Depressive Suicidal Black Metal. You probably listen to Billie Eilish, right? Well—wait, is Billie Ei—no, she wouldn't even be alive. You probably listen to Evanescence, right?"

"Right," she replies, not confused.

"So it's like that, but real. It's made by people who other people think have Mental Illnesses, but really—that is, if you actually take the time to think—you'll see that so-called-Mental-Illness is an advanced form of social engineering created by the ruling class to repress exactly these kinds of free thinking artis—"

—Our manager materializes in our "office" again. This time it appears he's had a few drinks. For courage? Or am I just that conceited?

He makes like he's about to say something questionably appropriate, but then closes his mouth and reconsiders. Then opens again. Then closes. Kind of gnashes his gums, actually. Jumpin' Christ, did he take meth? He finally asks me:

"So, uh, Jhaegar, you're suicidal?"

"Well," I take a moment, "I suppose that would depend upon your individual perception."

"You need help."

[198]

I find Timsheil holding me back as I try to rip our managers eyes from their sockets…just kidding! That's a hateful stereotype that crazy people (not necessarily conceding to him calling me crazy) become aggravated once you call them crazy and usually resort to physical violence.

"Whatever do you mean?" I ask calmly, hands folded in my lap.

"I mean you're sick and I can't have you diseasing up the workplace. Hey Timmy, will you give him the number to your shrink."

Timsheil passes me (so prepared, these nutcases!) a pamphlet—eh, more like a brochure, really.

"Here you go, partner!" Subtitles: *No fair! Now Cleve gets to discuss his sexuality!*

"Dr. Cleve Blunderhaus?" I read/vocalize.

"Cleve's the best!" she replies.

"Yeah," chimes in our manager. "Dr. Blunderhaus monitors all our patients here."

"Yes, I'm very familiar with all your coworkers," Cleve tells me.

"Is that a man's name or a woman's?" I ask.

Cleve ignores my question. When I first got here, the receptionist told me I wasn't allowed to talk. I said something like, "What the fuck?" and she corrected herself (rather unconvincingly) that she meant to say—

"—What would you consider to be your greatest accomplishment, Jhaegar?" asks Cleve.

"Uhhh…I got the platinum on *Bloodborne*."

"Interesting." Cleve writes that down. "What would you say is your second?"

"Uhhh…I got it on *Dark Souls*, too…not *Dark Souls 2*, but *Dark Souls*, TOO, as in, 'as well'…fuck *Dark Souls 2*…but that was on Xbox."

"Interesting." Cleve doesn't write that down. "What would you say is your third?"

[199]

"What? Is this WatchMojo?"

Cleve writes that down. "And—fleshing you out here—what would you say is your sixth?"

I contemplate this for a while. Ponder it, too.

"I guess I haven't killed myself yet…permanently, at least."

They pop their eyebrows as they write. I contemplatively ponder if I should ask Cleve for their preferred gender pronoun. It's okay for me to mock Cleve, right? Cuz I enjoy wearing women's clothing? What does wearing women's clothing make acceptable? Also, they're so thin! How do they keep warm? What's just nuts, though, is those leggings? Like, yoga pants or just black leggings that are all mens's's favorite creation? Those are SOOO warm…like how? There's nothing there!

Cleve stares me down. I feel I need to tell them this, but how do you just bring that up? And if I do, then at what session? And do I need proof? Will Cleve ask me to drop trou and see what kind of panties I have on? Piss, I wish I was wearing a—no, I don't shut up! Bras are constrictive and oppressive and don't he—SHUT UP don't fuck piss!

"Why do you consider that an accomplishment?" Cleve asks.

"I guess I don't really do anything else."

"Do you not have any hobbies?"

"Well yeah, I cook sometimes. I like writing…sometimes. Movies are okay…well, not really. Most of them annoy me."

"Do you have a girlfriend?"

I point my finger (angrily, but not Mental-Illness-aggravated-ly) at Cleve.

"That's a hateful stereotype and, as a doctor, you should know better."

[200]

"So you have a *boy*friend then?"

"I…ya know what? I…" My head sags in defeat. "At one point…"

"Good. Good."

"I don't know how old I was. I don't know how old I am now, even. I just know I'm here and time doesn't matter when you're edgy and make constant asinine observations."

"Go on."

"I like to think he was gay, too. I mean, we're all kinda gay, am I right?"

Cleve just stares.

"But yeah—no, he was gay. Definitely. We didn't have sex or anything—I'm a self-proclaimed ascetic—no, antiseptic! Sorry. Words, ya know?"

Cleve writes. Sigh.

"He showed me his penis once—I was pretty freaked out. What was really stupid, though, was that we were, like…surrounded by women in bath towels, ya know? Cuz they'd always be going in and out of their rooms or they'd invite us over and be like, 'Ope! Shower time!' and then just do the whole thing cuz they were so comfortable around us and knew we wouldn't do anything—and not cuz they knew we—I mean, *he*—was gay, but cuz they just, like, trusted us? I guess we were trustworthy? It was just weird that out of that entire year, I saw his penis and never once saw any vagina, even though they were quite literally inches from my face the entire time…but now that I think about it, vaginas are ALWAYS inches from your face, there's just usually more material in between instead of a bath towel…and it's not necessarily that I wanted to see their vaginas—I mean, I—it's more disappointment I only saw a penis."

The record store salesman shoots me a blank look.

"Sir, do you want the album or not?" he asks.

[201]

"Can you just tell me if you think I'm a misogynist?" I ask back.

I—

I—

Shut up—

No, please—

***

I sit watching porn. None of this does anything for me anymore. Did it ever? Was I

hoping to accomplish something?

I close out of the Word doc. I do not save. Nothing worth saving. Nothing is worth saving.

I have six tabs open at once. I flicker between them constantly. Load new pages. Search new

topics. One has to do it. I need one of them to do it so I can go to bed.

"Amateur women shave their pussies," what the fuck is this? Why do I have to click this?

No help the camerawork is shit. Not Sven Nykvist, is he? Do women ever film porn? Always

these fucking men and every once in a while their hand will reach out to touch the (poor girl).

Accomplishing nothing. How can I watch this? I escape my computer. I go to the

bathroom. I turn the tub water on—all the way hot like I like. Like I "like." I just have to do this

now.

I do not know what I am supposed to wear. A degenerate, too, like everyone else. I just

want someone to kill me. I keep the gun in my drawer—all nine fucking bullets—but I cannot do

it. I'm always crying.

I lower myself into the tub. It is full and scalding now. My toes have started to bleed, but I find it comforting in its own way. The bow hooking the bikini cups floats in the water. I hold it in my right hand. I find this comforting as well.

I have begun to turn off the lights when I do this. What do they say? That the extraction of one sense heightens the others? I consider cutting my nose off. My tongue. My ears.

I want to rest here and feel this.

***

"Look man, I don't think you're a misanthrope, just buy the record or don't!" the salesman, shouting now.

So yeah, I buy it...and proceed to check it out whilst walking down the street (well, the sidewalk).

Personality (One was a Spider, One was a Bird). See? I'm not the only one who uses parenthesis. I guess it's my favorite album...well, it is. Dr. Blunderhaus told me I needed companionship to heal and I (understandably) told him that was also a hateful stereotype. I decided to buy myself a treat for undergoing that nonsense and figured, "Hey, I don't have this album yet, better buy it again," and bought it again.

Kinda strange that I'll try killing myself to this album in the future. Strange cuz...I don't know, cuz it's my favorite album and it always made me happy—like *happy* happy cuz it's just so sick and I'd always play it at 2 a.m. when I couldn't sleep and wanted to die and this would like...reel me back in? Sure. It just evened me out which makes it funny that I'd wanna kill

[203]

myself to it—kill myself to it cuz it's my favorite album and why would you kill yourself to anything else, but funny cuz this very album probably stopped my suicide countless times before.

So why didn't it stop me when I shot myself in the head (in the ear, sorry)? Or did it? That's why I'm still here? I don't know, I just wanna hug Luke Steele (singer) and cry as he pats my back and tells me some shit like, "That's what art's all about, man." Insert pithy quote on how art makes life meaningful.

Oh, yeah! I was gonna get a dog!

I step into the toy store. Run to the dog section (some people say plushies, but—ya know? Pithy quote time) and scan the available dogs for sale.

My eyes fall on a cute little pug with a red neckerchief kinda deal.

This is Roderick, the Dog

I pick up Roderick. He is kind of a Dog. I pet him a bit to make sure he doesn't bite and he tests out okay. A lady shopping with her children shoots me *The Look* for buying a stuffed pug, but frankly, my dear, fuck me in the ass...or...I meant...he's my dog and he's a good little dog and your shitty kids are probably gonna grow up to get killed by Rooz.

It's interesting how songs can take on multiple meanings in one's life. "You Won't Bring People Down in My Town" used to represent that one scene from that one movie I wrote that was hopeless, but I find it playing again in my head as I take Roderick with me towards the apartment I don't yet have. I wonder if this is for better or worse, as well as wondering if I have any other newfound powers in addition to muscles and private thoughts...or Newfoundland powers, had Roderick been a Newfoundland. He's a Dog.

[204]

Whatever. I sing the lyrics as I snap my fingers and dismantle reality. How am I doing this? Before me, cinder blocks and rebar and wooden planks and just everything swirl in a storm of creation. My apartment—my apartment *building* to be more precise—forms floor by floor, room by extravagant ro—

—SHUT UP, I'm not gay I'm not gay I'm not a woman either I'm just a just a I hold Roderick tight as I sit on my couch. I do this a lot nowadays. I was able to throw out all my clothes—no wait, I haven't bought women's clothes yet in this reality. Roderick's cooling me down—I can't use that song anymore, it's fine, I'll just forget about it. Just forget and hold my dog. It's fine.

"Bark," he says.

"Bark," I say back. Good dog. What a dog.

Roderick tells me that we're hungry and I need to get to work. I've always enjoyed women telling me what to do (there's this quaint little interview where some 70s feminist asks Dick Cavett why he likes—well, that she's impressed he has strong women on his show—and he's like, "Cuz I'm weak and like to be dominated," and I'm just like, "Same, Dick Cavett, same"), but Roderick's fine, too, I guess. He gets to be a tad demanding at times. I mean, I can take it, sure, it's just—I don't know. He's fine.

I commence the Indian Butter Chicken. Oh! Another quaint interview! Anthony Bourdain (rest his soul) and a local food critic ate Butter Chicken in Delhi and Tony's like, "Wow, this Murgh Makhani tastes amazing!" and she's like, "Right, Butter Chicken!" like wow, you'd really think that should've been switched around. But yeah, Dave Chappelle (sorry I'm just dropping all these names that don't relate to cinema) had a bit in a special where he made fun of Tony's suicide and like—don't get me wrong, I'm all in favor of suicide humor—but Chappelle just has

[205]

no idea. Like, he literally said something like, "Anthony Bourdain traveled across the whole world eating great food made by great people and this dude killed himself," and people laughed. That's not even a joke. And even the rest of it where he talks about some guy with a shitty life ("shitty") life he knew who didn't kill himself and compared the two? Like, hey man, leave Tony alone. You could make fun of him, sure, but not like that—it was just tasteless. Going back to George Carlin, it's all about the structure of a joke. Carlin knew how to make suicide funny—

—Sorry, Roderick's yelling at me to take the chicken out of the tandoor. I tell him it's an oven and he barks at—

—He was just the best. Oh, George…kinda nifty how I almost killed myself in a way he described in his show…though I think the commercialization of a suicide note lowers its inherit value, as in order to appeal to a wider audience, one must comprise and extract the more unsavory morsels of the one almighty Artistic Truth. Still, I wonder if he'd be proud. I like to think he would.

I like to think (also)(what) I could make (no) I also wish I could make this for a woman. Ya know? Like, "Hey babe, here's some Murgh Makhani I made for you," and she'd be like, "You mean Butter Chicken?" and we'd have a grand ol' laugh. Now THAT'D be nifty…and of course, now I'm horny. Roderick looks at me with those eyes and I feel his judgement. Piece of shit dog—

—He barks at me and I get back to cooking. He really is demanding. I find my erection growing stronger…it's analogous to my guilt at this point. I really need to come, but I don't know where. Roderick suggests I come in my food and eat—eh—sorry—old dominatrix fantasy of mine where she forces—doesn't matter—but it's like, what do you want me to do? Just bend my sauce pan over and let it have it? And it's not even my curry—cuz that's how I know I have

[206]

to torture myself—and I'm really trying to be good, I swear—but—I don't know. I need variety. For some reason, the word *variety* makes me even hornier—I think it's cuz it starts with a *V*. All I can think about is—shut up—Roderick, you too!

Curry's—I mean, Butter Chicken's done. I sit down to eat and notice I forgot to make chapati. Roderick tells me that's just like my stupid self and I tell him he's not a woman so he's not allowed to degrade me. Suddenly, I picture Roderick as a woman (human) and it's all fine. What would her name be? I hope it's—

—No, shut up. Leave me alone—no, shut up! Fuck fuck fuck just eat the—the Butter Chicken—Murgh Makhani—whatever. It's actually pretty swell, quite pleasant if I should go so far. Lot spicier than Lu's Curry, but—

—FUCK FUCK! Just eat it, juuuust eat it. Just eat the chicken and it'll all go away. It'll all go away. I pull Roderick close and set him on my lap as I eat. He's quite warm and comforting. I see why people enjoy dogs. I don't need anyone but him. He's perfect and he's my dog and he's just so perfectly perfect. What a Dog.

I eat my food.

I—

—The butter chicken and the hopes of a wife are gone, yet their scents still linger. Roderick tells me that hopes are just the memories of lives we wish we had. I tell Roderick he's a Dog.

I wish I could just eat food in peace. My erection hasn't gone away and I know I'm gonna have to masturbate soon—which in turn means I'm gonna have to punish myself soon—just not as soon—later soon—and now the idea of, "Well, who's it gonna be tonight?" as if it's some kind of fucking game show where women compete to be abused by me. Just a load of

[207]

nonsense and—ya know—how can women have boyfriends and husbands and shit when they know—they KNOW—that we're all just fucking nutcase fucks who—

—Jumpin' Christ, I just can't take it. It's basically just rape. I mean—it's rape! But only a sort of mental rape. You see, when I picture someone in my head, let's say—let's just say Indiana Jones—and I imagine having sex with Indiana...well, he didn't consent to that! Indiana didn't ask to be in my fantasy, but here he is! And every time I watch Indiana Jones—okay, let's go back to a real person, this example doesn't really work with a—so every time I see that girl in school, I'll think to myself, "Gee wow this girl sure is—"

—Wait, I've already talked about this. Sigh. Sometimes I go on a rant like this and I'm just doomed to repeat it cuz every time that subject appears in my life I have to "re-explain/re-rant" to myself. And like, I'll admit, I have to do it to really get the info down in my head—ya know? I'm not the best with mind stuff—but then I just get so pissed cuz it's like, "You're an idiot, Jhaegar! There you go again, wasting more time explaining stuff to yourself cuz you have no real friends to explain it to!" It's kind of like that scene in *Taxi Driver* (1976) where everyone who watches it thinks the line, "You talkin' to me?" is supposed to be so cool and whatnot? It isn't. It's debilitatingly depressing, cuz not only is Travis talking to himself, he's imagining that other people wanna talk to him and that he's so high and mighty that he can say, "What? What? You talkin' to me?" as if he's some kind of demigod. What's an even bigger waste is, while I'm explaining this to myself right now, I know that (ya know, either in two weeks or two months) I'm gonna hear someone mention *Taxi Driver* and go into this same rant, just nonstop, as if I don't already know it, as if I haven't already explained it to myself and my dog and...

Just screw it all...

[208]

I don't know. I go to my record shelf. Not sure how I already have a full record shelf—it's cuz I'm fucking—I don't know, DERANGED, I guess—but I have a full record shelf. I take Burzum or whatever self-loathing Edgelord—well, no, he's not an Edgelord, he's actually—just shut up shut the fuck up no one wants to hear you talk—and put on Screaming Jay cuz that's about how I feel right now.

Roderick asks me who Screaming Jay is.

"You know Oogie Boogie from *Nightmare Before Elm Street*?" I query.

Roderick shakes his head.

"Imagine him, but like a real person."

Roderick scampers off. What a piece of—just—I don't know, I wish he paid attention to me more—I just wish people'd listen!

"Well, how does it make you feel when they don't listen?" Dr. Blunderhaus asks me.

"What do you think? Aren't I yelling at you right now? BAD!"

My feet kick out on his gay little—no, it's not gay, I'm g—so it's therapy again and Cleve just doesn't know fucking anything.

"Here. I'll up your dosage for this next month—"

"—I don't want a higher dosage, I want different medicine! The one you put me on now says it's for *Eternal Pain*, I want the medicine for *Unfathomable Anguish*!"

"Unfortunately, Mr. Holdburn, we'd have to get that cleared by another professional."

"Uh huh. Sure."

"What I can give you is medicine mostly used for treatment of *Irrevocable Despair*—"

"—I'm not IN despair, I'm in—you fucking fucking fuck!"

"Now, Mr. Holdburn—"

[209]

"—That's not even my name!"

"Is it not? Then what indeed is

```
shut up shut up shut up shut up shut up shut up shut up shut up
shut up shut up shut up shut up shut up shut up shut up shut up
shut up shut up shut up shut up shut up shut up shut up shut up
shut up shut up shut up shut up shut up shut up shut up shut up
shut up shut up shut up shut up shut up shut up shut up shut up
shut up shut up shut up shut up shut up shut up shut up shut up
shut up shut up shut up shut up shut up shut up shut up shut up
shut up shut up shut up shut up shut up shut up shut up shut up
shut up shut up shut up shut up shut up shut up shut up shut up
shut up shut up shut up shut up shut up shut up shut up shut up
shut up shut up shut up shut up shut up shut up shut up shut up
shut up shut up shut up shut up shut up shut up shut up shut up
shut up shut up shut up shut up shut up shut up shut up shut up
shut up shut up shut up shut up kill me shut up shut up shut up
shut up shut up shut up shut up shut up shut up shut up shut up
shut up shut up shut up shut up shut up shut up shut up shut up
shut up shut up shut up shut up shut up shut up shut up shut up
shut up shut up shut up shut up shut up shut up shut up shut up
shut up shut up shut up shut up shut up shut up shut up shut up
shut up shut up shut up shut up shut up shut up shut up shut up
shut up shut up shut up shut up shut up shut up shut up shut up
shut up shut up shut up shut up shut up shut up shut up shut up
shut up shut up shut up shut up shut up shut up shut up shut up
shut up shut up shut up shut up shut up shut up shut up shut up
shut up shut up shut up shut up shut up shut up shut up shut up
shut up shut up shut up shut up shut up shut up shut up shut up
shut up shut up shut up shut up shut up shut up shut up shut up
shut up shut up shut up shut up shut up shut up shut up shut up
```

I'll make my own medicine—medicine ("medicine") doesn't even work, everyone knows

that, they just don't wanna admit it cuz it's easier for them to lie to themselves and say it's

working, say it's making them better—no pissing pill's gonna treat me for...for what I did. I

have to make it up to her—I know I'll never accomplish it, but I'm gonna fucking try! Fucking try and—so what if I kill myself—at least I'll have died fucking trying unlike all these other dumbass fucking no fucking dull witted pieces of—

—I'm in my bathroom now. I've closed the door so Roderick can't get in. I don't want him to see me like this.

I need to understand how she felt.

I need to—I can't just cause myself pain. That's MY pain. I need HER pain.

I need HER Unfathomable Anguish.

I stick my thumbs up by the bridge of my nose and scrape out my eyes.

Do my best Varg Vikerness scream as I toss them to the floor.

Sink my fingers into my cheeks and pull away the flesh. Rip the skin from my face. Yank out my hair. Peel back my scalp.

I peel it down to my throat and keep peeling. I unzip my body. I crawl out of my skin as my new "I" is reborn.

Underneath my blood and tissue, my unspooling muscles…a new form with a new face and new eyes…

And new breasts. And new hips. New lots of fun things.

I dismantle my old shell and am born anew.

The mirror…

Staring back at me is the woman I was meant to be.

***

[211]

My panties fit a lot easier now that I don't have a penis in the way. I consider playing with my vagina for a while, but (in the interests of being a willful and unbroken young woman) I decide to hold myself back (that is, until I inevitably snap and go to town).

Also, not saying women who play with themselves are broken—I'm actually pretty in to that (not them being "broken," jumpin' Christ—that they do what they want), I'm just saying that a woman who plays with herself—but who's really just a man in a woman's body—is probably bad—well, I mean—no, no, it's bad. I shouldn't do it. I'm trying to improve here.

On a positive note, I'm finally able to cross my legs in public without being judged—now it's just normal! The waiter doesn't treat me any different when he gets to my table and thinks I'm some loser boy and the other, uh, eaters here don't even notice…and I kinda feel my—no, can't, shut up!

Oh man (woman), what to order? I wish this had come with a woman's mind as well. What's a womanly appetizer? Am I just a misogynist for thinking there's such thing as a womanly appetizer? Emma Watson probably thinks so—whenever I'd order a salad in the past, I'd always get a shitty look (not *The Look*, but I would get those later when the check comes and I whip out my Sasha Banks Prepaid Mastercard) so am I not allowed to order, like, a steak now? Well, not "not allowed," but I'll just be judged?

Wait, wasn't this whole exercise for me to be judged?

"Aww Jhaegar, ya really are a fuckin' fruitcake," whines a familiarly sassy voice.

Satan (wow, she really cleans up—as in like 90s grunge stuff, but this woman is—

"—Jhaegar, shut da fuck up, okay? I can't hear what ya thinkin', but I know it's somethin' fuckin' nuts. Ya really gotta—oh, hey. Jhaegar, will ya ordah fuh me?"

[212]

I glance up from Satan's grimy cheeks and find the waiter, uh, waiting. I (it's my hopelessly lustful Jhaegar side) wanna say he appears jealous of us two lovely ladies enjoying an afternoon out, but I'm sure he's just irritated instead.

"Oh, yeah—we'll, uh," my mumbling's at least cuter as a woman, "we'll, um, uh—so like, uh…" Piss, think like a woman! "We'll have two Bloody Marys," I state as I burst into high pitched giggles—ya know, when two white women lunch at an outdoor café cuz it'll be "exciting?"

The waiter fucks off and I look back to Satan, already rolling her eyes and toying with her knife. I hope she stabs m—no, I don't!

She glances up to meet my eyes.

"Jhaegar, I think ya got a woman problem."

"Well, I, uh—"

"—Like, really bad."

"How'd you even find me? It's 2001, wouldn't you not know me yet?"

"I ain't bound by time an' space. I'm just a concept, ya asshole. I'm inside da hearts an' minds a people everywhere," as she covertly takes in my hips, breasts, and un-grimy, rather polished cheeks, "especially bo—women, like you…or so Rush Limbaugh wants ya ta think."

"Well Satan, I don't mind you being inside me."

Piss, I feel SO sassy now. I wonder if she got the—

—Satan splashes her Bloody Mary (evidently they were brought to us) in my face. It soaks my dress to the point where—oh fuck, don't—shut up shut up—don't look.

"Excuse me," I muster, "I have to go, uh, powder my—"

"—Sit down, Jhaegar, ya ain't goin' nowhere."

[213]

Other eaters look over at us—they're gonna think Satan and I are dating and that she wears the pants in this relationship and just has her way with—wait, why is this ba—?

"—Just tell me why you're here. I'm already a walking kink myself, I can't handle you at the same time."

Satan considers me. Reaches over and grabs my Bloody Mary. Now the other eaters REALLY think she domin—shut up!

"I recognize dat I can't—well, dat ya don't want my help—but I'm just here ta tell ya dat ya fucked somethin' up…in da system, dat is."

"Huh?" Guess I'm still as clueless.

"When ya killed yaself in my office—or ta be more precise, HOW ya killed yaself—well, how ya ALWAYS kill yaself, it just so happened ta be substantially worse dis time and it triggahed somethin'."

"Dog City?"

"Nevah Sleeps," as she sips from Mary—which is another interesting tho—

"—Shut up!" I yell.

"Losin' it, huh Jhaegar?" she asks without looking at me.

"I know I'm a lot of things, but I'm not fucking crazy, okay?"

"Didn't say ya was crazy," still not looking.

Satan finishes her drink and leans over the table to whisper to me. Thankfully (like I said), she's wearing 90s grunge so at least she wears a full shirt. Say what you want about grunge girls, they're actually quite modest. Funny how people deride them, yet they're the ones wearing skirts and crop tops and…white pants and—and—and—

"—Jhaegar," Satan says as she grabs my chin and swivels my face to focus back on hers.

[214]

"There ya go. Anyway, ya killed yaself wrong cuz ya didn't pay attention ta dat book ya think ya read an' I'm on da 'Outs' now. Dis'll probably be da last time I see ya, okay?"

"Sure?"

"An' I just wanted ta let ya know, dat even dough I give ya a hard time, what happened back den happens ta everybody an' ya shouldn't ruin da rest a ya life by drownin' in ya own

G

U

I

L

T

Clothes shopping is so much more fun as a woman. As a man, it's a disaster—either you go with your girlfriend and it's kind of alright cuz then you get to try stuff on for her and she can say what she likes and you just buy—but if you don't have a girlfriend? Jumpin' fuck. It's rough—and you can't go with your other guy friends cuz it's like, "Hey, man, wanna go to the store and try on some JEANS?!" Doesn't work like that. So what you do is, ya know, you go to the fucking store and everyone gives you *The Look* and you find yourself in such a panic to just get the fuck out of there that you end up buying shirts you don't like and shoes that don't fit.

And it's so much better as a woman cuz, like, if I was a Trans woman it still wouldn't work. Everyone would just know. I mean, sorry to say (like, I'm actually sorry to say), but you can tell, you always can, and me becoming a Trans woman would never REALLY change the fact I'm a man who'll never—just shut the fuck up, Jesus jumpin' fucking—no, shut up—okay, so it's just better as a woman. People give you a better look like, "Oh, look at her. She's so

[215]

confident. She's so smart. She has her own sense of agency and struts around unchained by civilization," and I'm just a fucking—shut up already!

Is it allowed to try on bikinis in a store? What if my vagina's really—I mean, am I supposed to just put that back on the shelf? For some other poor girl to get? Piss, I told myself I wasn't gonna do this shit, I wasn't supposed to come to the store and—

—I'm running, I'm just fucking running. They can't stop me if I'm not stealing any merchandise, ya know? Like, "Don't mind me! I'm just a smart, confident woman with a sense of agency running out of this store," and everyone who sees me'll know. They'll know.

Sigh life. Just from one mess to another. I get in my car (yeah, I have a car (Toyota, I'm a woman now, right?)) and drive off. I also cross my fingers that I don't zone out and end up in a ditch. It's become a more frequent problem as of late.

Am I even really a woman yet? I mean, a *woman*. I have the body, but I lack the mind. Honestly, if I had a woman's mind, all my problems would just—not that I have—they'd go right away, but I'm still a stupid MAN!

I attempt to think of conundrums I've encountered in the past and still come up with the man's answer. So, ya know, like—so riddle me this: what does a teenage girl think of when she's about to go on a date with her new boyfriend or first boyfriend or whatever? Cuz guys are thinking, "Gee wow, I can't wait to touch her ass, see her boobs and all that," cuz guys are fucking creeps. But are women creeps? Do they think, "Gee wow, I can't wait to touch his muscles," like what muscles? The kid's fourteen! Like girls already have sexualized features, but boys don't, so what do they look forward to?! Do girls think, "Gee wow, I can't wait 'til he sticks his hand in my pants without asking, I can't wait 'til he fucking squeezes the shit out of my boobs, I can't wait 'til he takes off my clothes and subjectifies—" —or is it objectifies? Who

[216]

fucking cares—and does that make them creeps? Or are they empowered? Is it a sign of early sexual dominance for them to realize they fill the role of the Pleasure Giver, thereby controlling their current man and all men from there on out? Does it help them realize that while men run the world, women run the men and possess all the real power? And like, if I told my proverbial (theoretical?) girlfriend this, she'd think I'M the creep, I'M the weirdo, and go on letting her quarterback boyfriend ass fuck her in the back of his Pontiac chuckling to himself about how he's gonna tell all his friends tomorrow and how she'll see those friends in class on a regular— shut the fuck up—basis and how I'm just as bad as he is and I'm no better and I just wanna fucking die and how I—

—I sail into a ditch.

I remain in my now smoking car thinking about life.

What do girls look forward to? Prince Charming? True Love's Kiss? Is growing up as a girl characterized by having all your dreams dashed away by realizing men are hopeless assholes? I mean, really?

When I wore that wedding dress in preschool—no, I never did SHUT UP!—fuck, it's getting worse...I don't know what I'm doing...when I bought a dress later and wore it I felt so cherished and desired and powerful. Is that what they look forward to? Does anyone look forward to anything? How the fuck do other people think? DO they think?

Oh, and tangent time: I'm not trying to blame women for all my problems. You'll read about some non-socially-revolutionary school shooter in the news and the media'll run it as, "Well of course he had to kill those kids, his GIRLFRIEND DUMPED HIM," or, "Gee golly well totally, have you seen WHO HIS MOM IS?" as if males have no impact on other males' lives and as if one isn't responsible for oneself—I think it goes back to some phony

[217]

psychological study (well, they're ALL phony) or Freud or Oedipus or whatever and they're all just a waste of time. Everything in life is...everything in life is my fault and no one else's. Nobody caused or impacted or influenced or whatever stupid term-ed my life and made me do what I—ya know—everyone down here digs their own grave—and fuck me, what's worse—shut up—(and this is probably the most "Nice Guy" thing for me to say) but everyone hearing this'll say I'm just a "Nice Guy" stereotype who, once he finds out you don't wanna have sex with him, will make you pay the sushi bill (literally don't care, I'm gonna kill myself anyway, I'll pay any bill I see) and it's like...why can't I just be a nice guy and not a "Nice Guy," ya know? Like, why has kindness been ruined in relationships?

Oh sigh, the car's on fire. Better get out—but really, though! Is the anger towards "Nice Guys" just the anger when the woman finds out their "Nice Guy-ness" was a façade and their true "Angry Guy-ness" is revealed? So how does one ever find a true nice guy? Is that another thing women are—oh piss, the seatbelt's jammed. Now all these anti-seatbelters are gonna be like, "See? I told ya HaHHahAhhAHAH!" ya know? Oh well. Guess I'll just die ("Guess I'll Die") cuz, I mean, not like it matters—oh wait! Like I said, is that just another thing women have to resolve themselves to? Like how men aren't Prince Charming and are just gonna conceptify them? So why BE in a relationship? Why be fake and together rather than alone and true? And— oh, it looks like I'm burning now (great film, by the way), whatever, I'll just be born again somewhere else. Fuck it. Who cares? Let the fire get me. I *like* dying.

The fire vanishes.

The comedic half of me says the fire went away to spite me, yet the confident woman (bodily) half of me says I made it go away. Hmm. That's kind of...nifty, I guess.

[218]

My seatbelt unjams. I rise out of the car—like, RISE out of the car. I levitate down the road.

Very nifty.

I wonder if that's where it all really started. Not with—uh, but with the preschool deal? Is that the origin of my madness? Does madness have an origin or is it a latent human quality? Do others experience these troubles? I mean, they'd have to, right? As much as I hate to say it, I'm just a human, a human like everyone else—and if I'm a human surrounded by other humans, would it not be acceptable to presume all other humans share the same thoughts? How could I be the only one?

You are becoming the Only One

Will you fuck off?

Dog City Never Sleeps

But wouldn't you think everyone should be like me and I'm nothing more than just an amalgamation of everyone else? When people scorn me, what makes them justified? Are we not the same? How could anyone be unique?

Dr. Blunderhaus sighs and takes off their psychiatrist (sociologist? Who fucking cares what they're called?) glasses and sighs.

"Ms. Holdburn, I think you need religion."

"I'm gonna put some dirt in your eye," I meme back.

Dr. Blunderhaus makes a pouty face at me. Am I making a pouty face, too?

[219]

"Aww, look at little Dog Junior," they say. "Gonna cry?"

* * *

One of my first girlfriends—oh hey, does that make me a lesbian now? One of my first girlfriends...well, uh...my first girlfriend said church was all a scam cuz when her parents asked her to pray and whatnot she just sat there and closed her eyes and felt like a schmuck. She really was a keeper. Now I'm here closing my eyes feeling like a schmuck, I just have no parents ("NO PARENTS!!" haha have you heard that song? I forget the other lyrics, all I remember is Batman just—ya know—"NO PARENTS!!"). Anyway.

I don't know what to do. I guess I pray for nothing. I wonder what others here are praying for? Haha—hehe—should I tell 'em? *Hey, hey you, guy! Did you know prayer is actually a form of sacrilege as it's antithetical to spiritual determinism? If God has a Plan for you and you're set on that Plan, why would you ask Him for something else? Does that mean you're a heretic?* Here, I'll try it on this guy.

"Hey, guy, did you know—?"

—He stares into my eyes and says:

"Did you know that suicide is the ideological pinnacle of an egalitarian civilization?"

"What?" I stammer, probably beaming.

He stares back into his lap:

"It overcomes that final human prejudice we have towards death that will pull us into the ascendance of the God-AI. But I doubt you care—(sigh)—life's not 'meaningless' per se, but I'm beginning to believe humanity lacks free will to even decide in the first place. Everything is

[220]

nothing—and people tend to view the word *nothing* with a negative connotation, meaning that *nothing* really is *something*, much like words are gendered or even—"

"—Or even characterized by Comedy or Tragedy," I finish. "You're a Dazai fan, huh?"

A tiny light glimmers in his eyes.

"Who isn't? But *nothing* really has a positive connotation. *Nothing* does not mean a negative absence of *something*, a sort of silent indication that one may not have a substantial answer, but it is really a positive status of no being, absolute zero, not even the idea of a *something* to qualify a *nothing*. Just nothing."

"Do you wanna have sex with me?" I've never had sex as a woman (or, ya know, in general) and I've always drea—this man is more than worthy!

"No, thank you."

"Oh, okay, uh…my name's Jhaegar, what's yours?"

He glances at me. Seems perturbed. I should probably come up with a female—

"—I mean, my name's Bathsheba."

"Mitchell. Nice to meet you," as he shakes my hand.

Oh, hey! I think I—

"—Wait, aren't you Jewish?" I ask.

"Yeah," he mutters hanging his head.

"Tough break."

"Eh, they did it to themselves."

"Sorry, I only got so far in your note. I had to kill myself, too."

Mitch seems slightly taken aback. Oh piss, is it something I said?

"Excuse me—?"

[221]

"—Uh, here, uh—write this down, you'll need this," I try to save myself. *"Rationalism leads to Nihilism and Nihilism leads to denial of reason, thus any rational life leads to irrational self-destruction."*

"I knew that," he spits, full of scorn. Oh piss, oh piss, oh—

"—Oh, sorry, I, uh—I thought I had to help you or—like time travelling affecting the future or—?"

"—Who the hell are you?"

I run—I know I have to stop running and get in the robot at some point—but I just run out of there. Screw Mitch, I don't need him anyway.

But death really is nuts, isn't it? Cuz we just think, "Oh, it'd just be like nothingness." Well yeah, but the idea of *nothing* is only qualified cuz everyone alive possesses the notion of *something*. With death, it wouldn't be *nothing* as we know it as the absence of *something,* but *nothing* as we don't know it as *NOTHING*...like, it wouldn't only be vanishing, but having our capacity to understand our vanishing vanish as well...it's not watching T.V. in a dark room and all of a sudden the power goes out...it's watching T.V. in a dark room and all of a sudden the power goes out, yeah, but also the room disappears and whatever held the room disappears and the empty space that now fills where the room was disappears and YOU disappear as well as not even being able to PERCEIVE that you disappeared along with the very concept of "disappearing" disappearing. Have you ever tried to imagine dying, like actual death? You can't! It's just like—like—jumpin' Christ, I hate everything!

Other church goers shoot me some side eye. Oh wait, it looks like I was banging my hands on the pews. Where'd Mitch go? Where'd I go? I'm back? Screw it all. I hear everyone pray for salvation from the End of Days. What a bunch of losers, pretty sure the End of Days

[222]

didn't happen…or did it? And why would you pray for that anyway, no one's coming to save you.

"Why would you pray for that?" I ask some lady.

She balks at me and turns to dust.

Like—oh fuck, did I just vaporize her?

Other worshipers notice and panic. I raise my hands and vaporize them, too. I guess they'll find out if there's *nothing* or *something* or whatever other fucking option after all.

I find I'm levitating again. Did I come back to church just to kill these people? What does that make me? There's a few worshipers left and I'm tempted to inform them this's still technically a part of God's Plan, but I decide to vaporize them instead. Actions speak louder than words (or so they say (or not say?)).

Sigh—no, piss, I shouldn't've done this. Just let people do their own stupid shit. I know I can revive everyone here. Wait, can I? Why won't I? Then what's wrong with—shut up!—just— I'm sorry, I thought this would make it better—what am I—get these breasts off of me!—just— I'm sorry, I don't know what I'm doing.

I float out of there.

***

I cry in my bed.

No one's coming to save me.

I'm—what? I'm being pulled, like I'm being

[223]

***

I cry in my bed.

No one's coming to save me.

I cannot be fixed. It is time to

***

Just shut up! Shut up! Just—

—I'm—NO! I get out of bed.

Piss, I can barely hear my own—SHUT UP!—it just never ends, ya know? Just going and going and going like a big fucking storm in the ocean and I'm just plucking dust from the air or something—probably that *or something* what the fuck am I even saying anymore? My ear never stops ringing and—fucking forget it. Forget it all. Wonder what Audrey Hepburn's doing right now? Don't be a Thot, be an Audrey—wish I could dress like her—imagine me with all those monochrome perfections or whatever they're called and I'd be so classy and cherished and and and and and I need to put on some music go away go away oh nice, of course it's

"Grief" by Earl—just like—ya know? Fucking stupid song, actually—kind of edgy—not Billie Eilish edgy, but still edgy—piss, am I edgy? Probably, but I'm like *Sátántangó* edgy. Fuck, who knows? Everyone wants me to kill myself anyway. They'd all like it—this must be where I title my suicide note, "Please Feel Bad I'm Dead." Oh, look at you, Jhaegar, so meta. And I	but I did wanna kill those people—they had it coming—like—PISS FUCK SHIT—that *Joker* movie's trash and it's a hateful stereotype that I don't need to subscr—SHUT UP I didn't do anything wrong, they deserved to die and everyone on this planet has it coming, they all fucking do—if you're at least sixteen years old then you're guilty—hey, like Billie Eilish, everyone loves her, right?

[224]

fucking hate that, too, like in movies where they just HAVE to say the title. Like, gee fuck, I didn't know I was watching *Harry Potter and the Chalice of Dildos* until you mentioned it, thanks. But you know what? Yeah, let's just be a perfect being—I hate myself anyway so it doesn't matter. Do suicide notes usually have titles? What was Joker—sorry, "Arthur's" stupid note called? "How to be a Whiny Fuck in Three Movements?" Mitch's—fuck Mitch!—shut up!—just go away please please please please no not Mitch McConnell

What a joke—everyone should just kill themselves—if they really are as edgy as they want us to believe—and not even Anti-Natalism, just full on global suicide. Then we'd finally be morally flawless in the eyes of God and the perfect being again, right? Ah, fuck everything. "Those people deserved to die cuz they were awful," God, what a fucking loser. And this is the best we can do? This is the best representation of me? He's a whiny little punk who's mad at—and the three act structure? FUCK! It's so just horrifically realized

"Don't make sense, goin' to—" —you know where that's from? That's a real song right there, and why can't you believe suicide's on your "fucking mind?" Why can't you? Like really? What's so illogical about it? Piss, just shut up! These fucking rants don't mean anything, I just—I just do it cuz I have no one to talk to and I just wanna seem smart— but, "Oh, well, smart is actually a term meant for— really should say intelligent or

shit piss, man, my fucking stomach, like it's fucking boiling. How do people live—is this what Kurt Cobain felt? I don't know, how can I have these problems when I'm like twenty-five, what would I look like at sixty- five? Except when you cross over, there isn't—ya know, I wish that was true. Would I just be a blob when I'm that old? I feel like I'm halfway there now. I just—I just wanna scream, but nobody cares. If

ya know? The virgin Incel pasty white young male coming to shoot up the school with all the boys who were mean to him and the girls who rejected him, like what do you think, man? Look at your hobbies. What would you even have done with one of these girls had you gotten one, teach her to play Dungeons & Dragons? Or what— take her to your shitty comedy show—and by the way, to the people who didn't know that was,

[225]

erudite or—" —see? God, just fucking shoot me—and I do mean God cuz I just want Him to do it, I want Him to punish me for all my stupid fucking nonsense and just let me go home—and what's really worthless is now that I'm thinking about this song and having a bad time, I'll forever be reminded of this time when I hear that song so it's effectively ruined now (just like everything else) and oh, fuck, jumpin' Christ, here it comes—like that one coworker girl I had who liked him, too, so NOWWWWW I have to be reminded of— will you just leave me alone already fuck—is this maximum suffering yet? Dr. Blunder—no, fuck, the counselor, not—just LEAVE LEAVE LEAVE LEAVE LEAVE like did you study the cinematography how can people be so utterly dull

Jhaegar screams outside the counseling office and no one gives a shit, did he ever really scream? Sigh, this fucking—oh fuck—my hands, I keep coughing gore into them— like GORE—aww, fuck Al Gore, no one cares about your planet, it's gonna die anyway. But it's like—is my stomach acid already eating me? I just wanna— I just wanna—I jab my razor into my belly—and I'm a whiny loser, too, so I barely stick it—no SHUT UP—I don't need to stick anything anywh—and how do you think they felt? The acid pours out of my body, it scalds my hands—is this even real? My hands—my hands! Typing burns them worse, honestly— honestly, I think I welcome this— get her out of here, jumpin' fuckin' Christ on Pasolini Cross it's almost like

like, all his dream? Fuck you, you're what's wrong with the world. Literally every remedial indication that it was a dream was present—well, shit, the only thing that was missing was the wobbly *whooshing* noise as the screen bubbles and transitions— oh just go to Hell—ya know, I would, but I can't tell if it's worse off down there than here—I mean, I'm just trying to maximize my suffering, aren't I? Oh piss, what am I thinking? I haven't masturbated at least four times today, what's wrong with me? What would Al Gore say? I'd be able to keep up if it wasn't for my HANDS ABOUT TO FUCKING FALL OFF from working and typing and TYPING ALL FUCKING DAY they don't get it Kendrick Lamar said Earl was lik

[226]

or I guess, *is* like the best in the game right now—at the time—in the future, I don't know, they're alive, right? Whatever. I have too many issues for it to matter. Don't you love that, too? That if you're *sick* then that's just your whole life, that's all you have and will ever be, just a fucking roach others have to deal with— why won't they stop looking at me? What did I even do this time, haven't I paid enough? I can't—I don't wanna watch that, it hurts me. All I ever do is work and work to try and make it bett—please don't make me. It's

it's almost like it's oily— everything's just slipping through my fingers ("Slipping through my—)— SHUT UP! Piss, it's like that fucking—shout out to my non-existent Indian wife— Kachumbar or whatever it's called—this one lady like adds six tablespoons of oil to it and it's like WHY? Why would you do that? That's so unnecessary I love how now my food's drowning in sewage, thanks. And I can't do anything about it, I can't go anywhere. Anytime I go out there's always some stupid checker lady who compliments my hair like,

piss on a fuck, they're inside me— SHUT UP! Leave me alone, it's not my fault— I didn't ask to be a boy— why can't you let me be a girl, I thought I controlled everything? I can barely see anymore, either, it's all just a blur. I don't know where I am. I think I'm crying. No, I'm not in fucking India you fucking—no, don't be mean, you don't have to—ya know? Like unbottling—I just want her to hurt me— shut up, just—just leave me alone—I can't—I have to stop seeing, I have to stop seeing, I have to stop I claw at my face like I

just fuck 'em anyway, fuck 'em all, and ya know what? Mental Illness doesn't control my life—first off, I don't have a Mental Illness, it's just social engineering designed by the upper— just shut UP! Please, leave me alone. I didn't do anything that everyone else didn't already do. Why am I being punished? Why do I feel guilty? Why can't I just get over it? Why won't they stop commenting about my hair, isn't my ear bleeding? Why is everything broken—I was

[227]

filth, it's not love, it's degrading—it proves you're a fucking degenerate, Jhaegar, a fucking de-Jhaegar-ate and you know it. You're the reason those girls have to do that, you're the reason they're trapped in their lives, cuz sickos like you keep watching that shit, cuz misogynist sexist pig motherfuckers like you can't get enough of that poor girl getting utterly railed in her "All the young girls must love you" like fuck off, I just wanna die, they don't wanna—they don't have to fuck—no, shut up! Just leave me alone, I don't wanna see them, I just wanna buy groceries and for my car to work and to get this stupid shot and to get fucking shot, no I'm not sick or a roach or a disease, we're not sick it doesn't control our lives it doesn't control me did before—I'm still wearing my stupid woman body—I pull at my breasts and—no, shut up! It's not go—I rip at my—dig my fingers into my skin. Stupid girl at the checkout counter—just cuz you bought stamps from her doesn't mean she wants to fuck you, Jhaegar, you fucking misogynist Incel worthless fucking—my eyes my eyes my eyes my eyes just take them off I can't see them anymore such a good kid. I'm sorry I hurt everyone so just let me die to make it better—I can't get better, I can't—it's all everywhere now, they're burrowing deeper inside my—SHUT UP! PLEASE! PLEASE HELP ME! PLEASE the mitochondria is the powerhouse of the cell, why do they even teach you that stuff? Is that like a mitoclo—whatever the fuck? You piece of

***

I stop myself.

Looks like I am pacing like a psycho again. Is that what I should call these bits? "Pacing like a Psycho."

Seems to fit well enough.

[228]

Roderick stares at me from his spot on the couch. I still cannot believe he asked to be in the script. I wonder wherever he could have learned to be so selfish.

I pet him. It is not his fault. He controls the movements, but not the destination. Then again, who does?

Is this a sin of incontinence? Does that make it acceptable?

***

I am awake.

I have a penis.

What a drag.

***

I don't hate women, I'm just obsessed with them.

But yeah, I guess I have all these women's clothes now…gotta get rid of these. Start two piles, okay. I set aside a few pieces I really like in the "Keep" pile (these leggings!) and the ones I can do without in the "Sell" pile, chastise myself, then put everything in the "Sell" pile. Having these lying aro—no, just shut up! I have to get rid of these.

Driving driving driving driving driving stick a finger in my (under my? something?) waist or whatever and make sure I'm wearing boxers. I am. Can you resell panties? I don't— piss, I brought them, didn't I? They're gonna think I'm a creep.

[229]

I step into the second hand place that's conveniently still (already?) here. I pass the lady my clothes and try to act like they're my girlfriends or something. She doesn't believe me, but nods like she does. She's nice.

She also tells me to have a look around while she sees what she can buy. I mosey down the aisles looking at other fu—no, bad Jhaegar! Go to the men's section! What if she—ya know? I'm sure she saw you—don't worry about it. If she doesn't care where you got them, she won't care what you buy next. There's a really cute—no, Jhaegar, just just just—

—She calls me up. Quite fast (like everything else in my—

"—Mmk, Mister. These were all I could buy."

She holds up my favorite leggings.

"But those are my favorite leggings!" I groan.

She (once again) pretends I'm not a creep. "Sorry, Mister. These are all I can take. No one's really buying anymore now that the world's ending."

"Wait, what?"

"I can give you five bucks, or did you want them back?"

I consider her. I was gonna buy supper at my favorite restaurant with all my earnings (as if I'm at the casino), but I guess—

"—Yeah, I probably should—I mean, yeah. They're yours."

"Mmk," she says. "And you're right. They do hold my crotch nicely."

I try to get that thought out of my head as I drive. The pile of unsold women's clothing repeats that sentence over and over again. She did have a—can I just fucking die already? I can't get it—them—it—out of my mind…being a woman didn't help at all. I was supposed to learn and become sensitive or emphatic or whatever and I just spent the whole time ranting and raving

[230]

like I always do—and I'm not blaming women, by the way. Not everything's their fault, Freud, ya know? It's my own stupid probl—I ALREADY FUCKING SAID THIS! I just wanna wear the leggings again—no, please stop. Just please stop. Just drive. Just drive, it's fine I throw the clothes out the window while I drive cuz I'm just driving and it's all just just just all just fine and clothes really freak me out too you knoww

or I guess people who wear clothes freak me out? Like why are you wearing clothes? What are you hiding? And worse, what are you hiding behind your smile? Behind your eyes? If clothes cover the nakedness of the body, what do faces cover? The nakedness of the soul?

Sigh, I really gotta kill myself…

Everyone keeps looking at me—and I mean *Looking* at me as I walk and I—I'm walking now? Where am I? Why am I out here? I'm wearing women's clothing again—but not the leggings I like—and I'm just out in the fucking open like an idiot and jumpin' fuck I'm so fucking sick, man. I didn't ask to—I didn't ask to

But you did ask for it

Did you not?

"Excuse me, sir, are you okay?"

Am I okay? Who's okay? Who the fuck's okay you fucking fuck fuck? Do you have any idea what I had to go through to get—shut up! They've had troubles, too. You don't have the worst life ever, Jhaegar, just cuz it's yours, doesn't mean it's special and I—they all need to suffer. Suffer like I did. They shouldn't—they shouldn't get to be happy, they don't deserve it, they didn't earn it. They all did the same thing I did and they're just okay with it. I so much as look at a woman and I can't even sleep at—you did more than look at her, you—shut up! Who's

[231]

even talking? Where was the other voice? Why isn't anyone else screaming? Why is it just me? Is no one else guilty? And—oh, of fucking course! Here come more so-called-Mental-Illness stereotypes, here come more *Looks*, cute little fucking couple kissing each other's cheeks and smelling their faces and sixty-nine-ing their noses like they're fucking inhaling each other's spirits or some fucking—giving me the, "Gee honey, what a creep, good thing I've never objectified a woman like this asshole," look you fuck you FUCK

They do not know what writing this cost us

They don't know fucking anything those elitist asshole fucks I bet he marks his phone calendar about when she's having her period so he can stay away from her cuz she's *annoying* or *needy* or some other stupid shit he's gonna make up and she'll just be okay with it and—FUCK FUCK FUCK FUCK—I'D MARK MY CALENDAR so I could COMFORT HER and BE NICE but NOOOOO then I'm a SIMP and a NICE GUY and a fucking bleeding again from my eyes now why my eyes? Why my eyes? It's always fucking something fucking

Kill them

I stereotype all over the park as the guy calls me "Crazy" and I sink my fingers into his throat. I say some juvenile comment about "Society" or how "Others did this to me" while I do it and picture the girlfriend thinking I'm some sort of hero white knight saving her from—I kill her, too—I flick my eyes and beams of coagulated blood burst forth and zig zag towards her with a hellish whistle of steam. They puncture her lungs and pump her full of (shut up) pump her full of gore until it's gushing out her mouth as she wails—

[232]

—Viviiviana (I can't call her Vivi anymore cuz we're breaking up) floats her hand over to mine.

"Hey Creepy…Jhaegar?" she says, barely a whisper yet not weak. "I'm not trying to shit on you, but I think you really need help. I'm done with all the things I can do and nothing's changing. You need someone who's trained in this sort of thing—and yeah, I know I don't dress the part, but self-care is—it's hard for me to say, too, but—"

"—You don't love me," I whisper (very weak). All the lights are making me sweat. All the—and everyone's laughing. Anyone can enjoy the carnival but me.

"No, Jhaegar, I do. I DO. But…I don't know what I can do anymo—"

"—You hate me."

"Nobody hates you."

I can't get out of here. I can't get out of here. I can't get rid of this anger. I just want someone to hurt me.

"So what do you think is really wrong, Jhaegar?" Dr. Blunderhaus asks me.

Is killing my doctor also a stereotype?

"I wanna cry," I tell them.

"And why is that?"

"Just been one of those lives…"

I laugh. I also cry—like, laugh-cry cuz I'm walking through stereotype alley right now and it's my prerogative.

I rise. Tell Cleve:

"'I think I've had enough of your rants, Jhaegar.'"

[233]

What do you get when you cross a mentally ill loner with— —I can't, I'm sorry, I just can't—that's such a shit movie and honestly just—just bad. Funny enough, Arthur's (his names fucking *Joker* by the way, what's this "Arthur" shit?) motivation for his actions are that people exploit the mentally ill...well what the hell's that movie doing? EXPLOITING THE MENTALLY ILL! Is he not aware (rather, is the dipshit filmmaker) not aware that while Arthur rallies against exploitation, the film ITSELF is exploitative as it simply rides on the current glamorization of depression and self-righteous shallow concern for mental health? No, I bet they're fucking not. They're too busy counting all the money YOU fucking assholes paid to watch—

—This...this...inescapable Do-Gooder ideology...while it hurts everyone, guess who it fucking hurts the most? This yuppie shit about talking about your problems and them just *magically disappearing* doesn't work, doesn't work whatso-fucking-ever. Paying some disinterested, unenlightened, 3rd party "Professional" hundreds of dollars to sit there and pretend to listen to your nonsense only makes THEIR POCKETS fatter and OUR MINDS looser, more damaged and fractured than ever before. What doesn't kill you only leaves you weaker—like what? Hasn't anyone ever broken an arm? What's it leave? A scar! A physical scar! Now what do you think mental attacks leave?!

And you can't even fucking get out of it! If you stray from the narrative—if only slightly—you'll get crucified by all these Do-Gooders who suddenly don't do so good anymore, who then tell you you're trash and you need help and they're right and you're wrong and DON'T EVEN LISTEN when you try to tell them that the reason you're sad has NOTHING TO DO with the—fuck it, just forget everybody, no one would listen anyway, you'll just get the same *Looks* and they'd fucking do the nodding thing too and be like, "Right, right, right, right, so how does

[234]

that make you feel?" and, "Well this is just Straight White Rage cuz you don't have any real problems so why're you upset?" oh my fucking—

—So you end up going through your entire life subscribing to this phony ideology you don't remotely believe in, cuz you know everyone else believes it, and the only way for them to even acknowledge you is to at least let them "win" this one argument. Let them say I'm sick. Let them say I need help. Let them think they're fucking important and I'm just pond scum they're so righteous to so much as glance at. The "Sickness Fallacy" kills you in the long run, but maybe someone can eventually use it as a Trojan Horse?

And one more fucking thing: the idea that the Do-Gooders want to help us is quite possibly the most sanctimonious, hypocritical, plain piss Yuppie nonsense thing I've ever heard. They don't want so-called-Mentally-Ill people to get better, they want them to SNAP. Break racial and gender barriers all day, but never go near a mental health one, that's what they think. They want Joker to brutalize people cuz they enjoy it, too, even more than us—matter of fact, it's their enjoyment that makes us do it in the first place, ya know, at least we'd feel important for once. At least then we feel seen. It's just a big exhibition to them and the only way they can continue to sensationalize our plight is by kicking us while we're down and shoving the same old platitudes down our throats. "It gets better." "Think of all the love in your life." "God has a plan for you." Well guess fucking what—?

—Okay, I don't—I'm just killing Cleve right now. Fuck it, right? Don't mind me. Mx. Mental Health Awareness Month forgot that Mx. Jhaegar Holdburn née Shy but Sassy Lady has a history with impulsiveness and emotional volatility.

Whatever. I sit back down on the couch, covered in someone's blood. I say someone cuz, while one would assume it's Cleve's, I only choked them and am known to bleed sporadically.

[235]

Curiosity takes hold. I glance at my former doctor's body. What mysteries lie beneath those clothes? Thankfully, death and dismay (as per usual (not my fault, I didn't ask for it)) has cleared my head and I decide not to be a total creep. Better a murdering rapist than a raping murderist, as they say.

Sigh, I didn't rape her. I didn't rape anybody (though you've masturbated), but that's not rape. That's only rape to me—by my lunatic perspective! I didn't—I didn't mean to do anything bad, I didn't know—but that's not an excuse, it's not a real excuse, there can't BE an excuse. No excuses. I'd never hurt anyone, I only wanna hurt (SHUT UP) myself. Why don't my actions align with my morals? Are there other Jhaegars inside me? Which is the real Jhaegar? Do others feel this way? Why can't I follow my own piss shitting rules?!

You don't have any rules, you're a murdering rapist. Remember? Remember how you're evil, Jhaegar (I didn't do anything nobody else already did), you're fucking EVIL. You deserve whatever stupid nonsense the universe has coming (why am I this traumatized?) for you in this life and the next and the next after that and the next and the next until (I'm the one who did it, not the one it was done to) the whole rest of reality dissolves and only you are left, Jhaegar, only you and (can you imagine HER trauma, you fucking asshole?) you and your suffering.

I honestly don't know if I even remember what I did to her. It's been so long and I've thought about it so much that I can't distinguish truth from embellishment. Am I making the memories worse cuz I hate myself? Or am I hiding the pain cuz I'm guilty and don't wanna admit what I did? What did I even do? I can't remember. I don't wanna remember. I want it to go away.

I teleport to the bathroom. It must be Cleve's (like personal, not even office) bathroom cuz there's more Mental Health Awareness Month calendars. Wait...this thing says EVERY

[236]

month is Mental Health Awareness Month…does that mean I AM in their office? Why are their family photos in here then? Why is "their" such a confusing pronoun? (Maybe it's cuz—) —and why would there be family photos in any bathroom anyway? And why are they all gender ambivalent? And's that even the term or is someone Tweeting I'm homophobic?

And typical: toilet paper roll's out—not even just about to be out like a top tier hero would leave, but classlessly, sloppily, unoriginally out—and the fucking music, some country shit—and not REAL country, don't get me wrong, I like REAL country like Johnny Cash and John Denver and Charles Manson, but not this faux twangy pop country garbage, this "I was fuckin' a hooooorrrse right in da azzzzzzz, cuz when ya fuckin' horses ya ain't ever gotta azzzzk!" shit. Who un-ironically listens to this?

I don't know, it's somehow always the best song (or worst, I guess) to make you sad. Broken Bells is always playing or The Doors or—do I like The Doors? Were they supposed to be a positive or negative association? Who knows and why does music have to ruin—well, really, why do I have to ruin everything? Why can't I just think normally for a week? Just a week at this point, I could turn my life around in a week.

Yes, yes I can be happy! (I shit blood into the toilet bowl) Sigh life, but ya know? I'm not gonna let that or Twangy Bangy get to me. I'm gonna be happy! (I shit blood into the toilet bowl) Never mind! I'm gonna be SAD!

(Nothing)

Sigh life again.

I'm going to New Jersey.

[237]

***

I wonder if the stereotypical New Jersey "Hey, I'm waulkin' 'ere!" girl even exists. Are they all just regular women? I must investigate. I'll just dink around in Newark and get...(my asshole clenches)...get worse. Definitely get worse and not find a nice New Jersey girl. I'll...find Joe Pesci or something.

But yeah, I "Waulkin' 'ere" down the streets of Newark, Marissa Tomei lookalikes on every corner—before I even get close they yell they're, "Waulkin' 'ere," and I retort with, "Hey, I'M waulkin' 'ere," and they retort back and it never ends and I—

"—Um, hey man?" says someone. I sense a distinct lack of New Jersey.

I turn to find I "Waulkin' 'ere"-ed right into some poor gal—

—Gwyn? Gwynevere?! And her Blue's Clues hoodie?!?!

"Check where you're waulkin'," she says (not with a New Jersey accent, just a mocking one).

"Gwynevere Clamshell?" I ask.

"It's *Hunking*. You know me?"

"We dated after college...also, you're, like...not alive yet..."

"Don't come after me, man, I can't control that you superimpose me and those other chicks on everyone you meet."

"Um, hehe, what do you mean by—?"

"—I also can't control that you get off to women narcing on you, like for the fact that you're like thirty but still daydreaming about your old GFs who left you cuz, like, you refused to grow or something."

[238]

"I'm only twenty-five."

"Uh huh. Well it'll be the same when you're like thirty."

Piss, she knows me so well. I take the plunge.

"Do you enjoy my muscles? Do you wanna go on a date? I'm manly now, right?"

"Nah, I'm good. Yeah, I'm obligated to go on your date, like, I'm only here for you. And nah again, you're still like a little kid. And bonus answer cuz I know you love those: yeah, you will later akin me being, like, I guess, celestially forced to go on a date with you to being rape tonight when you're home alone cutting yourself in the bathtub."

"Alright, where to first?"

"You pick."

"But, I—" (—shut up, Jhaegar, you're a si—) "—want you to dominate me and wear the pants so I can wear your pants so pick a place."

"Mmk man, but if you, like, enjoy being hurt in the mode of women controlling you and forcing you to do whatever they want, the only way to TRULY hurt you would be to actually force YOU to do what YOU want."

"I love you."

"I know."

"Overrated movie."

"I've heard."

Vivi—I mean, Gwyn grabs my hand and tugs me down to earth.

"I'd ask you how you learned to do that," she says, "but you're kinda lame now and you honestly don't even know."

"But I don't."

[239]

"You grow strong. The Doggening approaches."

"I thought it already happened?!"

"Probably did, man. Didn't you trigger it or something when you were in the Don John?"

"Huh?"

"So where are we going? My pu—"

"—Shut up! You're not saying that!"

"You want me to say it—"

"—No, I don't—"

"—My pussy's too wet, baby, I need you t—"

"—Fucking—just shit—shit shit shit, why do girls even wanna go on dates?"

(We stand around or walk down the street or grab a beer or whatever)

"Whadya mean?" Gwyn asks. Eager and attentive.

"Cuz it's just so unfair for women! Have I ever told you about the—?"

"—Yup."

"Oh, okay. But yeah, I actually had a new thought recently. So: what's this shit with men being told they need a good woman to clean them up and turn their lives around? Why is that a woman's job? To fix a man's life? And you wouldn't hear that the other way around, you never hear, 'Hey girl—ya know, *you're trash, Eddie*—you need a swole hunky man to clean you up and turn your life around.' Since when did women become humankind's custodians— *human*kind's mind you, not *man*kind's, cuz that's the line of thinking that got us into this mess in the first place—and it just makes me wonder again: so what DO women hear? Do people tell them, 'Gee golly honey, all you need is a piece of shit guy who's life you can clean up and turn around,' like what? No! Do you actually do that? Don't! Stop! Live your own life, Gwyn!"

[240]

"Wish I could, man…"

"Real question?"

"Oh yeah?"

"Do women ever get guilty enough that they do this to themselves?"

"Do what?"

I gesture to myself.

She chuckles. "No—I don't know—like, you're controlling my actions, so I'm just like a man walking around in a woman's body—just less fun for you—so I don't have an answer."

Super sigh.

"Sor-ry!" she jeers all cute and sassy-like.

"Yeah…"

"So like, how 'bout that date?" she asks.

"There's a shitty diner here I forget the name of that's pretty decent."

"Mmk. Let's go there."

"Sor-ry," I say sassier, "I can't. I have to take you to a movie."

"Why?"

I pull out my First Date Venn Diagram. Above one circle is listed "Get Dinner" and above the other is listed "See a Movie." The circles also never intersect (sorry, it's Jhaegar specific).

"Well, ya know?" I pretend she knows as I point around the diagram. "You can either take a girl on a Dinner Date or a Movie Date. While both are similar introductory activities, they have stark, often forgotten contrasts. So Dinner Date: Dinner Date means, 'Hey, I like you and think you're cool so let's grab dinner or supper or whatever you fucking call it and talk and

[241]

discuss how cool we think we are while we wait to get food and have the inevitable time after eating while we can continue to discuss how cool we now know each other are…is?…while we wait for the bill to either have me pay or we can split if you're feeling really radical and/or I brought up Hillary Clinton and am guilting you into paying for yourself.' As you can see, Dinner Date's lead to increased knowledge in your date, maybe a legitimate connection, and most likely: fun. Now take Movie Date: Movie Date means, 'Shut the fuck up, we're gonna sit here for two hours (or three hours minimum if it's a movie I picked) and we're not gonna talk or learn or grow close cuz we're just gonna watch this random fucking movie neither of us have any stake in.' Movie Dates, while safe, are dull and emotionally cheap. It's like…like only a real schlub would take a girl to the movies on a first date…notwithstanding that some men (and women, sorry) are actually quite into film and if their partner isn't (which they never are) well, then fuck me! What teen girl wants to sit around and watch *Make Way for Tomorrow* (1937), huh? Or are we gonna hold hands while we dissect the postwar generational trauma of *I Live in Fear* (1955)? No. I'm gonna be stuck watching *Doctor Whatever His Fucking Name Is* (2016) and then she's gonna be like, 'What a great movie, did you like it?' and I'm gonna cry and it just—it just—it just doesn't matter. I'll tell her, 'Oh yeah, for sure,' cuz that's the safe second answer after I already picked the safe first answer of going to a fucking movie."

"Okay…so Dinner Dates are better, yeah?"

"Yeah," I tell her, "but I'm a sack of shit."

"So Movie Date, huh?"

***

[242]

EXT. MOVIE THEATER - DAY

Jhaegar and Gwyn approach a movie theater, hand in hand. Walk towards a ticket booth. Pass several posters…

…one of which is for a film titled, 'SHE BLED FROM HER EYES.'

>   JHAEGAR
>   Wait, what?

>   GWYN
>   Man, what now?

>   JHAEGAR
>   (confused(perennially))
>   This was my script—IS my script
>   in the future. How'd they steal it
>   already? I…

Jhaegar leans in to study the poster.

>   GWYN
>   You done narcing yet? Your
>   palpable Straight White Rage is
>   wrecking my energy.

Jhaegar's face morphs into shock as his tracing finger lands on one fine detail.

>   JHAEGAR
>   I have writing credit for this?!

>   GWYN
>   Cool, I guess.

>   JHAEGAR
>   That's just—that's just amazing!
>   I don't know how I—ya know?
>   People keep saying I'm affecting
>   reality and—oh piss…

>   GWYN
>   Yeah, man?

>   JHAEGAR
>   They let Kelly Reichardt direct.

[243]

                    GWYN
          Sure.

                    JHAEGAR
          This means they massacred my boy—
          daughter, actually—girl. Cuz the
          story was all about slow burning
          erotic lesbian horror.

                    GWYN
          Cool. Then what's it about now?

                    JHAEGAR
          Gender roles in a fading rural
          community.

                    GWYN
              (wishing she were dead)
          Shit…

INT. MOVIE THEATER - DAY

Jhaegar and Gwyn (well, Gwyn does—Jhaegar doesn't believe
in popcorn) munch on popcorn as they wait for the movie.

Gwyn groans. Irritable.

                    GWYN
          You don't believe in popcorn—?

                    JHAEGAR
          —Shh! The film's starting!

INSERT - THEATER SCREEN…

Showing a scene of CORYN and ILYA, two college aged girls
(now severely lacking any subtle slow burning horror or
romance), gardening together.

Coryn uses a trowel to dig a few holes. Drops a seed into
each hole and covers them with dirt.

                    ILYA
          Hey.

                        [244]

                    CORYN
          Yeah?

                    ILYA
          Could I use your trowel?

Back in the theater, Jhaegar whispers in Gwyn's ear…

                    JHAEGAR
          Ya know, I don't like where this's
          going, but I can least appreciate
          Reichardt's immediately creating
          conflict—I just personally like to
          let it simmer for a bit—and create
          a little, uh—and, I mean, you know
          Coryn's gonna say "No," ya know?
          But just…I don't know, when I
          wrote it, I strove to create a
          nightmarishly isolated atmosphere
          to show that Coryn was emotionally
          and mentally withdrawn from her
          peers an—

                    GWYN
          —Man.

                    JHAEGAR
               (defeated)
          Okay…

INSERT - THEATER SCREEN…

Coryn nods at Ilya.

                    CORYN
          Sure.

Coryn passes Ilya her trowel.

Ilya now digs holes and fills them with seeds.

Coryn doesn't longingly watch her. Instead she takes a
water pail and sprinkles her new plants.

Back in the theater, Jhaegar bites his nails. A rather severe look taints his usually sardonic expression.

Gwyn glances at him for half a second and, recognizing the danger in this action, directs her focus back to the film.

Yet it's too late, Jhaegar can't resist…

> **JHAEGAR**
> Ya know? Uh…I don't know if you've read my review of *Little Women—*

> **GWYN**
> —Nope—

> **JHAEGAR**
> —But this is exactly the issue I'm trying to tell people about. There's nothing intrinsically wrong with a feminine storyline, but a feminine storyline—a feminine work—is inherently experiential cuz feminine life is inherently experiential, ya know? I mean, just look at your own life.

> **GWYN**
> Watch the movie, man. You can blog about it later.

> **JHAEGAR**
> Babe! I mean, honey! I mean… Gwyn! Why're you so upset? Or do you actually like Reichardt—I mean, it's okay, I just think it'd be better if you liked Josephine Decker—

> **GWYN**
> —If you wanted to talk, you should've taken me to dinner.

> **JHAEGAR**
> I know! But, but—

                    GWYN
          —And like, you're such a freak
          about Indian food, you'd think
          you'd be jacked to show it to—

                    JHAEGAR
          —But I can cook Indian at home—

                    GWYN
          —Uh huh. And when're you
          inviting me home?

                    JHAEGAR
          Well…actually, uh—

                    GWYN
          —Uh huh. You don't even know.

                    JHAEGAR
          No! No, I—!

                OTHER PATRON (O.S.)
          —Hey faggot in the front! Shut
          the fuck up, I'm trying to write
          an essay on Reichardt's visual
          language!

Jhaegar twists back in his seat to face his new challenger.

                    JHAEGAR
          Oh yeah? Well, you won't get far,
          asshole! This scene's about all
          you're gonna get for the next two
          hours!

                  OTHER PATRON
          Don't you have a Kenji Mizoguchi
          film to go jerk off to?!

Jhaegar tries to counter, but his voice fails him.

                  OTHER PATRON
          Yeah, I see you, bitch!

Jhaegar twists back to face the screen, ashamed and
distraught.

                       [247]

Gwyn glances at him again and rolls her eyes.

                    GWYN
          You really do get off on your own
          suffering, don't you?

Jhaegar sinks lower in his seat. Remains silent.

They watch the movie without speaking. The longer they
watch, the more Jhaegar forgets his troubles and that usual
wry sparkle returns to his eyes.

                    JHAEGAR
          What if they had a tinnitus movie?

Gwyn SIGHS.

                    JHAEGAR
          I mean, uh, I don't have tinnitus
          …but, I, uh, know a guy who
          does. What's interesting, is that
          it would act as non-diegetic sound
          for the audience, yet is truly
          diegetic sound for the victim.
          Wouldn't that be cool? Such a
          reversal—and what an opportunity
          the filmmaker would have to
          discombobulate the audience
          through the way I'd implement
          it…like every poignant moment of
          repose or chilling moment of
          silence would be ruined by that
          fucking ringing…but yeah, people
          always say Mentally Ill people are
          crazy, but I think it's rather
          just irritating to be honest—like
          tinnitus—like your life's ruined
          so you just wanna ruin other
          people's lives—I don't know—
          doctor's don't know fucking shit,
          by the way. Just all fucking
          useless like everyone else. You go
          in and ask for help on ANYTHING
          and they'll be like, "Okay, take
          this steroid (cuz it's always a
          steroid) twice a day for two weeks
                    (MORE)

                    [248]

                    JHAEGAR (CONT'D)
          from the bottle of ten I've
          prescribed you and then it'll be
          gone," and I'm like, "Okay, it's
          not gone," and they're like, "No,
          it's gone, that'll be three
          hundred dollars," and I don't
          know. Fucking idiots…but a movie
          like that could never get made,
          ya know, too original. Too
          Chinatown—you ever hear about the
          Chinatown effect? Phenomenon?
          Whatever. What's really stupid,
          though, is that I'd be so good at
          filmmaking. I think I'd actually
          have something original to bring
          forward…and I mean, as Orson
          Wells would say, "Ohhh the FRenCH
          CHAMpppainnggeeNNEE!"

Jhaegar GIGGLES and pats Gwyn's shoulder, as if she gets
the reference and thinks he's witty.

                    JHAEGAR
          Just kidding. He'd say, "All you
          need is one," and I think that's
          all I'd need, too.

                    GWYN
          Jhaegar?

                    JHAEGAR
          Yeah, huh?

                    GWYN
          You're fucking crazy.

                                        CUT TO:

EXT. CARNIVAL/MALL - NIGHT

Jhaegar sits on a bench while sticking a needle in his arm.
He pumps LIQUID TURMERIC into his body.

                                        CUT TO:

                         [249]

INT. APARTMENT - NIGHT

Jhaegar lounges on his couch. Stares at his phone. Eyes out of focus, lost in a haze.

                                                            CUT TO:

EXT. CARNIVAL/MALL - NIGHT

Jhaegar's eyes roll back as yellow-brown veins of turmeric pulse below his skin, creeping towards his brain.

                                                            CUT TO:

INT. MOVIE THEATER - NIGHT

Jhaegar watches the movie alone. Gwyn's nowhere to be seen. No one AT ALL is anywhere to be seen.

                                                            CUT TO:

EXT. CARNIVAL/MALL - NIGHT

Jhaegar's consciousness wanes. He crumbles off the bench.

                            ***

Dig Doglius (the First Dog) travels through a forest dark for the straightforward path had been lost.

Jhaegar Holdburn (the Last Dog) floats behind Dig Doglius, incorporeal and transient.

Dig Doglius comes to a fork in the path, the same fork that comes to all Dogs. The final step. The only decision.

The path to the left represents The Dog, while the path to the right represents The City. The path of The Dog is the path of bliss, of youthful resplendence and psychological ease. Those of The Dog lead a heteronomous, or rather, a "Doglike" existence. Yet, this is also the path of naïveté and ignorance, the path of shortchanging one's potential in exchange for mindless peace.

In contrast, the path of The City is the path of erudition and growth, the path that ends in leadership and resilience. Yet, the path of The City paints a bleak vision, one in which the ultimate question posed to oneself will be: "What for?" This path corrupts Dogs into becoming jaded and arrogant as those of The City, in pursuit of a higher so-called intellect, sacrifice their Personality over decades of what is inevitably proven to be fruitless effort and self-defeating pride.

Like all Dogs to follow, Dig Doglius was faced with this choice. The Dog? Or The City? Unjustifiable joy or shattered idealism?

It was at this point that Dig Doglius realized the presence of the Third Path. While he could travel forward upon the left or the right, a third option, yet unknown to him as it remains unknown to so many Dogs today, opened his eyes. While Dig Doglius had two options forward, he also had one behind.

This was the path of Dog City.

Dig Doglius realized that rather than choosing one way of life he could choose both and neither, working backwards away from the mentally crippling attitudes of an organic civilization and instead towards the spiritual ascendance achieved only through irrational self-destruction. For, as Dig Doglius began to know, rationalism leads to nihilism and nihilism leads to denial of reason, thus any path one could take that leads to Universal Truth could only end in one's immolation.

At this point, Jhaegar Holdburn's incorporeal half-spirit floats down to Dig Doglius.

"So Mr. Doglius," he asks, "why does Dog City Never Sleep?"

[251]

"Oh. That's from your undiagnosed depersonalization disorder."

***

I exhale and glance down at my—guessing the turmeric fumes from my Murgh Makhani sent me on another one of those trips. I didn't even put that much in here (I've been leaning more towards—

—Wait, fuck—I didn't put that much in cuz I didn't make this, who opened this restaurant? There are Indian people in Sioux Falls? Did a bunch of whites open this? Did I open this and I—I don't know, I take a bite of the food. It's good, not great, but good. Could use more salt. I recently discovered the power of salt and how it actually does affect one's dish despite my previous belief that it was all just celebrity chef showboating. I would've added more salt.

Looking up, I find Glass Pipe and Turmeric Pill sitting across from me. While I'm pretty sure I killed both of them, this would actually be the first date I've been on (I know it's not a "date," but just whatever) I've been on in years so I let it slide.

I ask Turmeric Pill how it's doing.

"I'm fine, sweetie," it says.

"You can kiss her on the cheek if you want," suggests Glass Pipe.

I lean over the table and kiss Turmeric Pill on the spot I'd associate with her cheek. As I do, the Pill's shell splits and a manifesting fist of turmeric forces itself down my throat.

"Ha! Finally gotchya, bitch!" shouts Glass Pipe.

I—I don't know what's happeni

[252]

***

"Lover Release Me" by Brazilian Marissa Nadler plays from unseen speakers.

Fuck me in my—oh hey, it's called Bossa Nova!

I wipe my forehead. The heat from the lights makes me sweat like crazy and white people just—just shouldn't sweat. The carnival/mall is substantially more carnival-like this time around, so I'll just—ya know, cuz I think I hear the falafel guy polishing his falafel maker or something. Wait. They have falafel makers? He tells me to relax and that me and my Dad are just gonna forget about his falafels anyway so we can go ahead and stick to the—

—Though there's no mirrors in front of me, I see I'm looking at myself—some sort of out of body nonsense, I don't know—or maybe just a mirror, I don't—I do realize my face keeps changing—well, maybe not changing, but morphing back and forth uncontrollably. Young Jhaegar then Old Jhaegar (provided you think twenty-five is old—I mean I think it's old, but then again I thought I would've died by now) then back to Young Jhaegar.

"We've been here for eight years," he says.

"I know."

You can walk out of here right now.

You may not

Jhaegar snickers.

We can escape this.

[253]

You would escape into a void

"Unless I get on with my life, huh?" Jhaegar says. He snickers some more. Massages his temples, head collapsing into his hands.

Stay and you may yet dream

"A dream is a mind state," Jhaegar says. "It's all reality so long as my mind believes. I'll wake up here, I'll wake up there, it's all the same."

Buried in your mind you know it's not real.

You know we're unfulfilled.

Fulfilment is a lie perpetuated by the Successful

Jhaegar grins to himself, very slight. Aware of his own hopelessness.

"If I leave, I will die, will I not?"

There is no response.

No response.

"This Jhaegar will die, and would not the original be restored?"

Yes...No

[254]

"So why preserve the original?"

It is Real

"'What's more real than dreams?'"

I do not like this either

I don't know which one I am anymore. The watcher one or the watc—oh, super sigh. Am I an Invisible? But what am I now then—if "Jhaegar" can't see me? Am I the invisible Invisible?

"You're just trying to save yourself," says "Jhaegar."

I am trying to save US

"Jhaegar" leans back into the bench he's lounging on. Looks around as women materialize waiting in lines, riding rides, chatting with friends. Dozens of other "Jhaegars" materialize as well.

"Yes. I think I'll just stay here."

"Jhaegar" (Jhaegar Jhaegar Jhaegar) reaches into the pocket of a coat he's now wearing. We're no longer in the carnival, now we're at the mall I guess. He stares directly at me and points a gun at my head.

I start to tell him that I didn't mean t

[255]

***

There are no questions. That's what really gets me. It's not the idea that there aren't any answers and we're alone in the universe and it's human curiosity that ultimately wears us down. Saying there are "no answers" implies there are questions to be asked and that's the thing: there are no questions to be asked. Nothing worth finding out. Nothing to make a difference. Nothing that matters. There are no questions.

***

I cough out the chicken and reach for my drink—of course it's—well, I mean, not "of course" it's milk. It is milk, it's just that people always give you a hard time for getting milk like you're some kind of loser. Okay, it soothes your mouth and stomach from spicy foods, it builds strength and whatever, like, sorry I didn't order a soda and kill myself like everybody else. Jumpin' fuckin' Christ.

I'll just stay here—rant about Indian food forever...no...I leave the restaurant and see I'm back in New Jersey—or always was in New Jersey, the restaurant just used to be in Sioux Falls for the time bei—I don't fucking care. I'm somewhere, aren't I?

But yeah, it appears I'm levitating again. All these New Jersey girls gawk up at me like I'm some kind of Messiah. Reminds me of the end of *Taxi Driver* (it's my favorite movie, yeah, I'm gonna keep referencing it) where Betty hardcore wants Travis, but cuz it's probably all his fantasy, he rejects her to show how—ya know—like cool he is or something and how "He don't need no girl" or I don't know. Fuck film and fuck art and no one cares anyway. *Taxi Driver*'s

[256]

actually pretty overrated—just Paul Schrader jerking himself off and writing his personal sob story like every other "artist." Does anyone ever write about someone else for a change? Know what? I'm gonna kill the President so Jodie Foster'll be impressed with me (there's a lesbian, less-be-impressed with me joke in there somewhere, but I just can't anymore) and who's even President? It's Bush now, isn't it? Sigh…

I snap my fingers and appear at the airport, ticket in hand (wouldn't wanna wait in line and yeah, yeah, I know I could snap my fingers and appear in D.C., but I actually like flying on planes and no, it's not for the infinitesimal chance of being in a crash, I just think planes are nifty) and I'm gonna kill Bush and Dick Cheney'll be president and America'll be even worse somehow…well, I don't want it THAT bad, maybe I should just kill Dick Cheney—okay, I'll kill them both—and Colin Powell, just for fun.

I stroll through the airport looking for my gate. I remember to eat at Cinnabon, puke in the bathroom, then go buy a banana for five dollars. As I munch on my banana, I contemplate how I'm kinda like a banana myself…I'm not, though, it's just that my mind's really deteriorated lately. I could be kinda like anything to be honest.

I don't know what to do. I don't wanna kill George Bush anymore. I still kinda wanna kill Dick Cheney, but I don't think the trip's worth it just for that. I'd kill myself, but we all know I'm—plus, I'd just end up somewhere else. I'm never gonna leave this nightmare-dream-whatever…but yeah…I guess I enjoy it in its own weird way…I'll just remake Vivi and make Gwyn a Latina or something and have a cruise episode where they're both there and Snowelda and Buggins—ah, it just doesn't fucking matter. I'll get there when I get there, no use in trying to predict how much more I'll descend.

[257]

Sigh. Why are Vivi and Gwyn so underdeveloped? Or are they developed and I just think they aren't cuz I hate myself and know I'm a misogynist? Am I a misogynist? Did I even date Vivi and Gwyn or are they just mirrors? In my defense, are Buggins or Rooz developed? But wouldn't it just be sexist to defend myself? Can anyone be underdeveloped if everyone is just me? Is wearing cool hoodies even a personality trait?

I don't know. Maybe it'd just be better if I got "better." Whatever "better" is…might lend an air of consistency to the whole thing. But—I—I'm just gonna be stuck here anyw—well, that's cuz you chose to be stuck here—what does "better" even entail? Is that more Dog City shit? I hate everything.

Well, I guess…

I rise and head for my gate. The plane ride'll clear me up—I'll just—it'll be fine or something. I still don't wanna go to D.C., though…I'll go to…I'll go to California…not for any, uh, reason, just cuz…I guess movies are alright and all you need is one and it's only 2001 so the Spec Boom is strong (right?) so maybe I can get something…also, I think I might be a demigod now, so I definitely should get something…but, I feel early 2000's audiences won't accept *She Bled from her Eyes*…then again, fuck 'em, I'll just be like Tommy Wiseau and do whatever I want. Shout-out to Tommy Wiseau, by the way.

I snap my fingers to change my ticket for California and the moment I do I crash to the floor (I was levitating). I find I can't levitate again, but also find I don't care.

I wonder what Roderick's doing right now. Should've brought him with. He's kind of a Dog, isn't he? "Bark woof," as they say.

Right as I thought that, a passerby turned around and shot me a look—not *The Look* oddly enough, but a look nonetheless.

[258]

Jumpin' Christ…let's just get to my gate.

I sit down at the—is this even called a "gate?" I don't know airport terminology. I sit down at the sitting place where you wait for your plane—it's a nifty place to get into a rant or whatever, but I—I don't have the energy anymore. Rant to yourself or something, yeah, "Insert Your Own Rant," and you'll be fine.

INSERT YOUR OWN RANT:

A girl—well, a young woman—sits down across from—okay, not "across," but across and a few seats over—from me. She promptly pulls out her phone and types away. Wonder what she's typing? I hope she's happy and talking to her cool friends about how cool they all are—I don't know, she has a maroon sweatshirt on and you can't get much better than cool ladies with great taste in sweatshirts...and she has, like, black leggings or tights or—hers are more like runner ones, I guess. And a nose ring! She's like a—hope she doesn't notice me, I'll look away in a second—but she's like a Hippie X Cool Girl X Anything Else. Her name's probably Bailey.

Oh well, I'll give Probably Bailey some mental space, she doesn't need me ruining her life, too. This is, yet again, a good place for a rant...but I don't care anymore, I'm a changed man—

—I cough up a few flecks of blood. Sigh. Just, uh...just better I don't think at all.

...

...

Calling my ticket, that's nice. Time to get on—well, get "in" the plane ("Evel Knievel can get ON the—") —sorry, I'm sorry. George Carlin deserves better.

...

...

Rather empty, wasn't I one of the last groups to get called? I don't get the window seat, but I do get the aisle seat instead (my boon comes in handy, doesn't it?) and some other guy gets the window. Our middle seat has yet to be taken. Scary stuff!

...

...

[260]

I see Probably Bailey coming down the aisle. Oh, please no. Don't make me—well, don't make HER have to sit next to me, just give me a fat guy ins—okay, not a fat guy. Just give me another normal guy inste—

—Oh, thank God (uh, I mean, thank somebody else), she moves past us. She may only move so far as the next row behind, but that's okay (hey, she also has the Window Seat Boon!). She also doesn't have anybody else sitting by her yet. Ha! Maybe we'll both get fat guys?

The door or hatch or whatever closes and the plane people start checking everything. Oh? Okay, I've never actually had open seats by me before. Gee golly gee. I steal a glance at the dude in the window seat and we share a nod of relief.

"Whoa, I've never gotten the whole row to myself!"

What?

Probably Bailey's talking.

The other dude (I'll just call him Other Dude) glances back to see her.

"Well, lucky you, congratulations!"

"Yeah, I know," she says. "Didn't think I was gonna relax."

Jumpin' jumpin' jumpin' do I say somethin'? Why did HE get to say something, he's way older than her. Was he a popular kid back in school? I—I—I—I—

—I glance back at her.

"We're pretty lucky up here, too, we gotta free middle seat."

"Right?!" she says to me. "Just look at us go."

I turn to face ahead again. *Look at us*…she said US—shut up, Jhaegar! It's just small talk! She doesn't wanna marry you!

[261]

Other Dude faces forward as well. Probably Bailey gets back to her phone. Small talk is over and I can calm down.

Wow—well, at least I'm not sitting next to her...I mean, imagine she had the window seat and I had the aisle seat next to—oh my—what if it was the MIDDLE—next to—what a nightmare. I'm glad I have Other Dude.

She has a nice voic—

—the lights flash on and off.

The captain comes on the intercom and says our flight'll be delayed like twenty minutes—they have to check the plane for—ya know, cuz it's probably broken and they don't wanna scare us.

...

...

...Checking checking...

...

...

Twenty more minutes? What?

Other Dude steals a glance at me and we share a nod of confusion. We stare forward again and question oursel—well, maybe he doesn't, but I do. I—

—He cranes his head backwards.

"Looks like our luck got the better of us," he says to Probably Bailey.

She glances up from her phone and hits Other Dude with a fake laugh—ya know, to be nice?

"Yeah, I guess so!" she says.

[262]

He turns forward. She goes phoning. I—do I say something, too? No, no, shut up, Jhaegar, she doesn't wanna hear you talk.

…

…

…TWENTY MORE MIN—

—HOW?!?!

WHAT'S WRONG WITH THE PLANE THAT—

"—Attention passengers: I apologize for the lack of technical jargon I'd usually pretend you understand. This plane's messed up, you're all gonna have to get new tickets on better planes, please return to the terminal in a large discombobulate mess and see the one Flight Attendant Lady Person who's gonna reroute you all. Thank you for flying with us and please remember, the local time is Too-Late-to-Find-Another-Reasonable-Transfer."

Nifty. What a start to my "new life." Fuck riding planes, I guess, so I snap my fingers and try to teleport to California—of course it doesn't work anymore—my arms have returned to normal skinniness, by the way—double by the way, please don't call people like me "Skinny" or "Thin." I prefer "Lean" (well, I actually prefer, "Human Being," but I know that's asking too much) so yeah, if I can't fat shame you, you can't skinny shame me, alright?

I get in line at the terminal/gate/something. There really is only one lady here to reroute us all. Here's to another twenty—probably forty minutes. I—

—Oh my jumpin' fuckin' Jesus fuckin' on a Christ Cross…

Probably Bailey waits in line right behind me.

Do I—NO! Don't fucking say anythi—SHUT UP—don't say anything. She doesn't like you, she's not a "prize" you have to claim, asshole! She's just waiting in line, waiting in line like you, not WITH you, but LIKE you (which she DOES NOT)!

Sigh. She—DON'T LOOK—her maroon sweatshirt looks SOOOOO soft. Like, Curl-Up-And-Watch-Evangelion, soft. Do you think she likes Evan—no, she probably has real hobbies! I mean, look at that nose ring? She probably hikes and's from Oregon and's never touched a T.V. remote in her life. What a Queen—I mean, what a Normal Person. The line advances. We—at least I'm close to the fron—

—I glance back at her.

"So, uh, 'technical difficulties,' huh? Pretty sure that means, 'Broken Plane.'"

She looks up at me and smirks.

"Right? God, thought I had it there, but some part of me knew having a whole row was too good to be true."

"Weeeell," why am I holding that word so long? "Sorry about that."

"Sorry?" she says, raising her eyebrows.

"I'm pretty unlucky—comedically so, actually—so the reason the plane broke's probably cuz I was on it."

She laughs.

She LAUGHS.

A REAL lau—

"—Well, screw you, man. Couldn't you get on somebody else's plane?"

She puts her phone away…

[264]

"Yeah, no," I tell her. "I guess I take joy in misery—usually my own—but people keep telling me I have to 'change' or something, so I thought I'd try Other People's misery for once."

"Sure's working."

She laughs again, this time eyes looking down at her feet (she's looking at her feet!) until she looks up (but kinda off and to the side!) until she meets my eyes.

"Kind of expected it. I'm pretty unlucky, too. Nothing good lasts for long."

"Well, that's nice to hear," I tell he—YOU FUCKING IDIOT WHY WOULD YOU MAKE THAT JOKE TO—?

—She laughs again at her feet!

SHUT UP, JHAEGAR!

"Sorry—ya know, I—if we're gonna stand here—my name's Jhaegar, by the way." DON'T REACH OUT TO SHAKE HER HAND YOU CREEP! "What's your name?" I ask, just nodding once at her.

Probably Bailey nods her head as well. I wanna say she turns slightly red as if she doesn't like the question, but I also think it's just her maroon sweatshirt blinding me.

"Kinda—sorry—kinda weird, but my name's Jaelyn."

"What do you mean, 'kinda weird?'"

Jaylin (I'll have to ask her how to spell it later) shrugs, but not really a—the upward shoulder movement thing?

"Cuz it's kinda this ghetto-y name and I'm this plain white girl? Like…I'm not a 'J-Lin,' I'm a 'Bailey.'"

...

...

[265]

OH NONONONO HOW LONG HAVE I BEEN STARING AT HER?!?!

"Oh yeah, I can see it," I tell Bailey. "You do look more Bailey-like. Bailey-ish?"

Must not have been too long cuz she giggles—GIGGLES?! "Right? Right, I know. Don't know what my parents were doing."

"So, where're you going—well, where WERE you going, Bailey?"

Bailey smiles. Her maroon-ness grows brighter.

"Going back home—don't know why I have to fly to California first to get to Oregon, you'd think they'd have a flight, but I guess not."

"Oreg—?"

"—Yeah, I know. Not very 'Jeylen,' huh? What about you?"

"Oh, I'm not sure to be honest—not that I don't know where I'm going, I just don't know what I'm gonna do when I get there."

"That's alright."

...

...

The way she said it...

"Okay," I say.

"Well, hopefully you'll get a non-stop there so you can find out in a hurry."

Oh, don't dig yourself in, Jhae—

"—No," I state. "I think I'll have to insist that my plane stops."

Bailey raises a hand to cover her mouth. An old couple behind her notices her laughter.

"What?" she says.

[266]

"Ya know," I continue, "all these airport terms make no sense. Like, I don't want them to tell me they're beginning the, 'Final Approach,' ya know? Or when they say, 'We'll be on the ground in fifteen minutes'…well, that's a little vague!"

"I—hahaha—I see your point now!"

I make a mental note to never show her George Carlin. She needs to think I'm original and don't steal from him regula—

"—Alright, you two are next," the Flight Desk Whatever Lady says.

Bailey and I settle down and approach the desk.

The Lady asks, "So where were you two's final destination?"

Holy mother of Jump…

We both attempt to explain and talk over each other and notice each other and stop talking then proceed to talk again and it's a mess and finally she kinda laughs (like, little laughs so the Desk Lady doesn't think she's crazy) and gestures to me ever so slightly.

"'Final Destination,' huh?" she muses.

We get it through to the Desk Lady that we have different flights.

"Oh," she says. "I apologize. I thought you two were together."

Before I explode, I smile and nod to Bailey to let her know she can get her new ticket first. I back up to a safe location and watch her talk to Desk Lady.

She thought we were together…

Well…that was nice of her to say that…confuse that? I don't know. She was a sweet gal…Bailey, not Desk Lady (though I'm sure somebody out there likes Desk Lady, too). I hope she has fun in Oregon or wherever her "Final Destination" may be.

[267]

Bailey gets her ticket and walks towards her new flight gate thing. I approach the desk to get my—

—Bailey stops and waits several feet away.

I don't know what I'm doing. I don't know what I'm doing. I don't know what I'm doing. What's happening? I see Desk Lady pass me a new ticket. What do I now—I don't know what I'm—she says something—I don't know—I don't—

—I step away from the desk and meet Bailey.

"Nice ticket," she says.

"Thanks. Yours is pretty nifty, too."

"We on the same flight again?"

I hold out my ticket to compare with hers.

"Aww, that sucks," she says. "Looks like I'm the one with the non-stop…I think?" She laughs that laugh of hers again and oh my—

—You should go to Oregon, Jhaegar.

"So do you live in Portland then? Or something?"

"More like 'Or Something,' you ever hear of Medford?"

"Not yet. What's the coolest thing to do in Medford?"

"I really like

You may not go to Oregon

What?

No. Go away.

[268]

"—and me and my friends also—"

`You need to leave her alone`

"Shut up!" I yell.

"…Huh?"

Oh, jumpin' fuckin'—

"—No, sorry, not you," I explain. "Sorry—I'm sorry, it wasn't—so what were you saying about—?"

"—I, um, me and my friends…"

Bailey gives me *The Look.*

Oh my—no, you piece of pissing shitting ruining every—whoever you are I'm gonna find you and beat the

`Call her a "whore"`

I—

"—You're a fucking whore, Jayline, or whatever the fuck your—"

—She gasps—eyebrows furrow—eyes—HER EYES!

Bailey turns and speed walks away.

I lurch for her.

"No, don't leave!" I shout.

[269]

Stop

I freeze in position.

What? Why? No, I was gonna get better, I was

You are yet Invisible to them

You fucking pissing shit eating

You must be the difference

You must own your Despair

Bailey's disappeared into the crowd—no, I'VE disappeared into the crowd. Waves of humanity ebb and flow around me. All I can do is watch.

I feel everything breaking.

INT. AIRPORT TERMINAL - DAY

Tears well up in Jhaegar's eyes.

He hears The Voice again, the one he's always heard, the one that haunts him wherever he goes.

> **THE VOICE**
> Forget her, Jhaegar. You may not
> follow her into happiness. Such is
> not your path.

Jhaegar thinks his responses back. Talks to The Voice without physically speaking.

JHAEGAR

You don't know anything. She liked
me! She laughed at my stupid
nonsense and it wasn't her fake
laugh she did to Other Guy.

THE VOICE

Yes. I am aware.

JHAEGAR

So why'd you mess it up?!

THE VOICE

I had to. There was no other
option in the interests of our
preservation.

JHAEGAR

"Our" preservation?

THE VOICE

I am afraid so.

JHAEGAR

And who are you then?

THE VOICE

I am God, Jhaegar.

JHAEGAR

What? No, you're not. God's a
pissy little yup who'd never leave
Heaven. You'd—

GOD

—I am not their God, I am YOUR
God.

Jhaegar says nothing. Stares into empty air.

GOD

Do not give me that look, Jhaegar.
It is unbecoming of us.

JHAEGAR

What do you mean, "us?"

[271]

GOD

I am your God. I created you in MY
image. For the most part, you and
I are the same, the only
difference being you live in the
realm of the Invisible, and soon I
will not.

JHAEGAR

This makes no sense.

GOD

That is fine.

JHAEGAR

Jumpin' Christ…

GOD

But you were made lower, yet
higher than the Invisible. I may
be a God, but you are yet a God
among them: not Invisible, but
Invisiblessed.

JHAEGAR

And for what reason did you "make"
me, huh?

GOD

Who mandates I must have a reason?
Cannot simply the joy of creation
be my reason?

JHAEGAR
            (actually yelling)
You can't just—!

GOD

—Please refrain from yelling. I
can hear your thoughts. Speaking
plainly, I AM your thoughts.

JHAEGAR

If that's so, why did you just
make me yell at you?

[272]

                    GOD
Nifty, is it not?

                  JHAEGAR
What?

                    GOD
People enjoy fun.

                  JHAEGAR
You're not "people," you're God.

                    GOD
To you.

                  JHAEGAR
Oh, my—I'm about—

Jhaegar's eyeballs melt, bones shatter, and his penis
transforms into an octopus tentacle.

He SCREAMS.

And in an instant, he's NORMAL again.

                  JHAEGAR
What the hell was that about?

                    GOD
I can be rather sadistic. And
masochistic. I suppose we enjoy
pain.

                  JHAEGAR
But you're not doing this just for
fun, you haven't been torturing me
the entire time. What's your real—
our real—angle here?

                    GOD
What do you think it is?

                  JHAEGAR
I don't know.

                    GOD
Yes, you do.

                    [273]

                    JHAEGAR
          You like the power game.

                     GOD
          No.

                    JHAEGAR
          It gets you off.

                     GOD
          Those stories are on a different
          drive.

                    JHAEGAR
          You DO do it for fun, but you're
          using some nutcase mind shit to
          make me think you don't.

                     GOD
          Jhaegar.

                    JHAEGAR
          What?

                     GOD
          I am trying to help you.

Jhaegar stares at his feet.

                     GOD
          I am trying to help US. Do you
          genuinely believe I created you
          for "fun?" After all I have put
          you through?

Jhaegar seems to pout.

                     GOD
          Why do people create?

Jhaegar somehow pouts harder.

                     GOD
          Jhaegar. Why do people create? Why
          did I create you? Why did YOU
          create you?

                     [274]

                         JHAEGAR
            …I don't…I don't know…

                           GOD
            Because it makes us feel—

God suddenly struggles to speak, not as if overcome by
emotion, but as if gritting his teeth with heavy resistance
against some unseen and incalculable force.

                           GOD
            —better, does it not? Like Travis
            talking into the mirror? It makes
            us feel intelligent. It makes us
            feel needed. Feel loved. But most
            importantly?

                         JHAEGAR
            No.

                           GOD
            Yes?

                         JHAEGAR
            I'm not saying anything.

                           GOD
                 (struggling again)
            It helps us get through life. It
            helps convince us it is all
            somehow worth it and not a waste.
            It helps us traverse our pain so
            we may hopefully leave it behind
            and move on to other things, to
            new experiences and not get mired
            down in the tragedies of the past.
            You know this, Jhaegar.

Once finished, God COUGHS, violently even. It takes a few
moments for him to wrest control of himself. Finally calm,
he CLEARS HIS THROAT.

                         JHAEGAR
            You would—I guess, "I" would—we'd
            never buy this yuppie shit.

                          [275]

GOD

He—W—I decided to give you the
Happy Ending.

JHAEGAR

I wanted *In Water*…

GOD

Your suffering is my suffering.

Jhaegar CLEARS HIS THROAT.

JHAEGAR

Our suffering is our suffering.

Jhaegar glances up to plead towards God. Searches for the
place He might be (though he may not be a "He" by the way,
God isn't necessarily a man), finally gives up and decides
on a space above a kebab stand.

GOD

Yes, you are in the right place.

JHAEGAR
(vocalizing)
But why are you doing this then?
Why are you making me suffer? If
you said this is the "Happy
Ending," why won't you let me be
happy?

GOD

Because if you suffer, Jhaegar,
then I do not have to.

Jhaegar's eyebrows furrow in confusion.

GOD

If you suffer, then I can move on.
If I laugh at your misfortune and
smile through your misery, then I
may finally forget my own. That is
why I have to leave you here: so I
may go.

                    JHAEGAR
              (fighting tears)
      But everyone said I was special,
      everyone said I was some kind of
      "new being" or something...I'm
      Invisiblessed...

                    GOD
      And you are.

                    JHAEGAR
      But...but Bailey...

                    GOD
      I know. I love her, too.

                    JHAEGAR
      You're just—

Jhaegar cuts himself off. Manages to break free of his
frozen position and walks away.

                    GOD
      She was the first person to speak
      to us in five years. Five years,
      Jhaegar. Do you know what that
      felt like? Those five minutes of
      aimless chatter with her are some
      of the most precious minutes of
      our lives.

Jhaegar walks faster.

                    JHAEGAR
      I have to find Bai—

                    GOD
      —And then our new tickets put us
      on separate flights and I never
      saw her again. She got in her
      plane right away. I had to wait in
      the terminal for mine—I waited
      thirteen hours—and all I could
      think about was her. If she knew.
      If she could have even
      comprehended the impact she had on
                    (MORE)

                    [277]

GOD (CONT'D)
us. What she would have done
differently. Would she have called
us a creep?

JHAEGAR
Shut up.

GOD
Would she have smiled one of those
special smiles we always seem to
get? Those, "Mental Illness
alert," smiles?

JHAEGAR
Don't ruin my memory. Just go
away.

GOD
I will very soon, Jhaegar, and
that is the point. Once I have
finished your story…OUR
story…I will never have to think
about you ever again.

JHAEGAR
If you're gonna leave, just let me
see her—

GOD
—I cannot do that.

JHAEGAR
Why?

GOD
You have to be sad—lugubrious,
even—because sad things make us
happy, remember?

JHAEGAR
Maybe you're the one who needs
help.

GOD
We never needed help. We just
needed to move on.

[278]

                    JHAEGAR
          I hope you'll be happy when I'm
          dead.

                    GOD
          Alas, you will never die.

                    JHAEGAR
          Oh, I'll "live in the hearts of
          millions," won't I?

                    GOD
          Most likely just hundreds.

                    JHAEGAR
          What a waste…

                    GOD
          I have to leave now. Is there
          anything you would like to say to
          me before I go?

                    JHAEGAR
          I hate you.

                  M. PRICE
          Goodbye, Jhaegar.

A hollow THUMP reverberates through the air.

Jhaegar continues walking for a few steps.

Then he collapses on the ground and sobs.

                    ***

Is this what freedom feels like? Just walking around an (actually, there's some pretty

interesting films about—) —shut the fuck up, Jhaegar (I see that hasn't gone away). Sigh, I don't

know what to do. Am I really gonna get on this stupid fucking—and stop cursing! You only

[279]

started really cursing when you deteriorated more than usual. You're fine now. It's—ya know, it's all PG Era from here.

I don't know—it all just seems like a nightmare. Like, college was only a few years ago, but it feels like fifty. And my youth? My childhood? Even further? Memory's so weird—it's a lot like dreaming. When you have a dream, you don't know how you got there and you don't know where you're going, you just have a momentary episode of experience and sensation. It never occurs to you that you're in this dream and by all appearances, it's in current, real time, despite the fact it's essentially coming out of a sort of mental void—ya know, like empty space empty space DREAM empty space empty space and you wake up. Isn't that the deal with memories, too? I have specific memories of being at college or anywhere else…but nothing really before or after cuz I forget all the endless times I woke up and showered and went to class and—ya know—besides the additional idea that I don't use anything I learned at college or continue communication with anyone I met at college to even substantiate my past presence at college. I'm just left with a bunch of disjointed, isolated experiences.

And to me, they're all nightmares.

I was told that when you sleep, you're constantly dreaming and it's only the last two minutes or so you actually remember as a "dream," cuz your short term memory is total trash as you continue to experience a new "dream" built upon the bones of the previous "dream" and so on until morning. Comparing this to memories: I remember specifically what I just did in the airport, yeah, but will I a day from now? A year from now? Or will I categorize this memory as another nightmare defined by my interaction with Bailey? Another thing I heard is all reality affects your dreams—as in your mind can't conjure anything on its own. If you see a pedestrian

[280]

in your dream, your brain registered them as a pedestrian when you were at Burger King or Disneyland or whatever. What I wonder is if reality affects dreams, what do dreams affect?

When I was a kid, I'd always have dreams about monsters chasing me through my house and the only way I could wake up was by jumping off our balcony...suicide...and if I didn't do that, they would get me. Killing myself was the only way I could wake up and escape the terror of my mind. Does that mean from my earliest stages of development, I was seeing suicide as a comforting self-defense mechanism?

What really bothers me is that "last two minutes" part...so what are the other eight hours? What's happening that I can't remember? If suicide was my learned habit, you'd think I'd be killing myself anytime I encountered monsters...which can't ONLY be the last two minutes of any given night. So for every time I jump off my balcony and wake up in my bed, how many times do I jump off my balcony and just respawn right back at the top?

I don't know. I notice I must've stopped at that kebab stand from earlier cuz the remains of some kind of tandoori chicken deal mock me from my lap—"mock" me cuz I'm pretty sure they were covered in turmeric and I—I just can't anymore. I was also planning to insert a snappy *Cowboy Bebop* reference (cuz it's 2001 and I don't think it's creepy to like anime yet), but I— I'm quite discombobulated. Obfuscated.

But yeah, I'm on the (no, it's ovulated!) plane now (the new one).

At least I have the window seat, that's nice. Ya know, complain as I will about my life, I ALWAYS get the window seat—well, no, sometimes I get the aisle seat—I think I got the aisle seat last time I flew—but I never have to deal with the middle! Is that the secret boon of my life? All this suffering for the sake of somewhat convenient air travel? Whatever.

[281]

Some chump sits next to me. Guess he doesn't have the boon. Just forget—everything's gonna be forwards and backwards and whatever you want, Godard…and speaking of French people I disdain, I actually feel like I recognize chumpy.

"Are you Fig Dunkis?" I ask him.

Fig shoots me the side eye.

"Maybe. What's it to you?"

"I've been meaning to ask, is 'Dunkis' spelled with one S or two?"

"What do you mean?"

"Never mind," I say and look out the window.

It appears we're flying. Wonder how long I talked to Fig. Hopefully not too long. Oh well, planes make me happy—pretty sure I can use that word now cuz God or whatever's fu— left and I don't think it'll affect anything anymore.

Know what? Screw it, let's play around with Fig. I wanna tell him crazy stuff about the future and—

—What? Fig's already staring at me.

"Acute Altruism," he states.

"Fig?"

"You won't die, but they will."

Fig nods and presses two fingers to his ear.

Something inside me tells me I should copy. I do and find my ear's bleeding again (ear's there, just bleeding). All other feelings fade as my hearing focuses.

[282]

Familiar voices. Familiar laughter—giggles, even. I glance down the row and can't see (not saying Fig's fat, but—) —I turn around and find nothing important there either. Investigating up front...

I see the backs of four Middle Eastern men (not saying being Middle Eastern's their only quality) who seem to joke around with each other. I stare intently and it must cause some kind of telepathic signal to go off or something, cuz one of them turns back to look at me...

It's Ziad...HELL Ziad...

A spark of confusion twinkles in his eyes, as if he's having some sort of reverse déjà vu. His friends turn back to look at me...

It's the Three Als...the HELL Three Als...

One of them taps another one's shoulder and points at me. Says something. They all nod in consent.

Haha. Hehe. Hohohohahaha I don't even know if I'm laughing on the inside or the outside. Does it matteehehahahaha, hohohohnonono, oh no.

Ziad and the Als notice my laughter and turn red, panicked expressions on their faces. Ziad nods at all three of them in turn and I get the feeling he's telling them to "get ready" or something.

Hahaha oh sigh. Just let it happen. Hahaha. Hehehe. AaaaaHaHaHaHahahahahaaaaah.

Sometimes all you can do is laugh.

M. Price may or may not live in the American Midwest. If one should find Price walking alone in the park, please feel free to leave Price alone. Some people say Price is something, but others say Price is definitely not (but defiantly yes), and whether it can really be known, who can know? All we know now is that you will never get this time back.

M. Price's favorite pizza is pineapple (not Hawaiian as Canadian bacon is for the Goys (Hilary Hahn's favorite pizza is pepperoni (or so I've been informed))).

STONKS.

(and oh yeah, for business inquiries (clown shows, children's birthday parties, offerings for Azathoth) contact pleasefeelbadimdead@gmail.com or just harass me on Twitter @mpriceisdead)

DOG ALERT

Be on the lookout for *Please Feel Bad I'm Alive,* the soulless and even mediocre(r) cash grab sequel to *Please Feel Bad I'm Dead.* Also be on the lookout for the third one...but probably not, as I'm sure (I mean, let's be honest) you'll have given up on me by then.

Or just make a bacon carbonara…it's your choice, really.

DOG ALERT